The Tragical Tale of
BIRDIE BLOOM

The Tragical Tale of
BIRDIE BLOOM

TEMRE BELTZ

HARPER
An Imprint of HarperCollinsPublishers

Library of Congress Control Number: 2018958457
ISBN 978-0-06-283583-3 (trade bdg.)

Typography by Torborg Davern
19 20 21 22 23 CG/LSCH 10 9 8 7 6 5 4 3 2 1

First Edition

For Jerad, Ellie, and Violet

FORGOTTEN FOREST

FOULWEATHER'S HOME FOR THE TRAGICAL

TRAGIC MOUNTAIN

SLEEPING GIANTS MOUNTAIN RANGE

BEASTLY VALLEY

CASTLE MATILDA

BLACK SEA

MERRY MEADOW

SNAGGLETOOTH ISLES

PIGGLESTICKS

DEEPEST, DARKEST BOG

CONTENTS

ONE *Unhappy Birthday* 5

TWO *A Book Worth Saving* 15

THREE *Something's Buzzing* 30

FOUR *The Worst Mail Day* 45

FIVE *When It Rains, It Pours* 56

SIX *Something to Chew On* 74

SEVEN *A Witchy House Call* 86

EIGHT *A Triumphant and a Rat* 100

NINE *The Oldest Tragical of All* 119

TEN *Impossible Customer Service* 137

| ELEVEN | *Eight-Legged Wonders* | 155 |

| TWELVE | *The Healing of a Boy* | 170 |

| THIRTEEN | *A Bothersome Jar of Peanut Butter* | 188 |

| FOURTEEN | *A Terrible Choice* | 201 |

| FIFTEEN | *Worse than Wild Hogs* | 213 |

| SIXTEEN | *A Rotten Twist* | 229 |

| SEVENTEEN | *A Magical Cloak and a Foul Secret* | 244 |

EIGHTEEN *Come One, Come All to the Annual Witches' Ball!* 260

NINETEEN *Down in the Bog* 281

TWENTY *When Everything Falls Apart at the Bristles* 300

TWENTY-ONE *An Extraordinary Explosion of Glitter* 321

TWENTY-TWO *Something's Brewing on Tragic Mountain* 336

Hello. [1]

---

1. It is a pleasure to meet you. Truly. Life as a book is not as easy as one might think. A book waits. A book waits some more. Sometimes a book waits for years. And then one day, a reader much like yourself happens upon it. Plucks the book right off the shelf and opens it up. I am glad you have chosen me.

You, perhaps, are wondering if you have made the wrong choice. But wait! Don't put me back![2]

---

2. I promise there is much more to me than a single line on every page. So much, in fact, that I sometimes cannot say all that needs to be said within the story (especially when that story happens to involve a *witch*). So I have given you notes. *Foot*notes. Not because books have any grand delusions of skipping about the way humans sometimes do, but simply because they are found at the bottoms of the pages. Also, considering you have already gone and found my footnotes, I doubly like you. You are not only a reader—you are a very smart reader! We shall get along splendidly.

I do not think our meeting is by accident. Indeed, books pride themselves on being found by the right reader at the right time. I am certain that reader is you. As such, before we proceed even a sentence further, I urge you to hold tightly to me.

There are two reasons for my request.

First, you may have noticed my front cover. Surely you have heard the old saying that you should never judge a book by its cover? In my case, that's entirely true. And though I'm not exactly proud of telling a fib from the get-go, I had to. Otherwise, I never could have traveled from a kingdom as far away as Wanderly. So here's the fib: this story is not *really* a tragical one. In fact, it's quite the opposite of that. And that's what makes it so grand . . . but also a bit dangerous. You see, where I come from, there are some people—people in very important positions, no less—who want to pretend that stories like me *don't exist.*

The second reason you must keep a tight grip on me is because there are several scary parts (you didn't already forget about the witch, did you?). Although it is quite tempting to toss one's book into the air out of sheer fright, it is far better to stick together.

So how about we give it a go? There's no need to be shy. Books were made to be held tightly.

Ah yes. You're a natural!

Now that we are properly situated, let us pop into the haunted cabin of one known as Agnes Prunella Crunch. Today is a special—No, awful . . . No, special . . . Oh bother! I suppose I shall let you decide for yourself precisely what type of day Agnes is having. . . .

ONE

UNHAPPY BIRTHDAY

Witches aren't the celebrating sort.

But birthdays, as you well know, are different.

Not even a witch forgets her birthday.

And so, on September 5, as she had been doing for seventy or eighty or who really knows how many years, Agnes Prunella Crunch settled into her familiar rocking chair. She pulled the rickety table with the oozing slice of mud pie on it a bit closer.[3] She scratched her favorite wart at the tip of her exceptionally large nose. She kicked off her smelly, striped socks and wriggled her bony toes in front of the cauldron that emitted a puff of

---

3. Mud pie was Agnes's favorite. Lest you nod eagerly because you love it too, let me inform you that Agnes's mud pie was not the sort you order in a restaurant. It was not even the sandy sort you might make on the playground. It was the real deal. Real, stinking, goopy mud with a few juicy worms tossed in for good measure.

green smoke every now and again.

It was time.

Oh yes. Agnes nodded. *It was time.*

Agnes tilted in her rocking chair. Agnes tilted so far she might have tipped right out had she not spent years teaching her rocking chair to float. She wrapped her fingers around the cover of a ginormous book and hoisted the book up off the floor and onto the squishy lump of her belly with a soft grunt. She eyeballed the cover. It gleamed back.

The Book of Evil Deeds, it hissed.

At least that's what it would have done if Agnes or any other witch worth her salt had written it.[4] In fact, if it had been Agnes, she would have thrown in a few additional perks like a front cover nasty enough to chomp off whole fingertips when properly slammed, or pages guaranteed to deliver paper cuts every single time. Imagine that!

But as the only book in all of Wanderly written just for witches, Agnes considered it better than nothing. And it did say "evil" on the front cover, which practically guaranteed that even if the other 2,793 pages had been filled with spells ranging from the embarrassingly easy (how to light your cauldron without a match) to the utterly useless (how to polish your witchy boots in

---

4. But this, of course, was impossible. Like every book in Wanderly, *The Book of Evil Deeds* was penned by a carefully trained scribe and personally inspected by Wanderly's infamous ruler, the Chancellor. This was likely why most witches tossed *The Book of Evil Deeds* out with yesterday's dinner carcass.

a snap), the last spell, the final spell, simply *had* to deliver.

Especially on, of all days, Agnes's birthday.

Agnes wriggled her fingers; she squiggled her nose; she inhaled a deep, raspy breath. She turned the page and . . . her floating rocking chair crashed down against the dusty floorboards with a jarring thud. Her eyes darted back and forth across the scrawling script. She began clawing at the bottom corner of the page to see if another page had become stuck, and perhaps this wasn't really the last page after all?

But it was.

And it contained one measly spell.

One measly, awful spell titled "**How to Transform Your Hair to Slime Green.**"

Hair?! The last page of *The Book of Evil Deeds* was reserved for a hairstyle? Day in and day out, week after week, year after year, Agnes had dutifully completed thousands of banal spells to arrive at nothing more than a hairstyle?

Agnes didn't need a new hairstyle! Over the years, she had honed her ratty strands to a nearly perfect shade of purple and didn't see any good reason to change it. Not to mention slime green was last popular over a century ago. What Agnes really needed—what Agnes wanted more than anything—was to find some way to make witching fun again!

It is a terrible thing to feel that one has wasted years. It is a more terrible thing to feel that one hasn't any plan for the days to come. So, Agnes did what any respectably infuriated witch would do: she slammed *The Book of Evil Deeds* shut. She growled at it. She tossed it down toward her witchy foot and gave it a sharp, swift kick.

At well over two thousand pages long, however, the book kicked back.[5] Even worse, as it careened off Agnes's now throbbing big toe and boomeranged about the room, it finally landed—*squish!*—atop Agnes's mud pie.

Agnes's birthday was going from bad to cursed!

Oh sure, there had been a few bright spots, like that morning's visit to Fairy Fifi's Woodland Boutique, where Agnes enchanted the entire stock of ball gowns to dance the ogre's shuffle instead of the waltz, but even that wasn't what it used to be. It was a perfectly evil curse. It should have been glorious! It should have been thrilling! Fairy Fifi's resulting scream had been a record-breaking eleven! But all Agnes felt was utterly and completely . . . bored.

At this point you may be jumping up and down in your seat, wondering why Agnes doesn't just try something new? Perhaps apply those top-notch potion-making skills to becoming a scientist. Maybe adapt those impressive broomstick acrobatics to life as a trapeze artist. Or do something completely wild like become a schoolteacher. This would be the perfect sort of advice if Agnes hadn't happened to live in the kingdom of Wanderly.

---

5. Fear not, dear reader! Books rarely lash out of their own accord and instead use their hefty weight merely for defensive purposes.

In the kingdom of Wanderly, stories ruled all, and the citizens were required to live "by the book." You tell me how many witches you've seen waltz through a storybook in a frilly pink dress while humming a merry tune with a bunny rabbit underfoot? Considering Agnes would rather eat her smelly sock than do any of those things, that doesn't seem significant, but it was. Very much so. Because Agnes wasn't supposed to do *anything* other than what some storybook witch had already done. But what if not all witches were the same? What if Agnes were different? What if Agnes had an idea that no storybook witch ever had? Whether by accident or by calculated avoidance, those were the sorts of questions the Chancellor never bothered to answer.

Which meant Agnes was stuck.

Stuck on a rotten birthday, in a haunted cabin, all alone.

To be fair, the haunted part wasn't all that bad. Yes, the shelves on the walls sagged with jars full of hopelessly witchy things: rolling eyeballs, venomous snake fangs, and frog legs that still twitched. Yes, the ceiling was enchanted so that, no matter what time of day, it looked to be the unsettling hour of just past midnight, and, okay, fine, the black cauldron that bubbled endlessly over the hearth was guilty of throwing out a sharp crackle of lightning and a deep rumble of thunder from time to time. Still, somehow, Agnes's cabin oozed with its own sort of coziness.

Coziness, however, couldn't answer prickly questions. Coziness couldn't dole out appropriately wicked advice. Coziness couldn't solve the fact that Agnes didn't have anyone to talk to. Of course, Agnes didn't want another witch's company for some sappy, chatty-chat sort of reason. Blech! Agnes just wanted to find out if there were any other witches who were similarly stuck. If there were any other witches who had fallen into a bit of a slump. If there was some easy fix Agnes just hadn't thought of yet.

But that was never going to happen for the simple fact that in Wanderly—unless for the purposes of hissing, cursing, or plotting—witches didn't talk to one another. Ever.

Indeed, it was one of the ten governing provisions of the Witches' Manifesto that all witches were bound to. Lately, Agnes found herself wishing she'd never signed the thing, but when it was presented decades ago, the provisions had seemed ridiculously straightforward.[6] The brand-spanking-new cauldron and year's worth of bewitching dust the Chancellor tossed in as a signing bonus hadn't hurt, either.

But how to get around that aggravating rule now?

Agnes narrowed her eyes.

She thought.

She thought harder.

At long last, her nose hairs prickled. Agnes's nose hairs always

---

6. For example, what witch in her right mind would ever giggle instead of cackle? And if a witch couldn't commit at least three evil deeds a year, was she even a witch at all?

prickled when she had a deliciously clever idea, because Agnes could find the help she needed without uttering a single, audible, punishable word. Agnes didn't have to *talk* to anyone. Instead, Agnes could *write* a letter.

Agnes's cauldron bubbled to attention. It spit out a jagged piece of parchment and a quill. Agnes brandished the quill and stabbed it into the paper in erratic, jerky strokes. For once, Agnes wasn't intending to be terrifying; she was just rusty. Other than those few occasions where a potion required an annoyingly specific list of ingredients—too many to hold in her witchy head while slinking through the Dead Tree Forest—she hadn't much reason to ever set pen to paper.

Agnes had forgotten how much she disliked the business of writing. Writing was slow; writing forced her to think about her words rather than letting them fly forth, delightfully sharp edges and all. After what seemed like ages, Agnes threw her quill to the floor and held the finished letter—her letter—high in the air. She checked it over, which took approximately three seconds. This is what Agnes's letter said:

> Hello. Have you finished The Book? NOW WHAT?
>
> Ms. Crunch

If you are thinking this is a woefully short letter, you are right. Still, it was likely more than any other witch had ever written before. Not to mention, in the kingdom of Wanderly, the power of words—even a very, very few—could simply never be underestimated.

Agnes sealed the letter shut. She snuck a look around her haunted cabin. The daddy longlegs in the corner blinked at her. The fly buzzing noisily about froze in midair. The jar of various creaturely eyeballs rolled in her direction. Everything was watching her. Gawking at her. As if to say in one collective, hushed voice, *Are you* really *going to do it?*

"Of course, I am, you ninnies!" Agnes crowed.

And she tore the letter up into itty-bitty pieces.[7] She lifted the pieces onto the palm of her grimy hand. She closed her eyes and envisioned a terribly old crotchety witch, the sort of witch who might have had time to finish *The Book of Evil Deeds* and cook up a plan B after discovering the book's dastardly uselessness.

Agnes warmed her breath over the letter's pieces. They rose from her hand—up, up, and away! They whirled and twirled and spun! They headed straight toward the chimney where, to Agnes's great surprise—and before she could execute even a half twirl of her crooked finger—the pieces were promptly swept

---

7. When most people tear something into itty-bitty pieces, they intend to toss it into the garbage can. Agnes, however, wasn't about to submit anything of *hers* via the Wanderly Post. Not when she had a far superior form of transmission in her own magic. Unbeknownst to Agnes, this was quite fortunate because the post people were notoriously nosy, and the contents of letters were often riffled through two, three, and maybe even four times before making it to their final destinations.

into the black night . . . not by her own magic, but by a big whooshing gust.

Agnes frowned.

She dashed toward the chimney. She knocked her bubbling cauldron aside so that bits of green goo sloshed to and fro. She hiked up her skirts and thrust her whole head through the opening. She drew in a sharp breath. It was not a wayward traveler come to ruin her day. It was not even an unlucky bit of foul weather. It was none other than the Winds of Wanderly.

The Winds of Wanderly were no ordinary winds.

Agnes had heard stories about the Winds of Wanderly. Hushed stories. Secret stories. Stories that seemed like poppycock, if you asked Agnes. If the Winds had something as fantastic as hands, why would they use them to unlock doors and set the Chancellor's woebegone prisoners free? If the Winds had an achingly beautiful voice, why would they dive deep into a shadowy forest to call a single, shivering child home? If the Winds were *really* that remarkable, why would they dabble in the lives of Wanderly's citizens at all? Regardless, none of that mattered much to Agnes. Because of all the very many stories floating about, not one of them had ever once involved a witch.

The Winds of Wanderly couldn't want anything to do with her.

But where were they taking her letter?

Agnes tried to appear nonchalant. Though the hairs were standing up on the back of her neck, she plunked down into her familiar rocking chair. She forced her gnarled thumbs to twiddle as if she hadn't anything better to do.

Still, she listened.

She listened as the Winds of Wanderly continued to race around outside her cabin. She listened as the windows rattled and the rusted metal knob on her door twisted back and forth, back and forth, almost like the Winds wanted to come inside for a spell. She listened as the brittle leaves of the Dead Tree Forest rose up and clattered all about as if there were perhaps a bit of life in them after all.

And as the witch sat, she did something she hadn't occasion to do in a long, long time. On that night, the witch *wondered*.

TWO

A Book Worth Saving

Far, far away from Agnes, inside an impossibly dark house
perched atop a skinny, crooked mountain and surrounded
on three sides by the gnashing waves of the Black Sea, a young
girl stood in a line of seventeen other children.

Her name was Birdie Bloom.

Her knees were trembling.

She was hiding a book beneath the somber fabric of her black
gown.

Let me repeat, she was hiding a *book* beneath the somber
fabric of her black gown.

As I was saying, SHE WAS HIDING A—

Oh bother, it's no wonder you have such a blank stare on
your face. You are a reader. You are likely never caught without a book. At bedtime, you may even sneak extra chapters

of books after your parents have told you to turn off the light (don't worry, I'd never dream of telling). But the children who lived at Foulweather's Home for the Tragical did not feel the same way. In fact, the children at Foulweather's Home for the Tragical *hated* books.

You would too if you happened to be the bad ending.

And that is what the children were: nothing more than a house full of bad endings. The Chancellor called them "Tragicals."

While every other citizen in Wanderly dutifully modeled their lives off the books they read, being careful to avoid dark woods and sinister folks draped in cloaks, for the Tragicals, it was simply no use. In not one single book in Wanderly had a Tragical ever escaped; ever triumphed; or ever outwitted, out-run, or outlasted a villain. For a Tragical, every book always ended the exact same way: badly.

Even still, Birdie was hiding a book. Not because Birdie liked to be scared out of her wits, contemplating what villainous sort might one day sneak up on her (witches were the absolute worst when it came to sneaking up on people), but because the book she had was *different*.

She had stumbled across the book just that morning on a routine round of kitchen duty. She had thrust her hand into the butler's kitchen cupboard, expecting to find nothing more than a weary sack of flour, when she suddenly tipped forward and her hand wrapped around the book's spine. At Foulweather's Home for the Tragical, books were never tossed about willy-nilly; they always remained in an unwavering and upright position on the library shelves.

But Birdie had discovered a misfit.

A misfit book, nonetheless.

With no one at all to peek over her shoulder, she had been unable to resist cracking the front cover and had made three astonishing discoveries.

First, the book lacked the Chancellor's official seal of authorization. Birdie had never encountered a book without the Chancellor's official seal of authorization. Second, the book wasn't finished. It had no end. In the kingdom of Wanderly, where endings were deemed as certain as beginnings, Birdie had never even known such a thing could exist. Finally, as early as page three, the book spoke of something Birdie had never heard of before. It called this something friendship. The idea itself seemed so lovely and so wonderful Birdie might not have paid it any attention at all, except it happened to a girl who was terribly poor and terribly alone. A girl who sounded quite tragical. A girl who sounded just like Birdie.

And she knew right then and there she simply couldn't bear to put the book down.

Of course, Birdie would have stowed the book someplace other than beneath her gown had she known Mistress Octavia Foulweather would conduct a surprise inspection that very morning, but such was the life of a Tragical. Nothing ever seemed to go their way.

Mistress Octavia loomed at the front of the dining hall.

With her arms crossed, she drummed her fingernails along the sharp curve of her elbow. Everything about her was pointy. She *smiled*.[8]

And even the walls of the manor shuddered.

"I suppose you all assumed I summoned you for breakfast." She paused as the Tragicals looked over her shoulder to the impressively long dining table,[9] where eighteen bowls of cold blueberry mush[10] grew colder still. "Indeed, you are such greedy little things! No matter how many days in a row I feed you, you still expect me to do it again. What a burden you are for Wanderly! With not a single thing to offer but your deaths, you take, take, take!" Mistress Octavia's gray eyes flashed, and she bellowed with a force loud enough to make the flatware rattle, "THIEVES!"

Let us pause for a moment, because the children were not thieves in the way you might be thinking. For one, there was

---

8. Gah! Do not be drawn in by this falsity. Though smiles are typically a sign of affection and cheer, one simply cannot deliver what one does not have.

9. The table was not impressively long in the luxurious sense. It was, instead, impressively long in the lonely sense, because it was roomy enough to seat fifty-four children. There were, of course, only eighteen children at the manor, but they were required to leave at least two empty seats between them at mealtimes.

10. The blueberry mush was nothing short of an oddity. Nowhere in all of Wanderly did blueberry bushes grow in greater abundance than on Tragic Mountain. Unbeknownst to Mistress Octavia, the Tragicals found the mush to be utterly delicious—whether served hot, cold, or lukewarm. Mistress Octavia, on the other hand, found it to be disgusting, which was likely the reason she demanded it to be served to the Tragicals at every single meal.

not much available to steal. The manor was frightfully sparse. The furniture was aged and breaking. Everything was dim, dark, and dreary. But even among the shadows, not all was lost. Whether it was a stray button the perfect shape for rolling across the dusty floor, or an exceptionally long thread to twist and wind about one's fingers, the Tragicals still found things to treasure. Small tokens of joy in an otherwise miserable existence. Tokens that Mistress Octavia gleefully confiscated and, more often than not, destroyed right before their eyes.

Mistress Octavia drew to a stop in front of a little girl named Cricket. The Tragicals were forbidden to speak with one another, so Birdie never said Cricket's name aloud, but she made it a point to recite it in her head as often as she could. Birdie did this for all the Tragicals. She couldn't say why, except that if she knew the names of such objects as desks, chairs, and coatracks, it seemed, to some degree, important.

Mistress Octavia clicked the heels of her pointy boots together in smug satisfaction. "Caroline," she said. But ever so slightly, ever so subtly, the little girl—Cricket—shook her head. Mistress Octavia's eyes narrowed. "What?" she barked. "What is it?"

With her lower lip trembling, Cricket whispered, "That's not my name, ma'am."

Mistress Octavia tossed off two words that no Tragical had a single reason to doubt: "Who cares?" And then, "Empty your gown, *Caroline*."

Cricket did as she was told. She plunged her hands deep into the pockets of the black gown that swam about her small frame and turned them inside out. An explosion of paper burst forth! Not whole sheets, of course, but tiny snippets and odd-shaped scraps. Tiny snippets and odd-shaped scraps that must have slipped free from the butler's wastebasket and taken Cricket weeks to collect.

It took Mistress Octavia, however, less than a moment to shove Cricket out of the way, stab the sharp prick of her heel into the pile, and grind the paper bits into dust. She leaned in so close to Cricket the brass buttons on her cardigan nearly scraped the little girl's nose.

"Paper, is it?" she said. "And what was a child like *you* planning to do with such a precious and restricted item?"

Birdie could scarcely imagine what Cricket would say. In a kingdom that lived "by the book," there was perhaps nothing so valuable, nothing so powerful, nothing that held so much possibility as a sheet of blank paper. Though Wanderly's official storytellers—known as scribes—were allotted an unlimited supply of paper, every other citizen in Wanderly operated under various restrictions. Not surprisingly, a Tragical's annual distribution of paper amounted to a big, fat zero. Yes, zero, because allowing a Tragical to imagine anything other than their own bad ending was considered nothing short of catastrophic.

The Chancellor's reasoning was twofold: (1) Bad endings were a harsh reality that simply couldn't be written off. And

(2) if bad endings couldn't be avoided entirely, they ought to happen to those without anything to lose; to those who would not be missed; to those for whom nothing much was expected anyways. Consequently, the happy endings would be safely preserved for Wanderly's best and brightest, those whom the Chancellor called "Triumphants." After all, what hope could a storybook kingdom ever have if the heroes couldn't be counted on to prevail every single time?

Here, you may be shifting a bit uncomfortably in your seat, for how does one fall into such an awful category as having nothing to lose, no one to miss them, and not a single expectation? Does it have something to do with egregiously naughty behavior? Perhaps that offense your parents have told you ten (*ahem*, thirty) times not to repeat?

The answer is no.

The Tragicals were doomed for one reason and one reason only. A reason they hadn't a single ounce of control over: the Tragicals didn't have parents. The Tragicals were orphans.

Birdie winced as Mistress Octavia dashed her foot across Cricket's pile of dust, scattering it to the shadows. Loss was a way of life for the Tragicals, but it never seemed to get any easier.

"I am still waiting for your explanation, Caroline!" Mistress Octavia said.

Cricket's eyes were glued to the floor. As if her treasure was still there, just invisible. Her voice was a whisper. "I was saving those scraps for a ball. I was going to roll them up into a nice, round ball."

Mistress Octavia swirled her finger in Cricket's direction with the sort of panache that never failed to make Birdie cringe.[11] "Tragical children do not use balls! Tragical children do not play! What Tragical children do, Caroline, is they read. They read so they will never forget their roles, which is why you will be assigned to three consecutive nights of . . . library detention!"

Faced with the proposition of dark, sleepless nights, cradled by only the dragons[12] that prowled through Mistress Octavia's books, Cricket burst into loud, messy tears. Despite the presence of the seventeen other children beside her, *no one moved an inch*. They remained stiff as a board. They kept their eyes facing forward. They acted as if nothing at all was happening. There wasn't a single exchange of a sympathetic whisper, pat, or even a sideways glance.

---

11. Despite Birdie's fears, magic never once spun off Mistress Octavia. In the kingdom of Wanderly, magic was restricted to certain sorts, such as fairy godmothers, wizards, witches, and magicians. Not to mention, magic was strictly forbidden at the manor. It was the one rule the Tragicals were glad about, for they were certain if magic did happen upon them, considering they were doomed, it would only bring about *more* terrible things.

12. The dragons in Wanderly occupied a nearby chain of islands known as Snaggletooth Isles. Though most dragons were uniformly large, magical, ferocious, and in possession of a very sensitive sense of smell (they found humans most odorous of all), it cannot be stressed enough that the stories the Chancellor refused to acknowledge were just as important, if not more than, the ones he did. In short: not *every* dragon in Wanderly was the same.

Because of all the difficulties and trials the Tragicals faced, this was the very saddest: after years of being forbidden to speak with one another, the Tragicals had become extraordinarily good at *ignoring* one another. It began first as a means of self-preservation and then deepened to something much more troubling. Because day after day, hour after hour, Mistress Octavia's words chipped away at them. The Tragicals did not know how to *un*hear her; the Tragicals did not know how to avoid believing her. Whether they meant to or not, they began acting as if Mistress Octavia's words were true; as if they really were useless; as if they didn't have a single thing to offer. And so, they simply never tried.

Birdie was typically as guilty as the rest. But on that morning, a book was pressing against her heart. A book containing a new word: "friendship." From what she could tell, friendship didn't have much to do with being alone. Friendship was about being together.

But how?

Mistress Octavia whirled away from Cricket and on to the next child. Unfortunately, the next child was none other than Francesca Prickleboo. Francesca Prickleboo had perfectly plaited orange braids; a smattering of equidistant freckles across the bridge of her upturned nose; and shoes that managed to stay shiny despite the manor's abundance of dirt, dust, and cobwebs.

Francesca Prickleboo was the sort of girl who was bound, set, and determined to be *better*. Surely you have come across children like this in your world. You might recognize them as wanting to "have the farthest soccer kick" or "score one hundred percent on every mathematics test" or "turn at least ten somersaults underwater while holding a single breath." Unfortunately for Francesca, living at Foulweather's Home for the Tragical, there was not a single thing she could take ownership of other than her status as a Tragical. And so, Francesca dedicated her every waking breath to being just that: the most fabulous Tragical that Wanderly had ever known.

Without even a word from Mistress Octavia, Francesca stood with her pockets already turned out. Save for the sharpened pencil each Tragical was required to carry,[13] her pockets were predictably empty. Absolutely perfectly spotless. A Tragical who was content with nothing.

Francesca beamed. But then quickly corrected her expression to one of solemn despair because, above all else, Tragicals were never supposed to look H-A-P-P-Y.[14] She rocked back and forth on the balls of her feet. She tried desperately to catch Mistress Octavia's eye. But Mistress Octavia had already moved on. Mistress Octavia was merely one child away from Birdie. Birdie had

---

13. Given your keen intelligence, I know you have drawn to an abrupt stop here and wondered why a Tragical should be required to carry a pencil when they were denied even a single sheet of paper. Sadly, it was nothing more than Mistress Octavia's cruel attempt at humor.

14. Take heed: in the presence of Mistress Octavia, there are some words she deemed so revolting, it is best not to say them out loud.

to do something fast—something egregious enough to make Mistress Octavia forget all about her surprise inspection; something that would prevent Mistress Octavia from destroying her book.

Birdie scanned the dining room for ideas. But everything looked as terrified as she was! The candlelit chandeliers swayed overhead and flickered anxiously. The dreadfully thick black curtains that covered every window wrung their frayed hems together in what could only be described as distress. Even the eighteen bowls of blueberry mush that lined the dining table jiggled in unison and emitted hefty puffs of frost like smoke signals begging for rescue.

And that was when Birdie had an idea.

An idea that made her toes curl because it was so mutinous Mistress Octavia would not only have to punish her, she would have to punish her *immediately*. And though what that punishment might be made Birdie's spine tingle, it would have to be done. The book Birdie had found was too precious. The book was quite possibly the best thing she would ever stumble across. She didn't harbor any ridiculous ideas she could somehow manage to keep it forever, but even a few more days would be worth it.

Birdie set her jaw. She carefully secured her book with her left arm, keeping her right arm free for the business of mischief.

Then she sprang into action!

The mere sight of Birdie breaking free from the impeccably

straight line of Tragicals was enough to make Mistress Octavia snarl and whirl about. Her snarl deepened, however, to a more sinister expression as Birdie sprinted toward the dining room table, swooped up a bowl full of blueberry mush, and launched it at Mistress Octavia's perfectly smooth, perfectly taut, hairdo.

Plop!

Dribble-dribble!

Squuuuish!

The blueberry mush slid down Mistress Octavia's face. It crawled across her eyebrows and raced down the bridge of her nose. It dipped into her ears and splashed with delight across the once-spotless collar of her blouse. It was, in short, the most ambitious bowl of blueberry mush Birdie had ever encountered.

Mistress Octavia's chest heaved. Mistress Octavia's fingers curled upward as if they were claws. But when Mistress Octavia lunged in Birdie's direction, the force of her motion caused gooey globs of the blueberry mush to take flight once again. This time the globs soared off Mistress Octavia's head and splattered the line of Tragicals standing just behind her.

"Ah!" a little boy cried out when a hearty dollop landed on his nose and nearly left him cross-eyed as he tried to reach it with the tip of his tongue.

"Oh!" one of the teenage girls burst out when a spray of goo splashed like confetti across her black gown.

"Hey!" the boy named Ralph shouted when a thin streak

of mush landed above his upper lip, creating a very smart, very crafty-looking mustache.

And that's when it happened.

Apparently, the blueberry mustache was one hilarity too many.

At least when you happened to be an eight-year-old whose sense of humor had not yet been entirely snuffed out by the cruel reality of life as a Tragical.

It tumbled out. It tumbled free. Cricket *giggled*.

The sound was so foreign that everybody froze.

Cricket slammed her lips together. She scrunched her eyes shut so as to avoid catching another glimpse of Ralph and his ridiculous mustache. But giggles are rarely a solo event. They prefer, instead, to cluster together. It is a phenomenon as predictable yet mysterious as thunder following lightning. And so, it seemed, Cricket was helpless to stop it.

She giggled again.

And Mistress Octavia collapsed onto the ground in a fit of sneezing, hacking, writhing convulsions. The areas of her complexion that were not coated in blueberry mush erupted into great, big, itchy red hives. Without at all meaning to, Birdie and Cricket had perhaps discovered Mistress Octavia's one and only weakness: Mistress Octavia was gravely allergic to . . . laughter.

Mistress Octavia still, however, had a wee bit of breath left in her. Enough to say the only word she needed to say while gesturing wildly at Birdie and Cricket. "D-D-D-D—AHCHOO!—DUNGEON!!"

The butler, Sir Ichabod Grim, appeared almost immediately. The children never knew from whence he came; merely that he preferred to stay carefully tucked into the shadows and only stepped forward to do Mistress Octavia's bidding.

Sir Ichabod's life was nearly as dreary as the Tragicals'. He spent his days slogging up and down Tragic Mountain in search of blueberries; he spent his evenings boiling and mashing the blueberries; and in the time in between, he did nothing more interesting than folding a bit of laundry. Still, his right hand was marked by several mysterious calluses. The sort of calluses not accounted for by his activities at Foulweather's Home for the Tragical. The sort of calluses that shape a man whether or not he chooses to speak of it.

Sir Ichabod Grim never spoke much of anything.

Which meant he was either dreadfully boring or kept many, many secrets.

Birdie hadn't given much thought to which was preferable.

Though Sir Ichabod's eyes widened a bit at the sight of Mistress Octavia rolling about on the ground, he did precisely as he was told. He wordlessly plodded toward Birdie and Cricket. He did not bother to ask what they had done or inquire as to whether they deserved such a punishment. He merely wrapped his hands around a clump of black fabric near the base of each of their necks. He steered them toward the deep, dark belly of the manor while the heavy bronze medallion he was never without thumped hard against his chest.

Thump, thump, thump in almost the precise same rhythm as Birdie's pounding heart.

When one is used to absolutely everything going wrong, it is a monumental event when something actually goes right. But Birdie had done it! The book was safe beneath her gown. It would cost her a trip to the dungeon, but even that was made better by the fact that she wouldn't be alone. Cricket would be with her. Not in the same itty-bitty closet-size cell, but close. Perhaps even near enough to talk. And from what Birdie could tell, that was maybe the first step to becoming friends. Talking.

Of course, at that moment, Birdie hadn't a clue about what was zipping toward her in the dungeon. If she had, she might never have had the courage to enter, and then this would be an entirely different story if it even existed at all.

THREE

SOMETHING'S BUZZING

Birdie Bloom was having difficulty breathing.[15]

It wasn't the dungeon's fault. Certainly the dungeon was dark, dank, and drippy. It was fairly crowded with dog-size rats, shiny bulbous spiders, and assorted towers of junk draped in heavy white sheets that shivered like ghosts. It was outfitted with an entire row of round, open-air, iron-barred windows, which would have been lovely (as every other window in the manor was heavily curtained and even more heavily locked)

---

15. Did you expect to see Agnes? Surely she would never believe anyone would ask after a witch, but that is the special magic of a book. For the time being, we shall visit Agnes after two chapters spent with Birdie. But if you must know, Agnes was doing nothing other than spitting at the soupy clouds hanging over her haunted cabin and trying to act as if she hadn't thought even once about the mysterious disappearance of her letter.

except it allowed for the bucking, barking, banging racket of the Drowning Bucket to echo throughout.[16]

Indeed, any one of the dungeon's atrocities on its own was enough to cause difficulty breathing, but for Birdie, all of them combined paled in comparison to the gripping fear of trying to talk to Cricket.

Because what was she supposed to say?

Please don't furrow your eyebrows. I assure you, this was a very real problem. This wasn't the sort of problem that's resolved by tapping the shoulder of the person who sits in front of you and asking to borrow a pencil. The Tragicals spent their whole lives *not* talking to one another. But if Birdie was going to learn anything about friendship—if friendship was all about being together—this was the very thing she must do. Birdie jiggled a loose brick in the wall that separated her tiny cell from Cricket's until it slipped onto Cricket's side with a loud crash.[17]

She dropped down to her belly (as the loose brick was positioned rather low) and squished the side of her face up against

---

16. The Drowning Bucket was one of Mistress Octavia's favorite contraptions. It hung from the tippy-top of the manor and was suspended from a skinny wooden plank by a metal chain. It was sized perfectly for children and remained ever ready to plunge into the Black Sea, churning hungrily three hundred feet below.

17. No, the walls between the dungeon cells were not riddled with holes like Swiss cheese. They were quite solid. But Birdie had been sentenced to the dungeon twice before and had discovered the loose brick while trying to find a way out. At the time, it had seemed almost cruel (what child can slip through a brick-size hole?), but right then, it was just what she needed.

the hole. Her heart pounded. She swallowed at least ten times to be sure she could squeak out "Hello," because that's what she had determined she should say. It wasn't fancy. It wasn't exciting, but it was merely one word. Certainly Birdie could handle one word.

Birdie didn't expect to find Cricket's cell empty.

Empty?

Birdie blinked. She had walked alongside Cricket the entire way. Sir Ichabod had locked Birdie away first, but she had heard Cricket's footsteps shuffle into the cell beside her, and Sir Ichabod had slammed her door shut too. How does an eight-year-old girl up and disappear out of a dungeon cell?

Birdie pressed her face even closer to the hole, but it wasn't very large, and she simply couldn't see into every corner. She thrust her arm through the hole and grasped about with her fingers. To her horror, something grabbed her back.

"AH!" Birdie screamed at the top of her lungs.

"AH!!" another scream answered her.

Birdie flung her captured arm wildly to and fro, and Cricket came swinging into view. Her hands were gripped tight around Birdie's arm, and she was kicking her feet in every which direction.

When Cricket saw it was none other than Birdie, however, she exhaled a small puff of air and let go. She shuffled away from Birdie and settled into the middle of the cell. Birdie watched as Cricket carefully pinned the long fabric of her gown against her knees, presumably so it wouldn't drape along the ground and provide a convenient highway for the spiders.

Inside of her own cell, Birdie swallowed. Hard. Surely this was as good a time as a Tragical was going to get. "Why did . . . How did . . . Why would . . ."

Ugh. So much for hello.

Cricket brushed a few messy tendrils of hair away from her face. In a soft whisper, she said, "I thought you might be a villain."

"But you saw Sir Ichabod put me in here!" Birdie said, trying not to feel terribly insulted. "How could it have been anyone else but me?"

"We're in a dungeon," Cricket said, looking around warily. "Maybe a wicked witch crept through one of those windows. Or maybe you turned like those werewolves that live in Beastly Valley."[18] Cricket paused and leaned forward ever so slightly. "Why are you trying to break into my cell anyways?"

Birdie's heart thumped. Things had gotten off to an unsettling start, but that was okay. That was to be expected. They were Tragicals. But here, now seemed an opportunity to explain

---

18. Beastly Valley was the narrow bottleneck by which Tragic Mountain remained connected to Wanderly. Full of mud pits, winding tunnels, and mischievous vines, it was anything but an escape route. Not to mention it was the relocation zone for Wanderly's entire werewolf population. Containing werewolves might seem an arduous task, but not when the Chancellor enchanted them to remain in their beastly form so that they lacked any benefits of human problem-solving.

to Cricket that she wasn't breaking in but rather—

"Do you hear something?" Cricket said, pulling her knees more tightly to her chest.

With so many critters skittering around in the darkness, Birdie could hear lots of somethings. But Cricket was right. There was one something that stood out above the rest. One something that sounded *important*.

And it was.

Whoosh!

The Winds of Wanderly gusted up the side of Tragic Mountain.

Swish!

The Winds of Wanderly hopscotched along the dungeon's brick walls, swirling closer and closer to the iron-barred windows, thrumming with excitement, because of all the many nooks and corners and crevices of the manor, the dungeon and its open-air windows were the only places where the Winds could tumble and blow freely about. Where they could stir up the inch-thick layers of dust, and spin it like gold; where they could transform even a dungeon into a place of wonder.[19]

Alas, this proved entirely too much for Cricket. She gasped.

---

19. If this seems bewildering to you, let me assure you it was. Dungeons are not, even for the occasional moment, supposed to be full of wonder. Dungeons in a home for Tragicals are quadruply not supposed to be full of wonder. But you can't fix what you don't know about, and despite the grave seriousness with which Mistress Octavia viewed her job, she firmly drew the line at traipsing into dungeons.

She rolled up into a little ball so tight Birdie could scarcely tell where Cricket's head began and her feet ended.

Birdie cleared her throat. Here was something remarkable. A second chance to talk to Cricket! But what was she supposed to say? With a great deal of effort, she finally settled on the obvious.

"Um, it's the, uh, Winds of Wanderly," she said.

At which Cricket burst into a round of loud, wailing tears. "The Winds will destroy us! Our Tragic End has arrived! Oh, I didn't want to die today!"

Because of course that was the sort of thing Mistress Octavia planted in the Tragicals' heads. To be fair, the Winds of Wanderly didn't exactly make Mistress Octavia's job difficult. When the Winds rattled the children's dormitory windows as if they were dry bones and tap-danced upon the roof shingles, they hardly behaved like normal winds. And whenever something wasn't ordinary, the Tragicals couldn't help but think of *magic*. Magic come to get them. Magic come to hurt them. Just as they always feared.

In the midst of such distress, Mistress Octavia had never missed an opportunity to bend near and hiss, "The Winds of Wanderly want to have their way with you. Listen to them! If I didn't keep the doors and windows locked tight, they would tear you apart, limb from limb!" Mistress Octavia typically delighted in telling the Tragicals all about the nefarious citizens in Wanderly, eager to provide the children's Tragic Ends, but it was different with the Winds of Wanderly. With the Winds of Wanderly, Mistress Octavia almost sounded . . . worried. And so, on those nights when Birdie was feeling especially illogical, she liked to imagine the Winds of Wanderly weren't at all angry with the Tragicals, but with Mistress Octavia.

What if the Winds of Wanderly were on the Tragicals' side?

It was a delicious thought! An absurd thought! A thought that would have landed Birdie in a heap and a half of trouble. But nevertheless the sort of thought that was hard to let go of. And so, without at all intending to, Birdie had grown fond of the Winds. She had grown to look forward to their regular visits. And if anyone were to ask (which they never did), she would have staunchly defended this curious affection with the sole fact that of all the people in Wanderly who had forgotten the Tragicals, the Winds hadn't. When no one else bothered to visit them, the Winds did. And though it should seem a small matter, to simply be remembered felt nothing short of tremendous.

Birdie intended to explain as much to Cricket but was stopped by a sudden and annoying *buzzzzzzzzz*.

Birdie sighed. She wondered if she would ever get a decent go at a conversation with Cricket, but the situation grew altogether more incredible when Cricket popped her head up, opened her eyes two whole times bigger than their original circumferences, and began to jab her finger wildly at the air *behind* Birdie.

Uh-oh.

Birdie whirled around.

Her stomach flip-flopped.

Banging against the open iron-barred window of Birdie's cell was an egregiously hairy, excessively large, black hornet! A hornet with a stinger the size of Birdie's pinkie finger! The hornet's one redeeming quality was its plumpness, but alas, it was just determined enough to push, press, and slide its way through the bars of Birdie's window until it popped finally into her cell.

Birdie screamed.

Cricket whimpered.

The hornet *buzzzz*ed.

Thus began a chase so ridiculous that if Birdie's life hadn't been at stake, she might have found it quite funny. There are only so many places to run in an itty-bitty-size cell. The faster Birdie ran, the more she simply spun about in circles such that if she were to turn her head, the hornet always seemed to be *right there*.

Birdie was hardly used to such rigorous activity. Mistress Octavia preferred to keep the children in a weakened state, and Birdie simply hadn't the endurance to continue. Fortunately for her, the hornet seemed to be tiring as well. It took a break from chasing after Birdie and drew to a halt in front of her nose.

The hornet waited for Birdie's full attention and then wriggled its furry eyebrows at her. It defiantly placed a pair of arms (legs?) on its hips and blew a fine dusting of spittle that landed on Birdie's nose. Yuck! Birdie was certain it was the rudest hornet she would ever meet until she realized most hornets weren't known to have eyebrows, hips, or anything as sophisticated as manners.

And Birdie was more afraid than ever before. If the hornet wasn't an ordinary hornet, might it possibly have something to do with *magic*?

The short answer to that question was *yes*, but the hornet didn't leave Birdie much time to think about it. Instead, it revved up its wings to full throttle, sped to the top of the ceiling for a bit of momentum, and descended upon Birdie at full speed, stinger plunging straight through the fabric of her gown and into her heart.

The End.

Wasn't that awful?

That's precisely what would have happened in a normal Tragical story. In a normal Tragical story, the hornet's venom would have coursed relentlessly through Birdie's small body until her eyelids fluttered shut, and she breathed her last. Mistress Octavia would have thrown a party, the Chancellor would have bowed his head (however smugly), and the hearts of the Tragicals who still lived in the manor would shrink just a bit smaller, because the end really was as terrible as they had been taught.

But as I said, this isn't a normal Tragical story. And not a single one of those dreadful things happened to Birdie. To the contrary, the hornet exploded! Ha-ha!

Fortunately, the hornet did not explode in a terribly messy and unpleasant way, but into a neat little pile of ash not unlike the sort found in the bottom of one's fireplace. It didn't, however, stay that way for long—magic is nothing if not efficient. It lifted up, stirred up, and whipped itself into, of all things, a letter.

Birdie could scarcely believe it. For it is one thing to think one's Tragic End has arrived sooner than expected; it is quite another thing to contemplate that one has somehow, miraculously, avoided that end; but it is even another thing to confront one's end, escape it, *and* be offered a gift. No one ever gave the Tragicals anything. Especially not something as personal as a letter. This was hardly the fearsome result Birdie had always expected to result from magic.

Birdie brought the letter near. She cleared her throat and prepared to read it aloud when Cricket burst out, "Stop! Tragicals aren't allowed to receive letters!"

"But this isn't an ordinary letter. It—it flew in as a hornet. This letter . . ." Birdie paused. She took a deep breath. "This is a magical letter."

Cricket gasped. "Doesn't that make it a whole lot worse?"

Feeling the weight of such inconvenient things as Mistress Octavia's rules, Birdie thought back to that morning's inspection and Cricket's paper-exploding pockets. If Cricket were so afraid of rules, why did she risk breaking that one? What were those paper scraps *really* for? Was Cricket harboring a secret as wonderful as Birdie's book? Did they maybe have something in common?

Birdie leaned closer to Cricket. "Were you really keeping all that paper in your pockets to make a ball?"

"Those scraps were nothing like your letter," Cricket said with her cheeks flushed pink. "Hiding paper got me in trouble, but if you handle m-m-magic, you might get your Tragic End."

Birdie's heart thumped. "And you would care about that? About my Tragic End happening, I mean?"

The dungeon grew very, very quiet. Wasn't it true—hadn't it been written[20]—that no one could care for a Tragical? Wasn't such a proposition impossible?

"I dunno," Cricket whispered. And she looked utterly confused.

"Well," Birdie said, straightening up. "I don't think we need to worry about that anyways. If this letter wanted to do away with me, I'm pretty sure it would have done so while it was shaped like a giant hornet." And, without further ado, Birdie bent her head and read aloud:

---

20. Why, yes; yes it had. The Chancellor ensured there were oodles of books where this exact sentiment had been written down. And that was perhaps the Chancellor's greatest problem: as the leader of a storybook kingdom, he did not *really* understand books. He did not read books to find truth; he instead read them in an attempt to create it.

Hello! Have you finished The Book? NOW WHAT?

Ms. Crunch

Cricket frowned. "Is that it?" she asked.

Birdie gulped, because that *was* it if you were only reading the words. It wasn't it if you took into account the penmanship that was unmistakably stabby. Or the color of the ink that was a dead ringer for blood-red.

Cricket didn't wait for Birdie to answer. "Guess we should have seen it coming," she said, and sat back from the hole in the wall with her shoulders slumped.

Birdie blinked at her. "You thought someday a magical letter would arrive dressed up as a hornet?"

"No. Only that if it did, it would be an accident. There's no way that letter was meant for any of us. We don't read books. We hate books. Why would we ever want to talk about one?"

Yesterday that would have been entirely true, but that morning, Birdie had found a book she didn't hate. A book she had risked a great deal to protect. A book that seemed worthy of being referred to in capital letters as "The Book," simply because there was nothing else like it! What if whoever sent the letter had the same book as Birdie? What if, like her, they wanted to know about friendship? For truly, wasn't the timing astonishing and hadn't Birdie experienced the precise same reaction upon discovering the book, upon learning about friendship: "Now what?"

Perhaps the letter was the answer she was looking for. Perhaps whoever wrote the letter would become Birdie's friend.

But Cricket didn't know a single thing about Birdie's book or friendship. She wouldn't, unless Birdie found the courage to tell her. Birdie swallowed hard. She reached beneath the folds of her gown and pulled forth her book. It was warm from being held so close, and beneath her fingertips it felt as if the words were vibrating against the cover, as if the words themselves had wings and wanted to escape. To be set free.

Friendship, the book whispered.

Birdie didn't know if Cricket heard, but Cricket did bend down to peer once again through the hole in the wall. Her jaw gaped. "Why in the world would you be hiding *that*?" she asked.

"Because it's special," Birdie said. But her voice sounded very small. Books had always been her enemy. It was quite a difficult thing to overcome years and years and years of awfulness. And judging by the glazed look in Cricket's eyes, Birdie might as well have been talking in another language.

Cricket reached down and wrapped her fingers around the loose brick. She prepared to fit it back into the hole, upon which her conversation with Birdie would come to an end.

"Wait!" Birdie cried. "This book is about friendship—"

"What's friendship?" Cricket said, wrinkling her nose at the unfamiliar word.

"It's—it's—" But Birdie didn't really know yet. She hadn't finished the book, nor had she ever had a friend of her own.

Still, maybe there was something better than an explanation. Maybe she could show Cricket. Maybe Birdie didn't have to wait to find a friend before she could be one. Maybe she could start right now.

Birdie threw open the front cover of her book. She riffled across the pages until she came to the back. The place where the book was unfinished. With a determined tilt of her jaw, she placed her left hand along the spine of the book and grasped the corner of a blank page in her right hand. With a groundbreaking *riiiiip*, Birdie tore the page loose.

She froze and waited a moment with one eye shut to see if the ceiling might topple upon her head. But save for Cricket's horrified gasp, the spiders kept on spinning and the rats kept on scurrying. Birdie slipped toward Cricket's cell. She passed the paper through the hole and into Cricket's hands.

"Maybe this will help with your ball," Birdie said.

Cricket's hands trembled. "But what if it wasn't r-really for a ball?" she whispered. And then, before Birdie could answer, Cricket peeked in the direction of the book and added, "I've never seen a book so full of blank pages. What could be the use of such a thing?"

"Maybe some books are meant for more than just reading."

With a small and unpracticed smile, Cricket nodded. And though she still replaced the brick in the hole, she added, "Be careful with that letter"—almost like she meant it.

Birdie was certain it was a start, but she couldn't think on it too long, because for once, she had something to do. She had a magical letter to respond to. A magical letter delivered by none other than the Winds of Wanderly! Though Birdie would have preferred to know a bit more than just the sender's name (especially a name as, *ahem*, mysterious as Ms. Crunch), you and I both know it was much better that she didn't. For even a child as hopeful as Birdie mightn't have had the courage to write back to a wicked witch. In much the same way you may have a difficult time turning the page to see how Agnes reacts to such a shocking turn of events.

FOUR

THE WORST MAIL DAY

Agnes Prunella Crunch licked the last of the wriggling centipede legs off her knobby knuckles, then gulped from a jug of pumpkin juice and sat back in her spiderweb-encrusted rocking chair.

Two days had passed since her birthday, and for the most part, the morning had been acceptably rotten.

She had risen early and set off on her broomstick. She had managed to scare not one but *three* wide-eyed fairy godmothers on their way to Fatimah's Flight Academy (No Witches Allowed);[21] she had plundered a squirrel family's entire winter

---

21. Agnes found Fatimah's Flight Academy (No Witches Allowed) especially annoying. Everyone in Wanderly knew the hands-down best way to zip about Wanderly was by broomstick. It was simple; it was effective; for crying out loud, it was comfortable! But apparently, the broomstick had become so closely associated with witches that no one else wanted to touch one with a ten-foot pole.

cache of nuts; and she had happened upon a fallen tree log full of fungus and creepy-crawlies, which was the source of her scrumptious breakfast.

But there was also the matter of The Invitation.

The Invitation had crept beneath the door in the dead of night. It had tiptoed across the room and tapped Agnes on the shoulder. And when Agnes bolted upright, she had thought for certain it was a response to the letter that had been swept away by the Winds of Wanderly on her birthday.

But Agnes knew otherwise when seventy-six familiar witch cackles tumbled out and chased her all around the cabin, shouting insults and making raspberry noises. It had taken Agnes a full five minutes of whacking and shooing with the fiery tip of her broomstick before the blasted things got bored and skipped out through a crack in the window. The Invitation smelled as awful as it ever had—a combination of dirty socks and fish bones—but even that wasn't enough to make Agnes want to open it because she already knew what was inside.

She had, after all, received—and destroyed—the same exact invitation for the past thirty-odd years.

Agnes drummed her fingers against her squishy belly. She creaked back and forth in her rocking chair. As she suspected, the stony morning light hadn't done a single thing to improve The Invitation. It was as aggravating as ever. Still, she begrudgingly read aloud:

COME ONE, COME ALL TO THE ANNUAL WITCHES' BALL!

Have a plumb rotten time humiliating
your foes and enemies!
Lick your grimy fingers over a full buffet of scorpion
tails, tossed poison ivy, and fried daddy longlegs!
Make everyone sniff your witchy boots when you take
top prize in the Witches' Challenge!
The curses begin October 4 at
You Know Where.[22]

EVERYONE MUST PARTICIPATE OR ELSE!*
(*NOTE: This is NOT a Trick. This is NOT a
Forgery. This Invitation has simply been spell-checked
by the Council. Otherwise, it is an entirely authentic
witchy document.)

Spell-checked? Bah! Though properly spelled words were usually appreciated by Agnes, the Chancellor and his Council's increased meddling were not. Since when did they peruse witchy documents?

---

22. It is quite possible that, living where you live, you haven't heard of "You Know Where." Typically, when people title things in such a manner, it is because they are too awful to even speak of. But what else would one expect from a witchy hangout? Especially when that hangout is Wanderly's gloomiest, moodiest, shiver-inducingest castle? If you are still curious, however, I shall whisper the name very, very quietly: *Castle Matilda.*

One by one, Agnes cracked her knuckles. She despised social gatherings. In her opinion, such activities as synchronized cackling, glaring contests, and spending an entire night racking one's brain for the perfect insult was, in short, a bunch of hooey.

She also loathed when someone told her she *had* to do something. Truly, it was almost as if she had a reflex that made her do the opposite. This extended as far back as her mother's reasonable command of "Agnes, put some pants on, for goblin's sake!" when a four-year-old Agnes eschewed pants for an entire chilly month, up until a mere week ago, when Agnes saw a sign posted in the Dead Tree Forest that said (in an uppity tone, no doubt): "Stay ON the Path for the Protection of the Budding Botanical Life. There Will Be Consequences." "Consequences"? For *Agnes*? Ha-ha! She had rescheduled her entire afternoon solely for the purpose of trouncing all about the foliage. As predicted, she had suffered not even a tongue-lashing or finger-wagging, though there had been an abundance of pollen that had taken residence atop her clothes, and in her scraggly purple hair, and left her sneezing for days.

So, Agnes had never gone to the Witches' Ball before. She had never wanted to go to the Witches' Ball before. But the niggling question that had been bothering Agnes worked its way up from her small, stony heart and into her thoughts for the umpteenth time. The question that, no matter how much pumpkin juice Agnes tossed back, she could not seem to be rid of: *Why isn't being a witch* fun *anymore?*

She had even grown so desperate as to contemplate flipping back to the beginning of *The Book of Evil Deeds* and starting the useless set of spells all over again, just to have something to pass the time, *but she couldn't*. She'd become so sickened at the sight of the book she'd torn it apart from cover to cover, whipped the shredded paper into a bit of a snow flurry for kicks, and then smoked the whole thing in her cauldron.[23] Of course, she could have requested a new copy, but Agnes couldn't stomach asking the Council for a chicken bone, much less a book.

Agnes sighed. Maybe it was time to stop being such a hermit. Maybe it was time to do what those other obnoxious witches did. Maybe she wasn't at all bored of being a witch, but merely bored of being an underappreciated witch. Maybe she needed to win a *prize*.

Agnes glanced back at The Invitation in her lap. She zeroed in on the one line, and the one line alone that mattered: *Make everyone sniff your witchy boots when you take top prize in the Witches' Challenge,* she read.

She scratched at the bugs nestled in her purple hair. She pursed her cracked, raisin-dry lips. She contemplated her most evil and most impressive curses to date: turning frogs into the flies they loved to snack on, turning a maiden's lovely voice into a croaking horror, temporarily tingeing the sky a shade

---

23. Gah, this gets me every time! I simply can't bear to look! Sometimes it is a very dangerous thing to be a book. Please let me know when the scary part is over.

of phlegm green—Oh, those were all *fine*, but even without having once gone to the ball, Agnes knew fine wouldn't win a top prize.

I need something outrageous, Agnes thought. *Something no one would ever expect!*

Boom! Crack! Pop! Fizzle, fizzle!

Agnes bristled.

She whirled around in the direction of her cauldron bubbling over the hearth. Something was amiss! Though she'd enchanted her cauldron to toss out periodic blasts of thunder and lightning, this was different.

Agnes crept closer. She lifted her arms high in the air and flexed her long, bony fingers. Whatever wild and woolly beast that dared to pop out would certainly meet its doom in the clutches of Agnes Prunella Crunch!

Agnes hadn't a clue, however, what to do when the fluffy lemon meringue cupcake with the rainbow sprinkles floated down the chimney and hop-skipped merrily along the lip of her cauldron. Agnes's jaw gaped. The cupcake hadn't any teeth; it hadn't any claws; it smelled ludicrously sweet! What was it doing in *her* cabin?

Certain the cupcake had taken a disastrously wrong turn and was instead destined for some place annoying like a fairy godmother soiree, Agnes bared her crooked teeth and waited for it to flee in distress.

But it didn't.

In fact, the cupcake drew to a halt in front of Agnes's humongous nose, skirted around her, and continued to parade about her haunted cabin in a way that caused the jars full of witchy things to recoil, hide, and possibly even cower because they had never seen such a thing.

Agnes's eyes narrowed. No floating cupcake was going to brighten her horrid surroundings! She raised her hands and let loose a real satisfying zap that should have sent the cupcake whirring back up the chimney where it came from, thank you very much.

Instead, the cupcake shivered, shook, and in one obnoxiously glittery burst, transformed into a sheet of paper, which came to rest on the toe of Agnes's witchy boot. Agnes looked down. Agnes blinked. The paper had writing on it.

Someone had responded to her letter.

Agnes bent her creaking bones and plucked the letter up by its top right corner. She dangled the paper in the air, twisting it this way and that, examining it ever so carefully. Despite the letter's most peculiar entrance as a cupcake, Agnes couldn't detect a single curse, hex, or booby trap.

She flipped it forward, backward; she shook it all about!

But it was no use. The letter couldn't have come from a supremely crotchety old witch.

The letter was utterly devoid of magic.

Agnes's shoulders slumped. Maybe even a plan as clever as writing to a witch wasn't enough to get around the no-talking rule set forth in the Witches' Manifesto.

That didn't, of course, answer the question of who *had* responded to her letter, but if they didn't have a drop of magic, then frankly Agnes couldn't give a hoot.

"Bah!" Agnes exclaimed. "What a wicked waste of time this letter-writing business has been!"

She wrapped her craggy fingers around the letter. She was preparing for the deliciously satisfying *riiiiiip* that would mean good riddance, when she noticed the letter writer's penmanship. It was . . . round and chubby. Every *i* was neatly dotted, and not a single *t* was without its crossbar. And . . . there was something else too. The barest whiff of a scent that was vaguely familiar; a scent that smelled almost, unmistakably like—

Agnes yowled and drop-kicked the letter.

It catapulted off the toe of her witchy boot and up toward the ceiling. It bodysurfed through the frothy layer of cobwebs and spun wildly down toward Agnes's prized porcupine footstool. Instead of being pierced through, the letter sprang up in the direction of Agnes's popping cauldron. Certain her cauldron would finish off the job, Agnes licked her lips in anticipation, but her cauldron chickened out at the last second and belched up a smelly gust that sent the letter spinning right back to Agnes!

"Aiiiiiiii!" she shrieked.

The letter skidded to a halt. It laid itself, once again, on the toe of her witchy boot. Agnes eyeballed the letter that smelled suspiciously of *child*. Witches were experts at sniffing out children. It was the sole reason their noses were so large and horrid. But it wasn't for the purpose you might expect. Witches did not typically track children for the intent of wickedry, but instead, to keep a safe distance. Children always made a mess of everything. And the meddling little buggers usually traveled in groups, which meant incrementally more trouble.

Agnes ignored the annoying little twitch of her lip that sprang up once every twenty-two years or so when she felt a bit anxious. She supposed the letter would not go away of its own accord. She supposed it was best to roll up her sleeves and get it over with.

Agnes held the letter as far away from her face as her arm could stretch. She read:

Dear Ms. Crunch,

    Hello to you too! I sure hope you weren't waiting long to hear that, but I've never dealt with magical letters before or tried to send anything via the Winds of Wanderly. I'm not sure if delivery is an instant sort of thing or if it takes a few days.

    I also think I should be up-front about something. It's possible I received your letter by mistake. I say this for two reasons: (1) Not only is yours the first magical letter I've ever received, it's also the first letter I've ever received (magic and letters are both forbidden where I live), and (2) your letter was all about a book, and for a kid like me, that's sort of the last thing we like to talk about.

So, in order to clear up any confusion, here goes: My name's Birdie Bloom. I'm about ten years old. And I'm a Tragical.

Please don't let that last part scare you away. Most folks like to pretend Tragicals don't even exist, but I have to tell you—even though your letter buzzed into the dungeon like a deadly hornet and chased me around for a spell, it's now tied for first place as the BEST thing that's ever happened to me.

If you're wondering what you're tied with, funny enough, it's something I discovered on the same day I got your letter! That's for sure got to go down in the record books, considering some Tragicals never experience one good thing in their whole lives. Anyways, the other thing I'm referring to is a book.

I know. It doesn't make sense. I mentioned a moment ago how Tragicals hate books. But this book is different. I'm even wondering if it's the same book you referred to in your letter. If it is, I've got a question for you: How could I have finished the book if it's got no end?

Anyways, I'm dying of curiosity now. I can't help wondering if maybe your copy has more writing in it, or if, like me, you're wondering if it's not just a good book, but a true book? I didn't have a clue how I could find out such an answer on my own, but maybe we can find out together?

Of course, if you wrote to me by accident, it's more likely than not you'll want to forget any of this even happened. And I would understand. But if you do decide to write back, make sure to keep sending your letters by the Winds of Wanderly. If Mistress Octavia catches even a whiff of what I'm doing, she'll shred your letter up into itty-bitty pieces, and I'd feel just awful if you were waiting on a response from me.

No matter what, thanks for this. Receiving your magical letter is enough thrill to last me a whole lifetime. I know my lifetime's going to be shorter than most, but I think that's still saying something.

Yours truly,
Birdie Bloom

Agnes Prunella Crunch brought the letter closer.

She scratched her head.

She tapped the toe of her witchy boot.

Her first letter of the early morning, The Invitation, leaped suddenly off her rocking chair and smacked against her cheek. Agnes scowled and snatched it up. She held both letters out in front of her, one in each crooked hand. She couldn't decide which was worse.

But neither could she deny an idea was starting to brew.

A deliciously wicked idea, because she was, after all, a witch.

FIVE

When It Rains, It Pours

It was a typical Tuesday morning at Foulweather's Home for the Tragical.

Birdie and the other Tragicals had woken to the sound of Sir Ichabod shuffling in between their beds while shaking a knapsackful of rattlesnake tails in their ears. Shortly after, he had conducted a raffle to see whether it would be a morning upon which the Tragicals received breakfast. (It was not.) And just then, with stomachs grumbling, the children were nearly through with their daily trudging practice.

Trudging was serious business.

The Tragicals had to achieve the right slump. Their knees had to be bent just so. It is harder work than one might think to look wholly miserable (especially for the fifteen-minute duration Mistress Octavia demanded). It was, however, a wee bit easier today considering Mistress Octavia had roused them at two o'clock in the morning for one of her infamous Villain Drills, and several of them remained half asleep.

Villain Drills were not for the purpose of avoiding danger, but rather for the purpose of flocking to it. It takes a great deal of training to run headfirst toward one's doom instead of dodging it at all costs, and Mistress Octavia was convinced the sleepier the Tragicals were, the easier it would be to produce a response that was nearly automatic. It remained to be seen whether Sir Ichabod Grim agreed with her, as he too was a reluctant participant in the spectacle—being dragged out from his nook in the kitchen pantry and dressed up as anything from a scavenging pirate to a meddlesome magician.

In sharp contrast to the other Tragicals trudging beside her, Birdie was not at all tired. She couldn't be. After days, weeks, months, and years of everything in the manor being the absolute same, for once, things were different. She had a book. She had received a letter (a magical one!). To cap it all off, the other night while she was brushing her teeth, Cricket had brushed lightly against her and whispered, "Anything?"

To be sure, the word "anything" could pertain to, well, *anything*, but Birdie was certain Cricket was referring to whether Birdie had received a response to her letter. And it almost didn't matter that she hadn't, because the very thought—the very idea—that Cricket was hoping the same thing as Birdie, that they were doing something *together*, warmed her from her head to her toes.

This was the thought Birdie held near as the Tragicals trudged into the Instruction Room. While her classmates looked hopelessly at the walls painted in shades of black, blacker, and blackest, Birdie snuck a glance in Cricket's direction. While her classmates' gazes flickered briefly toward the drapery-clad windows they'd never once seen out of, Birdie even attempted to smile at Francesca Prickleboo (never mind Francesca's returning glare). While her classmates filled the space that was woefully empty, save for the collection of lonely little desks, Birdie instead counted the Tragicals themselves. There were seventeen of them (eighteen, including herself). Seventeen . . . Had there always been so many? Could there really be seventeen chances for finding a friend? Surely even a Tragical couldn't thwart those odds.

Of course, Mistress Octavia always managed to put a damper on everything.

She stood poised at the front of the classroom with her arms crossed and her fingertips drumming against her pointy elbows. She tapped the toe of her black, high-heeled boot against the stone floor; she tilted her head and—

Birdie leaned forward in her chair.

She squinted, trying to get a better look at Mistress Octavia's hair. She shook her head as if her eyes were a bit out of focus. But they weren't. She could see quite clearly. And the undeniable conclusion presented itself: Mistress Octavia's hair was *not* perfect.

For most every other individual in the world, a rumpled hairstyle was expected every now and again (thank goodness). But Mistress Octavia was obsessively tidy about her hair. She always wore it slick and smoothed back. Never once had a single hair toed the line of being arguably "out of place" (even when it had been covered with blueberry mush). And so, to see not just one but—Birdie counted them—1, 2, 3, 4, 5, 6, 7, 8, 9 unruly hairs was no small thing. It was its own miniature rebellion.

But why?

And then, Birdie noticed the air. The air in the manor was unusually heavy. It was almost even a bit damp. It was the sort of condition that caused even the slickest of hair to curl up and frizz. The sort of condition that, if Birdie recalled correctly from the book titled *Natural Disasters Never to Avoid*, was the precursor to a possibly severe *rainstorm*.

Birdie flipped about in her seat. Had any of the other children noticed? Were any of the others as mystified as Birdie by Mistress Octavia's hair and the inclement weather? But, as usual, her fellow classmates' expressions remained frustratingly blank. If they noticed, they didn't let on. They merely looked to be settling in for another long, mindless day of Oaths practice.

Mistress Octavia prowled up and down the classroom as if

she spent her evenings mimicking her ravenous wolf pack.[24] She looked each of the children hard in the face. Then she whipped her broken broomstick handle out from behind her back and whacked it against Cricket's desk without any warning at all.

The children jumped.

The Tragicals always reacted in such a way when Mistress Octavia brought forth her broken broomstick handle, because why couldn't she get a proper sort of pointer? Something that wasn't laden with splinters and snapped in a manner crudely enough to hint at a Stage 3 temper tantrum?[25] Not to mention, in Wanderly, only witches and housekeepers dealt with broomsticks. The Tragicals were terrified enough by the witches they routinely encountered in storybooks, and they needn't one additional reminder that likely half of them would meet their Tragic Ends at the hands of one.

Mistress Octavia jabbed her broken broomstick handle toward the blackboard, where she had written: "When faced with a fatal threat, I will not fight back or retreat under any circumstances." Directly below that, in large, glaring letters, was written: "DRAGON."

---

24. Mistress Octavia did indeed keep an entire wolf pack at her disposal. They prowled off-leash on the patchy grass surrounding the manor. They didn't know a single command, but they snarled and howled loud enough to properly terrify the children, and that was enough for her.

25. If temper tantrums were measured not by degrees but by age, a Stage 3 (the sort that explodes from a three-year-old) would likely be the worst.

"By now, I assume each of you has memorized the content of Tragical Oath Number Five. Indeed, for some of you, your sixteenth birthday looms just around the corner, and you will at last have the chance to commit your name to this very important document and pledge your allegiance to the good of Wanderly."

Birdie's stomach turned. Her stomach always turned when Mistress Octavia mentioned signing the Tragical Oaths, which she did as often as she could. The Tragical Oaths were, after all, the whole point of Foulweather's Home for the Tragical. The Tragical Oaths were comprised of ten requirements that made a Tragical a Tragical. The Chancellor insisted it wasn't merely enough to treat the Tragicals as such; they had to accept their roles (and thereby, their certain doom) by voluntarily signing their name to them. The payoff, however, was big. Every child who chose to sign the Tragical Oaths was released from Foulweather's Home for the Tragical.

As in they were set *free*.

At least that was what the Tragicals assumed. But for every Tragical who signed the Oaths, not one had ever returned to the manor. Not one had ever written a letter. Not one had ever been heard from again.

Mistress Octavia's broomstick slipped below Tragical Oath Number Five to point at the word "DRAGON." She licked her lips. Her eyes gleamed.

"During last night's Villain Drill, only three of you were pathetic enough to try to hide beneath your beds. But tell me, would the result have been the same if you found yourself face-to-face with something as terrible as a dragon? How will you compel yourself not to run away as Tragical Oath Number Five demands?"

In response to Mistress Octavia's question, one hand was raised high. It rippled proudly through the air like a parade flag. It belonged, of course, to Francesca Prickleboo. She waited on the edge of her seat with her lips pursed and her eyes glued to Mistress Octavia. But Mistress Octavia hardly looked interested. Her gray eyes continued to scan the room. And when another hand rose in the back of the classroom, she hastily shouted, "You!"

It happened to be the boy Ralph.

Birdie snapped to attention. The other children straightened up a bit too. Despite the Tragicals' painful habit of ignoring one another, Ralph was in a slightly different category. Ralph was the only child in the whole manor who had a single memory of life in the Beyond.[26] While all the other Tragicals arrived at the manor before the age of three, Ralph was deposited (kicking and screaming, no less) at the age of *seven*. Of course, no one knew what any of Ralph's memories were because the children

---

26. The Beyond was precisely as vast as it sounded. The Tragicals used the term to refer to anything outside the locked doors of Foulweather's Home for the Tragical. Though they had a full panoply of books, with quite extensive descriptions of Wanderly, at their disposal, I admit there are some things even a book cannot give full justice to; some things that simply must be experienced firsthand.

never talked to one another. Birdie determined, however, that his memories must have been rooted in something halfway good. Otherwise, he wouldn't have kept trying to escape from Foulweather's Home for the Tragical.

Ralph met Mistress Octavia's stare. "I wouldn't run away because I wouldn't be afraid."

The other Tragicals gasped.

Mistress Octavia's nostrils flared. "Not afraid? Not afraid of a *dragon*? Have you listened to a single word I've read during story time? Do you know what dragons do to young, scrumptious boys like yourself?"

Ralph swallowed. He stuffed his hands—which were shaking a bit—beneath his desk. "I guess there's two ways to look at it. First, if I'm taking my duty as a Tragical seriously, I ought to be glad to stumble across a dragon." At the word "glad," Mistress Octavia's jaw dropped. Ralph continued on, "Surely getting gobbled up by something as fantastic as a dragon is worth at least ten or twelve bad endings when compared to something boring like falling into a pit of quicksand. If I free up extra good endings for the Triumphants, they might even have to call me a super Tragical."

"A *Super* Tragical?" Francesca burst out, looking wildly around the room while fanning herself with her hand. Surely in all her years of striving, she had never imagined there could exist something so wonderfully self-explanatory as a Super Tragical!

The rest of the children began to twitter and stir.

They began to think.

Ralph *may* have nearly smiled.

And that's when the first roll of thunder occurred.

BOOM-BOOM-BA-BA-BOOM!

Thunder so loud, it sounded as if it was coming from inside the manor.

But that was impossible, wasn't it?

"Silence!" Mistress Octavia hissed. She fixed her eyes on Ralph. "There is no such thing as a Super Tragical. There is nothing super about Tragicals, and certainly nothing super about a single one of you. You are all nothing! It is the very reason why you were sent here, the very reason why no one comes for you, and the very reason why no one will care when you meet your Tragic Ends."

When Mistress Octavia was finished huffing, to Birdie's astonishment, Ralph's hand rose up again.

"What? What could you possibly have to say?" Mistress Octavia shrieked.

"I didn't, um, get to share the second reason why I wouldn't be afraid of the dragon. You see, you never said what color the dragon was—"

"What difference does something like color make? Isn't it enough to know that all dragons have row upon row of shining teeth?"

"Well, if it happened to be blue, that might make all the difference in the world. Because there's one dragon in Wanderly that they say has the power to—"

"ENOUGH!" Mistress Octavia brought her broomstick handle down against Ralph's desk with an explosive crack. But even that was nothing compared to the second round of thunder that was so deafening it hands-down *had* to come from within the manor and was—gulp—getting closer.

BOOM-BOBBITY-BIBBITY-BOOM-BA-BOOM-BOOM!!!!!

The Tragicals screamed. A few grabbed their chalk slates and held them in front of their chests like shields. The two youngest simply froze in their seats, threw their heads toward the sky, and wailed. Even the gangly teenagers (all three of them) folded up like pretzels and slid beneath their desks.

But Birdie stared at Ralph. She stared at the boy whose eyes were lit up from within because surely he *knew* things. Things he might be willing to share. Not that Birdie was interested in dragons—whatever color they happened to be—but in something she couldn't stop thinking about: friendship. Maybe Ralph could teach her what friendship looked like in the Beyond! Maybe he could teach her how to be a friend.

Birdie's thoughts were interrupted by Mistress Octavia's shrill cry of "SIR ICH-A-BOD! SIR ICH-A-BOD!"

As usual, Sir Ichabod arrived quickly. He slipped into the Instruction Room and shut the door softly behind him. His messy hair fell like a curtain across his eyes, and beneath the frayed hem of his sleeve cuffs, his hands trembled.

"Yes, my lady?" he whispered.

"Stop making such an obnoxious racket! It's completely disruptive!"

"That w-wasn't me, my lady." Sir Ichabod paused. He looked around. He looked around as if he expected something to sneak up behind him. "That was the thunder. C-come from inside."

Mistress Octavia's eyes narrowed. "That doesn't make any sense, you ridiculous fool! Now admit that racket was nothing more than you banging about your pots and pans, and be sure it doesn't happen again!"

"I . . . Well, okay . . ."

But Sir Ichabod was unable to finish because someone knocked upon the Instruction Room door.

Everyone, even Mistress Octavia, froze.

"Ichabod." Mistress Octavia's voice was a whisper. "Whom have you admitted to the manor today?"

Sir Ichabod stared blankly. For truly, who was ever admitted to the manor? Even though Mistress Octavia extended invitation after invitation after invitation to the Chancellor, he never bothered to show up.

Mistress Octavia waved her hand in the air. "Are all the children accounted for?"

Sir Ichabod counted the children because Mistress Octavia could never keep track of how many Tragicals were under her care. "All here," Sir Ichabod whispered.

Raising her voice a tinge higher, Mistress Octavia demanded, "Then who could possibly be knocking upon the door?"

A second and more insistent knock erupted. As if jolted suddenly awake, Sir Ichabod threw his skinny arms across the doorframe. He squeaked to the Tragicals, "Hide! You must all hide!"

Mistress Octavia, however, wasn't about to do any such thing. She charged toward the door. She raised her broken broomstick handle high over her head, ready to dish out a hefty wallop. But once she was within a few feet, the door bulged, and Sir Ichabod catapulted off the frame! He knocked a stunned Mistress Octavia flat against the ground, whereupon her arms and legs kicked wildly beneath him like a trapped roly-poly.

The door swung wide open.

The Tragicals waited in agony for the revealing of a horrid monster bearing two heads or maybe even eighteen arms—one to grasp each of them—because what could be more tragical than all their lives ending at once?

But the visitor did not have a head.

Or arms.

Or even legs.

Instead, puffing into the classroom like a steaming locomotive came a chain of black storm clouds. A chain that snaked around the room until every last inch of the ceiling was covered. The clouds sucked up their girth the way a child prepares to blow out candles on a birthday cake. In perfect unison, the clouds burst open and released a streaking, pouring, pounding torrent of rain.

Everything was drenched. Everything was flooded!

The Tragicals sat in stunned silence because none of them, except perhaps for Ralph, had ever witnessed water streaking down from up above. And certainly rain outside beneath a wide-open sky would have been glorious enough, but rain inside the manor—rain that had managed to come and find them—well, that was even grander!

Still terrifying, of course. But also grand.

In all her worrying over what magic might one day do to the Tragicals, Birdie had never imagined it would arrive in the form of letters and rainstorms. Things that made her knees buckle, but things that were also, maybe, *good*.

Was such a thing possible with magic?

A few of the bravest children rolled up the sleeves of their gowns and tentatively stuck their hands out from beneath their desks. They gasped as the water splish-splashed off their skin. Though the rest of the Tragicals stayed curled up into tiny balls, they kept their eyes held wide open. For once, they were watching one another, noticing one another, experiencing something *together*.

Birdie would have liked to watch too, but she hadn't forgotten her revelation about Ralph. With a shrieking Mistress Octavia temporarily trapped beneath Sir Ichabod, it was the best chance she was going to get.

Birdie lay low, on her hands and knees. She crawled in between the legs of the desks and sloshed through the rising water. She happened upon Ralph while he was chewing on a hangnail and looking sort of bored, like he'd not only seen rain plenty of times before, but magic, too.

Birdie's heart pounded. If Ralph was that familiar with something as impressive as magic, surely he'd know plenty about friendship.

"Hello!" Birdie said, a bit out of breath.

Ralph stared at her. He even scooted a bit farther away.

Which was a tiny bit awkward, but Birdie figured it was best to get on with it. Mistress Octavia wasn't the sort to stay trapped for long, and she would be all too eager to punish Birdie's attempt at conversation. "So, you seen this kind of weather before?" Birdie continued.

Ralph blinked. Birdie told herself that was better. Definitely better than a blank stare. She cleared her throat. She dove in. "You, uh, have a friend before, too?"

Friend.

The word was so big. It almost felt too big for Birdie to say aloud, but at the same time, it seemed the sort of word that should be said and said often. True words are like that.

But Ralph narrowed his eyes. He looked toward where Mistress Octavia had finally succeeded in shoving Sir Ichabod to the side and was engaged in a great cacophony of irate splashing at Sir Ichabod's expense. Birdie wished Ralph would hurry up already. They didn't have much time!

"Why do you want to know?" he finally said.

"Because I'd like one."

"Oh, well, that's great, then," he said with a shrug.

"But I don't know what one is exactly." Birdie paused and leaned forward. "I thought you might be able to help."

"You want *me* to be your friend?"

Birdie froze. Because she didn't want that. Or at least she didn't think she wanted that. Did she? Ralph got into trouble a lot. He came up with wild ideas like, well, being a "Super Tragical." He was a messy eater; he sometimes made a strange whistling sound when he did chores; and he was a—a—a boy. Birdie didn't know all the rules yet! Could girls even be friends with boys?

But in the end, none of that mattered.

Mistress Octavia had moved on from Sir Ichabod. Mistress Octavia had moved on in a big, bad way. Her skirts were hiked up over her knees, and her skinny ankles quivered as she pounded down the aisle of the Instruction Room, spraying water every which way. She took a flying leap and landed atop poor Cricket's desk. She stretched her broken broomstick handle up toward the ceiling and began to jab a rain cloud in the belly!

Pop! Pop! Pop!

The rain cloud under attack shuddered. It began to shrink. And quickly! In less than seconds it whittled down to the size of a bouncy ball before falling—*splat!*—against the ground as nothing more than a single raindrop.

With renewed vigor, Mistress Octavia seized upon the next rain cloud and began to jab harder. She was going to destroy them all!

Francesca Prickleboo rose up so suddenly, her chair clattered behind her. Birdie drew in a sharp breath, and even Ralph straightened up with interest, as Francesca waded away from the protection of the desks and into the dead center of the room where the rain pounded the hardest. She winced as the drops pelted her cheeks, but when she spoke, her voice was loud and clear, "I AM FRANCESCA PRICKLEBOO. I AM A TRAGICAL. AND TODAY I WILL MEET MY TRAGIC END AT THE HAND OF A MAGICAL STORM CLOUD." And she closed her eyes and threw her head back in a gesture of total surrender.

Mistress Octavia stomped her foot on Cricket's desk. "Shut up, you wretch!" she said. "No one's going to meet their Tragic End by a little spit of water. And if you dare mention that awful, horrible, forbidden word in my presence again, it will be to the dungeon for you!"

Francesca's face paled to a ghastly shade of white. A drop of rain splashed off the tip of her nose. In all of Francesca's years, never once had Mistress Octavia threatened her with the dungeon. "Is it— Do you mean— Is it the M-word?" she asked in a frantic, high-pitched squeak.

"ARGH!" Mistress Octavia shrieked.

And just at the moment Birdie was about to feel sorry for

Francesca, just at the moment Francesca's lower lip began to tremble, Francesca must have remembered who she was: a world-class tattletale. Without missing a beat, Francesca whirled around and shook her finger in Birdie and Ralph's direction. "Those two were talking! Those two right over there were talking a ton! And she even asked him to be her fiend!"

"Fiend"?

Oh dear. This is precisely why I encourage readers such as yourself to always keep a dictionary handy. But on the off chance that you find yourself without one, let us just say that a *fiend* is the exact opposite of a *friend* (and then some). Maybe now you'll believe your teachers when they say spelling is important. Nevertheless, Francesca's error may have worked out to Birdie's benefit. It makes me shudder to imagine the punishment Mistress Octavia might have dished out had she suspected Birdie of something as non-Tragical as friendship.

It was still quite bad though.

Mistress Octavia slithered off Cricket's desk. She *plip-plopp*ed over to where Birdie was huddled beside Ralph, and she wrenched Birdie out from beneath the desk by the tip of her ear.

"Stay safe," Ralph whispered. It came out sharp and fast. Almost as if it were nothing more than a deep breath, but it wasn't, was it? He had said it, hadn't he?

Two words.

Two syllables.

Something, however small, for Birdie to hold on to.

Of course, with Mistress Octavia's fingernails pricking into her shoulder, Birdie certainly didn't feel safe. Nor did she feel safe when Mistress Octavia tossed her in the direction of a sopping wet Sir Ichabod and commanded, "Take her to the dungeon! This time put Chewy into her cell. He's been cooped up for days and is simply *dying* for a bit of playtime."

And so, for the second time in one week, Birdie was headed down to the dungeon. Only this time she wouldn't have the company of Cricket. This time she would have something much, much worse. Because Chewy was Mistress Octavia's venomous pet scorpion.

(I told you it was bad.)

SIX

SOMETHING TO CHEW ON

Despite the uneasy peace Birdie had made with the dungeon on visits past, dungeons get a whole lot more dungeon-y when a scorpion is tossed into the mix. Birdie had tried every which way to get out of Mistress Octavia's punishment. She had wrapped her fingers around the dungeon's rickety banister; she had tried to plop down onto the middle of the dungeon floor; she had even tried to reason with Sir Ichabod Grim, but nothing worked.

Birdie blamed at least part of that on the dungeon door. Because when Sir Ichabod had reached into his pocket for the keys, his hand had instead fallen slack against his side. There was no need to unlock a door when it was already cracked open. And perhaps because Sir Ichabod was nothing if not methodical, perhaps because he conducted his daily duties like an automated machine, he had stood and stared at the door for a full thirty seconds. Had he ever once forgotten to lock the dungeon before?

Birdie might have given the peculiar matter a bit more thought had she not found herself in the throes of such a dire predicament. For one, despite Birdie's desperate protests, Sir Ichabod had mindlessly nudged Mistress Octavia's scorpion, Chewy, into her cell with the toe of his shoe and crept back up the four winding flights of stairs a whole five minutes ago. Two, her black gown was sopping wet, and every time she moved, water squeezed out from the fabric, creating a series of unfortunate puddles. That was nothing, however, compared to the chill. Indeed, her teeth were chattering so badly her whole head was beginning to ache.

Birdie shivered in the center of the itty-bitty cell, so Chewy couldn't conduct a sneak attack by creeping along the walls and springing toward her. She fixed her eyes on the corner where Chewy sat and glowered. Of course, it also happened to be the exact corner where Birdie had lifted the stone in the floor and gently slid her storybook beneath the day she and Cricket were in the dungeon together. Birdie hadn't wanted to leave her storybook behind. She wanted to keep it close to her. She wanted to pull it out at any spare, private moment and dive into the pages so that she could learn more about *friendship*.

But she also knew bringing her book anywhere near Mistress Octavia was a risk. So she had left it in the one location Mistress Octavia never set a pinkie toe in. And now. . . now that she was *so close*, that location was being guarded by a cantankerous scorpion.

"Figures," Birdie said. And she slumped down onto the floor and crossed her legs beneath her, because it had been quite a morning.

Chewy flexed his shiny head in her direction. Whether due merely to Birdie's motion or the fact that sitting on the ground made her seem more appropriately sized, the formerly comatose scorpion began to shimmy in place. He flexed the long stinger on his tail back and forth, back and forth. And then, much to Birdie's horror, he leaped spectacularly away from the corner and skittered in Birdie's direction atop his eight jointed legs.

Birdie dashed to her feet. She pounded them against the floor with reckless abandon, hoping the flurry of movement would frighten him. It didn't. And Chewy was surprisingly fast. He dodged in and out from between Birdie's feet without breaking a sweat. He pressed his legs into the floor and sprang up.

Chewy landed on Birdie's calf, and in less than a quarter-second, skimmed over her kneecap! She could feel each and every one of Chewy's legs wriggling along her skin. And his giant pincers—Oh, Birdie hadn't paid much attention to those before. But they were big. And sharp. And he opened and closed them as if warming them up!

Birdie trembled with fear. Tears streamed down her cheeks.

She remembered Ralph's words. *Stay safe,* he had said.

But how? How does a Tragical ever stay safe?

Chewy continued to charge over the folds of Birdie's gown. He skipped across the banging drum of her heart without flinching and gazed at her with his shiny, hateful eyes. Once he scaled up Birdie's shoulder, he pressed his stinger deep into the grooves on his back and aimed for the tender, fleshy part of her neck.

Birdie let out a great, heaving sob. She didn't know what to do! She had never read any storybooks about scorpions! She had never read any storybooks where children like her tried to survive anything! Should she fling Chewy away? Should she bop him on the head or poke him in the eyes? Did she have time to do anything at all?

CAW, CAW, CAW!

A shrill cackle tumbled into the dungeon.

Birdie and Chewy looked toward the iron-barred window.

A peculiar gray crow—its wings pumping furiously—hurtled toward them at an impossible speed. Birdie was certain the bird was going to crash headfirst. At the last moment, however, it tucked in its wings, flattened its body, and shot *between* the bars of the window like a silver bullet. A bullet aimed straight at Birdie's shoulder. Birdie watched in awe as the crow's open beak clamped around Chewy and slurped him up whole, as if he were no less formidable than a wriggling little worm.

Birdie was saved!

Today was not the day her Tragic End had arrived. There was still time. Her story was not yet over.

Birdie's knees buckled beneath her. She collapsed in a heap

while the strange crow executed a loose and lazy circle above her head. It cawed triumphantly one last time before exploding into a neat little pile of ash. At first Birdie worried Chewy had eaten the bird up from the inside out—and would emerge stronger and even more terrible—but then she remembered.

She remembered how her first letter arrived from Ms. Crunch. Surely if a letter arrived as a hornet, it could also arrive as a bird. Couldn't magic do anything? But what Birdie was really thinking, what was really causing her heart to pound, was the idea that perhaps friendship—*friendship*—could do anything because Birdie had been as specific as possible. Birdie hadn't wanted to leave any room for confusion. Without a doubt, Ms. Crunch knew precisely who and what Birdie was, and she had written back anyways.

The ash rose up from the ground. It spun itself into a piece of paper. Birdie held it ever so gently between the tips of her still-trembling fingers. With her cheeks flushed, she read aloud:

To the Girl with the Boring Letter (I refuse to use your name since it is ridiculously cheerful, and your parents should be cursed because of it):

Boo! I am a witch. I am not kidding.

I figured it was best to get that out of the way from the get-go.

You wondered if you got my letter by mistake—Ha! You think? I wouldn't even borrow a lump of coal from a commoner, let alone ask for a bit of advice from a Tragical Kid!

Still . . .

Maybe you getting my letter wasn't a total disaster.

Not because of any so-called interfering of the Winds (I'm not much of a believer), but because lately, I've been bored out of my mind. Frankly, bugging you might be better than nothing.

Because I live by myself. In the Dead Tree Forest. Everything here is as rotten as me. I can stomp my boots as loud as I want, chew with my mouth open every single meal, and I never once have to run a comb through my buggy hair. It's perfect! The flip side is: boredom is real, and life stinks if you don't find yourself interesting.

The most interesting thing I've done in two months is turn the scummy pond outside my haunted cabin blue. If you're impressed by this, stop it. It's shameful. It's a level one apprentice spell. BUT I'VE ALREADY DONE EVERYTHING ELSE!

Anyways, since magic is "forbidden" at your place, I doubt we've been reading the same book. Mine's called The Book of Evil Deeds, and it's got an end all right. Bah!

Consider yourself lucky yours doesn't have an end. That way you can make one up. That's probably breaking a million of the Council's rules right there, but what do we care? You're doomed, and I'm wicked.

Anyways, if you haven't fainted dead away in a corner yet, I'm curious about a couple of things. First, who is that Mistress Octavia character? Her name alone makes my teeth itch, and why's she so nosy about your mail? Second, why are you "about" ten? I thought all little rug rats loved their birthdays?

And finally, how is the weather over at your place? Mwah, ha-ha-ha!

Write back quick! I wanna know how my curse worked. Because if there's one thing about magic: forbidden or not, it always finds a way.

Never in a million years yours,

Ms. Crunch

(I bet you wanna know my first name. But I'm not telling. I still haven't made up my mind about you.)

PS: For as much as I'd like to take credit for the whole "hornet" thing, that wasn't my doing.

If you're wondering, your letter arrived as an obnoxious cupcake, so maybe the Winds have a sense of humor. Who knew?

PPS: I'm not trying to make you feel better (at all), but maybe the reason everyone ignores Tragicals is because the Chancellor doesn't exactly advertise where you're holed up. Bottom line: I don't have a clue where you live. If the Winds get lazy, I'm gonna need your address. Send it to me ASAP!

Birdie was shaking all over.

It scarcely mattered that she avoided her Tragic End via Chewy's stinger, because another end—a much more terrifying one—had just presented itself. Of all the doomed storybook endings Mistress Octavia gleefully read aloud, were there any worse than those that came by witches?

Birdie set the letter on the ground. She scooted decidedly away from it. But the letter did not sprout legs and pursue her. It did not turn into a poisonous dart aimed at her heart. It didn't do a single witchy thing except remain a complete and utter disappointment.

In all of Birdie's daydreaming—in all of her penny-rattling hoping—she never once imagined she was waiting to hear back from a witch.

A *witch.*

Surely there could be no worse friend in the world than a witch. Especially for a Tragical. Birdie very nearly wished she'd never received the magical letter in the first place. The witch had even sent a curse for crying out loud! A curse delivered by the Winds of Wanderly! Yes, the rainstorm had given her a chance to talk with Ralph, and the children got to feel the splish-splash on their fingertips, but what if the next time the witch did something else? What if she did something dangerous? And even though Birdie didn't have a clue what "ASAP" meant, what good reason could a witch possibly have for wanting her address?

What had she done?

Birdie looked up toward the iron-barred window. She closed her eyes and imagined the Winds of Wanderly swirling around her; the Winds of Wanderly lifting up her hand; the Winds of Wanderly whispering gently into her ear, *Yes*, the way they did the day she released her letter from the depths of a dungeon.

But everything was quiet.

If the Winds were there, she couldn't tell.

And despite receiving a letter, a letter from someone outside the manor, from someone who said she wanted to hear from her again, Birdie had never felt lonelier.

"All I want is a friend," she whispered into the darkness. "And I got a witch."

As if it had been listening, a rat poked its head out from the shadows and tilted its head in Birdie's direction. It ambled into the lone streak of dim light that fell across Birdie's cell. It drew near to Birdie.

Though Birdie typically did everything she could to avoid the abnormally large rats that called the dungeon home,[27] this one had a distinguished sort of appearance. Almost like a gentleman rat. He even had a plume of silvery fur that curled regally atop his head.

As Birdie and the rat scrutinized each other, she was hardly prepared when—with a surprising burst of energy—he leaped jubilantly into the air and landed right in her lap. Birdie stiffened. She'd never seen a dungeon rat do such a thing, and though she still couldn't imagine actually reaching her hand out to pet the fellow, neither could she keep the corners of her mouth from curving up ever so slightly. And she heard herself saying to the rat, "Have *you* come to be my friend?"

Even though rats don't talk, the rat seemed to shrug its tiny shoulders. As if to say, *Why ever not?* Not a moment later, however, the rat was back on its way, toddling away from Birdie and leaving her lap a little lighter and a little less warm. She didn't ever think she'd have occasion to wonder after a dungeon rat, but that's precisely what she did. And she wished it'd stayed a bit

---

27. Despite her daily striving to make the manor as awful as possible, Mistress Octavia could take no credit for the chilling size of the manor's rats. Indeed, their round bellies could be attributed to one source and one source alone; the very same source which Mistress Octavia found grotesque, and the very same source that arguably kept the Tragicals alive: Tragic Mountain's abundant blueberries.

longer, because maybe the rat was right. Maybe the only limit to who could be a friend was Birdie's thinking.

Why ever not?

Still, as unusual as a chummy rat was, a chummy witch was a thousand times stranger. Maybe even impossible. But perhaps Birdie couldn't know that for sure. Perhaps Birdie wouldn't know if the witch could be a friend unless she tried.

Not to mention the witch *had* arguably saved Birdie's life. Certainly the Winds of Wanderly played their part, but without a letter to deliver, there would have been nothing to slurp Mistress Octavia's wicked scorpion up. And instead of chatting with rats and pondering the oddity of friendship with a witch, Birdie could have been—gulp—lying paralyzed on the ground. Maybe even for days.

There was also that one part of the letter that kept bouncing about Birdie's heart. The part when the witch had said "we." Birdie had never been a "we" before. She didn't necessarily know if she wanted to be a "we" with a witch, but maybe the fact that the witch mentioned it at all was promising. Even if the witch didn't know it yet, maybe what she needed was a friend too? Living all by herself in a place like the Dead Tree Forest . . . It was hard to imagine the witch had ever had a friend before.

Birdie rose up and moved toward the stone where her book was hidden. She rolled the stone aside, lifted the book out, and pressed it tight against her chest. She opened up the front cover and flipped toward the back, where the blank pages ruffled eagerly, as if they were simply begging to be torn out.[28]

Birdie paused.

She wondered if this was how every book in Wanderly began.

Blank pages. Full of promise. Full of hope.

And if, like the Tragicals, the books found themselves weighed down by the scribes' words that pressed hard against them. Maybe the books themselves never set out to doom anyone. Maybe, if it were up to them, they would rather be a friend.

Friendship certainly is complicated, Birdie thought. *I do hope that it's worth it.*

And as she tore out another page of her storybook; as she brought forth her formerly useless nubby pencil and bent her head to knowingly write to a witch; as the dungeon crept near and peered curiously over her shoulder, no one paid a bit of attention to the book.

But that hardly mattered.

The book had never been more content.

The book was, at last, doing what it was made to do.

Because good books, above all, are meant to come true. And this book had been waiting a long, long while for someone just like Birdie. . . .

---

28. Birdie was not at all off in her evaluation. Even a book knows there are times when losing a bit of oneself results in a gain that is of far greater value. *But* I would be highly remiss (and highly unpopular among my fellow comrades) if I failed to mention the tearing out of a book's pages should be carefully reviewed on a case-by-case basis.

SEVEN

A Witchy House Call

Agnes Prunella Crunch eyeballed her cauldron.

It was nearly empty.

There were no evil potions boiling and toiling, and no enchanted bones simmering and filling the small space with a potent aroma. No, there was just one thing inside of Agnes Prunella Crunch's cauldron: a meager serving of split pea soup.

Agnes's stomach growled, and Agnes growled back at it.

Other than the soup's lovely green color, Agnes was hardly a fan of the humdrum dish. But she had to remain hungry. She had to keep her nose in peak operating condition. Agnes didn't want to miss even a single whiff of something swirling toward her haunted cabin, because there would be day upon day to sauté a handful of juicy worms, but on this day, she was doing something she had never done before.

Something new—something thrilling—something risky!

Agnes Prunella Crunch was awaiting a letter from a *child*. And in all her witchy life, she had never felt quite so knee-jittering about anything. Sure, there was a pocketful of thrill-seeking witches in Wanderly who purposefully sought out encounters with children, but Agnes had never joined their ranks.

Indeed, she still remembered the year she received the invitation to the first-ever Witches' Child-Wrangling Convention. Oh, it had intrigued her for half a moment. There was no act so likely to induce audible gasps as kidnapping a child and living (without resorting to pulling one's hair out) to tell about it, but in the end, she declined.

It was a good thing, because not only did a group of do-gooding fairy godmothers dismantle the entire event, but before they arrived, one witch actually got wrangled by a child, and both tumbled into a different realm! The last Agnes heard, the witch was sentenced to work long days in the lunchroom of a school that overflowed with runny-nosed, screeching children (some who were even quite nasty and made bets on how many spaghetti noodles they could toss into the witch's frazzled hair).

Agnes shivered.

She hoped her plan wouldn't backfire in such a way. A few days ago, plotting to kidnap a child had seemed the perfect way to make a smashing entrance to the Annual Witches' Ball and take her witching to a whole new level. It had seemed the perfect way to win the *grand prize*. It had seemed the perfect way to make witching fun again!

But now she wondered if she had been a bit hasty—if meddling with a child was simply too risky. She had tried to be coy. She had tried to reveal just enough to gain the child's trust. But was her tacked-on request for the child's address too obvious?

Send it to me ASAP!

Agnes tilted her head back ever so slightly. She dug in deep for another big, long sniff.

"Aiiii!" Agnes screeched. Her small, stony heart rattled in her chest. She smelled it. She had! The unmistakable scent of child was catapulting toward her cabin. But what emerged from Agnes's chimney was not a child, nor was it even a letter. This time it was a *butterfly*. A terribly radiant butterfly with splashes of red, orange, and yellow on its wings.

Even worse, it fluttered all about her cabin, which left Agnes in a terrible predicament. She desperately wanted to get her hands on that butterfly and mush it all up until it resembled a proper letter. But witches have two default speeds: they slink or they lunge. Agnes found that lunging produced an inconvenient gust of air that sent the butterfly whirling out of her grasp; slinking, on the other hand, was entirely too slow and left her clawing and grappling at the air in a fashion ridiculous enough to make her jar full of jawbones snap back and forth in hysterics.

Agnes huffed. She rolled up her sleeves, hiked up her skirts, and attempted to—ugh—walk like a *commoner*. It was terribly humiliating—she almost tripped four times—but eventually her knobby fingers clasped tight around the butterfly, and it exploded in one glittery burst.

Agnes collapsed into her rocking chair. She brought the letter near and read aloud:

Dear Ms. Crunch,

I'm going to be real honest and admit I don't have a clue how to start this letter. Everything sounds sort of awkward. I guess when it comes right down to it, it's hard for me to stop thinking about how you're a witch. An honest-to-goodness, real live witch.

But every time that gets me to the point where it's a little bit hard to breathe, I remember who I am. And I think how there's probably not another person in all of Wanderly who would have written a letter back to a Tragical.

So, really, I guess the only thing I ought to say is: thank you.

You also asked a lot of questions. I'll do my best to answer them. First off, you mentioned Mistress Octavia Foulweather. She's the lady who runs this place and the one who tosses us in the dungeon from time to time. You said she made your teeth itchy, which makes me think you've got smart teeth because she's worse than awful. She hates us so much it's hard to imagine why she'd ever want to be stuck with us, except she says there's no higher honor than fulfilling the Council's call.

Second, you asked about my birthday. There are a few reasons I'm not 100 percent sure of my age: (1) Mistress Octavia, as you can imagine, is not really the type to throw birthday parties; (2) considering a Tragical's days are numbered, the passing of time isn't really something to celebrate; and (3) until four days ago, every day at the manor was the same, so even if you're trying, it gets hard to notice when one day slips into the next.

Third, and this is the biggie, you are right. We definitely are not reading the same book. But maybe it wasn't an accident I thought we were. Maybe the book I have is one you'll want to read, too. Because the book I have is all about friendship.

This moment right here may be the one where you faint in a corner, but if you're still with me, I hope you'll let me explain. You mentioned being bored. Really, really bored. You mentioned how where you live, there's nobody else around. Maybe instead of bugging me by sending curses (which, by the way, worked, but wasn't all that terrible considering how baffled Mistress Octavia was), you might consider being my . . . friend?

If you wonder why I want a friend so badly, I'll tell you. Growing up as an orphan and a Tragical, I sort of thought being alone was as permanent as having brown eyes. But if friendship really is for everyone, then that means somewhere out there is a friend for me. And considering how we met, it's hard not to wonder if maybe that friend is you. Wouldn't that be something?

On the flip side, considering I'm doomed, it's equally possible I'm walking into a total trap and you're rolling on the ground cackling hard enough to get a bellyache.

I'M WILLING TO RISK IT.

It's maybe the one benefit to being a Tragical: we don't have much to lose, but just about everything to gain.

That being said, I'm not giving you my address just yet. And even if you don't have a lot of faith in the Winds of Wanderly, I do. In all my years at the manor, they haven't forgotten us yet, and Tragicals are nothing if not the forgettable type.

I hope you really will consider my idea about being friends (that is, of course, if you aren't cooking up plans to eat me). And don't feel bad if you don't know a thing about being a friend. I don't either.

Yours truly,
Birdie Bloom

PS: I'm real glad you mentioned my first letter arrived as a cupcake. Wow, a cupcake! Your last letter arrived as a ravenous crow, only this time it didn't chase me around, but slurped Mistress Octavia's pet scorpion right off my shoulder! The timing was pretty perfect, because I was on the brink of being attacked.

Despite what the letter predicted, Agnes wasn't cackling on the floor with a bellyache.

Not even close.

Agnes was dumbfounded.

It takes a lot to dumbfound a witch.

Especially a witch as ancient as Agnes Prunella Crunch.

With Agnes in such a state, it was perhaps the worst time ever for someone to knock upon her door (on average, Agnes received approximately one wayward visitor every 3.75 years), but so it goes.

BAM-BAM-BAM!

Agnes's cabin door coughed and sputtered out a heap of dust beneath the visitor's heavy hand. Quick as a whip, Agnes coiled her fingers toward her cauldron and conjured a loud round of thunder and several electrifying lightning bolts. Whoever was outside would hear such a racket and flee for their lives!

BAM-BAM-BAM!

Or maybe not.

Agnes sighed. Though she didn't feel a hint cackly, she tilted back her head and emitted her most gruesome, threatening, evil "YEHAHAHAHAW!" It was better than she expected. Certainly all that practicing late into the night when boredom was its thickest had paid off. She brushed her hands briskly together with a satisfied little smirk. She wondered if she might even peek out the window to see the sorry sap sprinting wildly away. But she took one step, merely two, when—

"YEHAHAHAHAW!" blasted right back at her.

Agnes's breath caught in her throat. Only a witch could produce a cackle like that, but why would a witch be visiting her?

Agnes slunk toward the door. She opened it a crack. The first thing she saw was a bloodshot eye blinking at her. Without waiting for an invitation, the brazen visitor smacked the door against Agnes's cheek, thrust it wide open, and strutted[29] into Agnes's cabin.

Agnes's small, stony heart sank. The last witch in all of Wanderly she wanted to deal with was Rudey Longtooth. Rudey tossed her stringy green hair over her shoulder. She shuffled her boots through the inch-thick layer of dirt atop the floor and brushed her big ol' nose along this shelf and that. She even went so far as to wrap her grimy hands around some of Agnes's potions and slosh them about.

Agnes stomped her foot. She slammed the door to her cabin so hard her jar full of cockroaches erupted into a hissing fit. "Stop touching my things!" she said.

---

29. As I mentioned earlier, witches default to either slinking or lunging. A strut does not fall into either one of these categories, but neither was the witch at hand a typical witch. The witch at hand sported a *badge*. The witch at hand thought this was meaningful.

Rudey whirled about to face Agnes. Agnes, as always, found it hard not to stare at the exceptionally long black tooth that stuck out of Rudey's mouth and burrowed into the soft skin of her lip as if she was a beaver with dental problems.

"Oh, are you worried about this?" Rudey asked. She lifted the potion high overhead and threw it down against the ground with a loud crash! "Oops," she said with an unbecoming snicker. Almost immediately, a purple haze rose from the floor.

"You numbskull!" Agnes said. "You don't have a clue what you're doing!"

Agnes tried in vain to keep her nose above the purple cloud, but it was no use. In less than two seconds, both she and Rudey had their feet caught up in a jig. Rudey had loosed a dancing potion, and despite their snarling faces and evil glares, the two could not help but join hands with each other and do-si-do around the room! Spurred on by the two pairs of witchy boots tap-tapping against the ground, Agnes's cauldron drummed up a merry pink glow, and the bones in her treasure trunk clacked out an irresistible beat.

"Ishkaboo-pishkamoo-sickycoo-fi!" Agnes yelled.

The purple haze spun about itself like a tornado and dove into an empty vial on Agnes's shelf. The two witches' feet skidded to a halt, and they hastily let go of each other's hands and wiped them on their skirts in disgust.

"Now, tell me why in the world you are traipsing about my cabin!" Agnes said.

Rudey snarled. She reached beneath her purple Council cloak and pulled out her shiny golden badge. She shoved it toward Agnes's face.

"Ha! Shows how much you know. Everybody who's anybody is talking about it. I'm the *newest appointed Council member*. I'm now your witchy representative, and I make trouble on your behalf. Since I'm the *newest appointed Council member*, I thought it would only be downright obnoxious if I paid each and every witch a little visit and made 'em shiver in their boots."

Though Agnes wanted to heave each time Rudey proclaimed "newest appointed Council member," she instead zeroed in on that one despicable rule that had been causing her so much trouble.

"Oh, yeah? What about Witches' Manifesto Rule Number Six—the one that says no small talking between witches allowed? Ha! Does this mean you have to go tell on yourself?"

Rudey Longtooth stomped her foot. "Don't be ridiculous! This is different. This is *Council* business."

"Who do you think you're calling ridiculous? Don't forget I've known you since you were six, when you were getting your kicks by lining snails up and setting their shells on fire."

Rudey paused. A smile flickered across her face. "Oh, that was a fair bit of fun, wasn't it? It still tickles me black to watch a snail—ha! A snail of all things—try to outrun scorching flames. But I've got bigger things to scorch now. All thanks to the Chancellor, because I'm the first witch EVER to serve on the Council."

Agnes directed her attention to digging the remnants of yesterday's dinner out from beneath her jagged fingernails. "Guess the Chancellor's even more harebrained than I thought," she muttered beneath her breath.

But Rudy heard her, and she lunged at Agnes. She wrenched the handle of her beat-up broomstick against Agnes's throat. "Watch yourself, witchy!" she said with a hiss. "The Chancellor knows exactly what he's doing. In case you haven't noticed, the Triumphants in Wanderly expect a certain amount of happy endings. Those won't come about unless people like us dish out the bad endings to those miserably waiting for them. In short: it's time to get *wicked!* And lucky for you, I'm here to assist with that."

Agnes met Rudey's stare dead-on. "The day I take advice from you is the day I start flossing my teeth morning and night.[30] Anyways, I'm over the Triumphants. They're obnoxious. Why should we care if they get their happy endings?"

"Because if we do that, if we follow those ten measly rules spelled out in the Manifesto, the Chancellor lets us get away with *everything else*."

---

30. When it comes to witchy insults, this may be the very, very worst. Witches *never* floss their teeth. Some of them even think dental floss was spun by fairy godmothers as a cruel and unusual punishment for all witchkind.

Agnes opened her mouth, but then closed it again. Rudey sort of had a point. It was nice not to have any manners. Nice not to follow any of the rules posted in shopkeepers' windows. Nice to let loose a whole bunch of disruptive spells and watch the commoners throw their hands in the air and squeal.

Rudey smirked. "Now that I've got your attention, let's discuss the real reason why I came: the Annual Witches' Ball. You've never gone. Not once. This year"—Rudey cracked her oversize knuckles—"you're *gonna*."

Agnes's head twitched. Her funny bone jerked. She fought to keep her witchy boot on the ground in light of the spasm in her big toe. As I mentioned before, Agnes had quite a volatile reaction whenever anyone told her she had to do something. Agnes's voice was low and growly. "And whatcha gonna do to me if I don't?"

Rudey clasped her hands against her chest. She tried to draw her lips into a pout, but her long tooth made it awfully difficult. "Oh, how adorable! You're getting worked up. Oooh, it's making me a wee bit scared, but that's good. Hold on to that. That's exactly the wicked the Chancellor's looking for."

"I don't give a hoot what the Chancellor thinks is wicked!"

"Well, you better start hooting because I'll report you to the Council. And if you think the Council's full of a bunch of harmless Goody Two-Shoes, you're wrong. The gal I sit next to during meetings—Octavia Foul-something or other—is as awful as they come. Her assignment is to torment a house full of little buggers all by herself! Can you even imagine?"

Agnes's jaw dropped.

Rudey rolled her eyes. "Oh come on, you're not gonna make me say it! Pooh, you're gonna make me say it, aren't you?" She heaved a great big sigh and expelled in one smelly breath: "*Children*. Ugh! Are you happy? Now I'm gonna have the heebie-jeebies all day long."

But Agnes wasn't confused about the meaning of "little buggers." Every witch had their own code word for dealing with children, and Rudey was nothing if not a simpleton. What Agnes was chewing on and rolling about her tongue like a dislodged piece of beef was that name; that name that kept popping up in the girl's letters; that terrible, awful name: *Octavia*.

A shiver rippled up and down Agnes's spine.

The sort of shiver that precedes an evil act.

The sort of shiver Agnes hadn't felt for a long, long time.

"Look, I've got about one thousand better things to do than sit in your piddly cabin. So let's make it real simple: be a witch and go to the ball."

But Agnes stepped in front of Rudey. "Funny, I didn't know attending tea parties sponsored by the Council was a requirement to being a witch."

"Oh, it's hardly a tea party. But you wouldn't know, would you? Maybe you're too scared to come see for yourself."

"Wicked witches aren't scared of anything!"

Rudey raised her eyebrow. "You said it, not me," she said.

With one last gnash of her black tooth, Rudey strutted past Agnes. As she did, she flung her hand against a shelf full of specimens and sent the whole lot of them tumbling toward the floor, clattering and rolling about.

Agnes's hands clenched into fists at her sides, but before she could huff and puff a curse Rudey's way, she was gone. The door to Agnes's haunted cabin slammed shut.

Agnes was, again, all alone.

Behind her, the cauldron's once merry pink glow had dulled down to a soft shade of blue. A stray dragon's tooth and an almost-ready-to-hatch spider egg sack rolled near the toe of her boot. Agnes scooped them up and plunked them safely back on the shelf.

Crunch, crunch, crunch, went her boots through the thick layer of gravelly dirt.

Creak, creak, creak, sang her old rocking chair by the cauldron.

Swish, swish, swish. The Winds of Wanderly tiptoed forth, rustling softly about in the darkness.

Yes, yes, yes. The witch nodded.

Yes, yes, yes.

Agnes brandished her pen.

She ground her pointed teeth.

She reached for a piece of paper and began to scrawl.

EIGHT

A TRIUMPHANT AND A RAT

It was only eight o'clock in the morning, and the manor was in a state of total chaos.

The chaos had begun the evening prior when Sir Ichabod plucked Birdie out of the dungeon at half past nine and Birdie emerged with nary a scratch. Even worse, according to Mistress Octavia, was the mysterious disappearance of Chewy. A fact that caused her to toss not one but three hot, buttered croissants so high and so hard that they stuck against the dining room's vaulted ceiling and hadn't ceased from drip-dropping specks of butter.

Travel through the manor had since become a greasy affair, and Sir Ichabod had spent the morning teetering from the top of several different ladders, none of which had been tall enough to reach the pesky croissants.

Moreover, instead of sleeping, Mistress Octavia had forced the Tragicals to traipse all night about the manor like zombies, peeking into every dark corner for a clue, any clue, as to the whereabouts of her "little pumpkin."

A "little pumpkin" Mistress Octavia promptly forgot all about when she received The Message a mere thirty minutes ago. The Message went something like this: *I'm on my way.*

Boom!

That was it.

You don't get a visitor for six years straight and then, all of a sudden, one is coming.

Now, you can only imagine how quickly Birdie stood on tiptoe to catch a glimpse of The Message writer's penmanship because *what if Ms. Crunch had found out her address and was coming to get them all?* Fortunately, the penmanship was anything but spooky, scary, and bone-chilling. In fact, it was so polished and sophisticated, Mistress Octavia insisted the Chancellor's assistant must have sent it on his behalf, which was why the manor was a flurry of activity.

Mistress Octavia wanted everything to be just so.

She wanted the place to ooze with dust and grime.

She wanted dirty spots on the Tragicals' cheeks, for goodness' sake, and why weren't their gowns riddled with more holes?

To Francesca Prickleboo's complete horror, Mistress Octavia mussed up her Popsicle orange braids and dished out two healthy scuffs on the toes of her shoes. "But—but I thought I was supposed to be a *contented* Tragical," Francesca protested.

To which Mistress Octavia chided, "Content to look miserable. You're far too tidy!" And so Francesca swallowed hard and had been diligently chewing her fingernails and using them to snag her black gown ever since.

Mistress Octavia paced back and forth in front of the Tragicals. She gripped her broken broomstick handle tightly.

"Now, children, I know it's Wednesday. Wednesday is always Dramatic Arts Day.[31] But I don't want the Chancellor to get the wrong idea. I don't want him to think this institution is all play and no work."

Birdie didn't know how anything in their dreary days could be considered play, but when Cricket cast a small and certain look in her direction, she remembered. She remembered the day Cricket had been forced to turn over a pocketful of paper scraps for fashioning a ball, and Birdie had been able to replace it with an entire *sheet* of paper. Of course, that had also been the day Birdie began her correspondence with a real live wicked witch, but try as she might, she simply couldn't bring herself to

---

31. This was hardly the same sort of dramatic arts class you may be used to; the sort where, on any given day, you may find yourself wearing a royal crown or an ogre mask, or zapping a wand through the air. Namely, the purpose of dramatic arts at the manor was: accept the role you are given. As such, the children had never once switched parts, never once switched props, and never once switched costumes. They played the same roles every single time. You can imagine precisely how lively such performances turned out to be.

tell Cricket. She couldn't think of a single way to smooth out the prickly edges of the word "witch." Worst of all, she couldn't imagine a single scenario in which the recent, hopeful spark in Cricket's eyes wouldn't be snuffed out completely.

Mistress Octavia continued on, "And so we shall be studying instead a subject more appropriate for a house full of bad endings; today I shall conduct a FOG class."

The Tragicals all groaned. Not out loud, of course. The Tragicals never did anything out loud. They groaned on the inside, because FOG stood for none other than "Ferocious, Ominous, and Gruesome." It was a hopelessly dreary subject consisting of Mistress Octavia presenting the Tragicals with the worst of Wanderly and then speculating precisely how many were likely to die in such a manner. So far, Birdie's least favorite scenario was stumbling into the den full of wolf-size fire ants.

Mistress Octavia narrowed her eyes. "Before instruction begins, I want the Chancellor to have a full and complete picture of my teaching. Therefore, you will be stationed in the Dark Hallway when he first arrives. Upon Sir Ichabod's signal, you will proceed to trudge into the Instruction Room as you have never trudged before. And take heed: if anyone should choose to engage in any mischief, punishments will abound."

With that, and an unnerving swish of her hand, Mistress Octavia disappeared down the hallway like a black tornado—whirling and wheeling about and making sure everything in her wake looked absolutely awful.

Birdie sucked up a breath. The five-year-old whose hair was thick with mats—Birdie was certain her name was Amelia—collapsed along the stone floor for a nap. The rest of the Tragicals, however—and most especially the ones who were near the age of sixteen—remained wide-eyed. Certainly the Chancellor had promised to visit before, but as far as they knew, he had never sent an official Message about such a visit. What would it be like to look into the eyes of the one who proclaimed to all of Wanderly they were . . . nothing? The one who demanded the production of book after book after book to flood throughout the kingdom and ensure it would always be so?

The sixteen-year-old girl at the front of the line, the one with cracked eyeglasses whom Mistress Octavia always referred to as Martha but whose actual name was Mildred, opened her mouth, but then pressed her lips together tight. She glanced down the long line of children—as if to say, *Come along, then*—and began shuffling toward the Dark Hallway.

You are likely wondering how the Tragicals knew which Dark Hallway Mistress Octavia meant, because wasn't every hallway at Foulweather's Home for the Tragical dark? Indeed! But the Dark Hallway did not earn its name for lack of proper lighting. The Dark Hallway was instead a place of "dark" reminders. Its walls were lined on both sides with glaring portraits of the Council members. And every time the Tragicals trudged by, they were to remember precisely how doomed their futures were and the people put in place to guarantee them.

And so, as they trudged along, no one but Birdie thought much of the loud gasp that exploded from the back of the line. The furrowed brow and twisty mustache of Magician Slickabee's portrait had caused just such a reaction on multiple past occasions. Birdie, however, paid attention because the back of the line was where Cricket trudged, and the gasp sounded unmistakably eight-year-old girlish, and Birdie was certain that gasps (however predictable) were the sort of thing a friend shouldn't ignore.

She was right, because Cricket had skidded to a jarring halt. Her face was ghastly pale, and her eyes glistened. Birdie followed Cricket's gaze to the place where Griselda Peabody's portrait usually sniffed down at them. Except Griselda was gone. Hanging in her place was a drawing. A drawing on the piece of paper that had been torn out of Birdie's storybook.

The drawing showed two girls in familiar gowns, one noticeably taller than the other. The girls stood side by side, holding their hands up to a cloud-filled sky. Falling down from the clouds, falling into their hands, was something much larger than raindrops. At first, Birdie thought it was great clumps of snow, but then she could see it was something even more marvelous. Paper. Whole sheets of paper. And every time the manor's walls heaved a contented little sigh, as if for once it was proud of what was on display, the falling sheets of paper appeared to wiggle and move. As if the drawing was more than just a drawing.

And it was. Because of all the very many dreary books and

terrifying illustrations that had numbed the Tragicals' minds over the years, they had never once seen a drawing so full of *hope*. It stirred them up from the inside. It made their very limbs tingle. As if, like the drawing, they too might be something more. Something more than just a Tragical.

Imagine that.

Though the children—not one—had moved even a muscle, a boy of about seven whispered aloud, "Do you—do you think that drawing's got something to do with magic? Like how those rain clouds came to visit?"

Birdie knew Cricket was responsible for the drawing, but that didn't mean it hadn't anything to do with magic. Ms. Crunch—a bona fide magic expert—had suggested as much when she wrote in her letter: If there's one thing about magic: forbidden or not, it always finds a way. Maybe magic didn't have to always show up by way of flashy explosion and dazzling skill; maybe magic could arrive even through the hands, through the imagination, of a little girl. And certainly this drawing—Cricket's drawing—changed things. And wasn't that what magic did best?

But not everyone was looking for such a change.

Francesca Prickleboo stomped her foot on the ground. She stepped in front of the long line of Tragicals. "Who did this?" she hissed.

For a moment, even she looked a tad taken aback at how very much like Mistress Octavia she sounded. Still, she continued,

"Of all the places to do something naughty, why would one of you choose to do it here, in a place of honor? And on the day of the Chancellor's visit? Who was it?"

Birdie's heart sank when Cricket's tears began to fall.

"I didn't do it . . . I didn't do it," Cricket said, shaking her head. "I mean, I drew it, but I never would have put it there!"

Upon Cricket's confession, upon sensing her distress, all the children silently, instinctively, moved away from her. They were Tragicals. That's what they did. And it's what Birdie almost did too. She had to fight quite intensely to force her feet to remain put, but keeping her eyes fixed on Cricket's drawing helped. Remembering that she was the one who had given Cricket the paper in the first place helped even more.

Friendship. Together. That's what it was all about.

When Birdie drew up alongside Cricket, Francesca's jaw gaped. "But she— She's nothing more than a troublemaker!" And then Francesca assumed the position that sent shivers down the Tragicals' spines. She threw her shoulders back, she tilted her head toward the ceiling, and she let loose her loudest, tattliest cry. "MISTRESS OCTA—"

But Griselda Peabody interrupted her.

Or rather, Griselda Peabody's *portrait* interrupted her. I don't mean that it floated eerily down the hall like a ghost. No, Ralph gave it a proper whack with the toe of his shoe and sent it sliding down the buttery-slick hallway until it came to rest against Francesca's calf.

"Oh, Mistress Peabody!" Francesca said. She swept Griselda Peabody's portrait up and into the cradle of her arms. "No Triumphant should ever be treated in such a way."

And a Triumphant Griselda was. On the other side of Wanderly—in a place teeming with emerald green forests and blue, cloudless skies, nestled atop the peak of Triumph Mountain and framed by a smooth, glassy sea—was the place that could not have been more opposite to Foulweather's Home for the Tragical. Instead of being filled with the bad endings, each canopied four-poster bed was filled with a happy ending, and at Peabody's Academy for the Triumphant, Griselda Peabody was in charge of it all.[32]

BOOM!

The foundation of the manor quaked. Birdie and Cricket reached out for each other so as not to stumble and fall. A collective shadow fell across the Tragicals' faces, because surely it was him. Surely he was there. In less than a moment, they would meet face-to-face with . . . the Chancellor!

---

32. Just as the Tragicals were not sent to Foulweather's Home for the Tragical on the basis of bad behavior, the Triumphants were not sent to Peabody's Academy for the Triumphant on the basis of good behavior (indeed, several of the children were dreadfully rotten). Instead, every year a pool of highly select nominees, ages one to fifteen years, was chosen to undergo an exhaustive battery of top secret tests designed exclusively by the Chancellor. An average of merely 1 percent ever passed—the results were never once discussed—but the Chancellor claimed the test's ability to identify Wanderly's best and brightest was (in his words) "foolproof."

Which didn't explain why, from two hallways away, Mistress Octavia burst out, "*You?* What are *you* doing here?"

And a curiously breathy voice answered, "I believe the more appropriate response is 'Hello, Griselda,' but I'm nothing if not gracious—that's how we *Triumphants* operate—so I'll give you a moment to collect yourself before I start docking points. I'm here for your triennial inspection."

"But it's been six years!" Mistress Octavia growled.

"Has it?"

"And where's the Chancellor?"

"Last I heard he was organizing his shoe closet—"

"What?"

"He's got a lot of shoes. But let's get started, shall we? I would prefer to be done five minutes ago, if you know what I mean."

The Tragicals gawked at one another. Francesca looked down at the Griselda she held in her arms. "What's going to happen to us?" Her voice came out as a whisper to no one in particular.

"What's going to happen to *me*?" Cricket echoed while choking back sobs.

Birdie gritted her teeth. "Nothing," she said. "Because Mistress Octavia and Mistress Peabody are never going to find out about any of this."

And before Birdie could lose her nerve, she strode toward a stunned Francesca Prickleboo, snatched Griselda's portrait out of her arms, and marched toward the wall where Cricket's drawing hung. But it was hanging high. Much higher than it first appeared. And no matter how much Birdie leaped with all her might, the tips of her fingernails barely grazed against the bottom edge of the drawing.

All the while, Griselda Peabody's voice snaked closer. "Oh my! Is this what you call proper accommodations? There are so few cockroaches here it's as if you employ an exterminator! Explain to me how this is preparing the children for the worst?"

Birdie felt on the brink of tears herself. She turned to Cricket and asked, "How did you manage to get this up here in the first place?"

"It really wasn't me!" Cricket cried out. "I'm telling the truth. I never put it up there!"

And that's when Ralph stepped forward. He drew near to Birdie and kneeled down before her. "I'll lift you up," he said.

Birdie gulped. "And how, exactly, do you plan to do that?"

"On my shoulders. Come on, it won't be scary."

"I'm not scared—"

"Then climb on."

"But—"

"They're getting closer! Hurry. None of us is tall enough on our own."

Birdie swallowed hard. Though she really wasn't scared of heights, how could she explain to Ralph that she was just getting used to standing beside another person, much less scrambling atop one's shoulders?

But then Birdie happened to glance at Cricket. Cricket was bobbing her head up and down, trying to encourage her. If Birdie didn't do it—if she didn't get that drawing down in time—what *would* become of Cricket? Mistress Octavia was bound to get sick of doling out dungeon appointments, and with Chewy long gone . . . What if Mistress Octavia finally resorted to the Drowning Bucket?

Birdie plunked her hands on Ralph's head. She swung one leg and then the second over his shoulders. Birdie and Ralph swayed awkwardly this way and that. They were a teetering, quivering mess, but slowly—very, very slowly—they rose. And, together, they became the tallest Tragical in all of Wanderly.

But the *click-clack* of Mistress Octavia's footsteps was nearly upon them!

"Hurry!" Ralph said. "Just grab it off the wall! They're almost here!"

Birdie was trying to do just that, but every time she lifted one corner up and moved to the next, the wall seemed to grab the drawing right back. It was as if the manor *wanted* Cricket's drawing to remain. As if to prove its point further, the wall up and flung off Magician Slickabee's portrait with such ferocity he went sailing across the hallway! A flabbergasted Francesca Prickleboo barely managed to duck as the portrait smacked against the opposite wall and slid miserably down to the floor.

Mistress Octavia Foulweather's and Griselda Peabody's

footsteps drew to a sharp halt.

"What was that terrible noise?" Griselda Peabody said.

"Oh, that? Probably just one of the children practicing faint-ing or maybe even spontaneous death." But Mistress Octavia sounded uneasy. And she did what she always did when things were going awry. "SIR ICH-A-BOD! SIR ICH-A-BOD!!"

And from somewhere among the shadows, Sir Ichabod appeared. He began shuffling through the Dark Hallway at full speed, until he saw what the Tragicals were up to.

Upon seeing Birdie teetering from Ralph's shoulders, a child-ish drawing pinned to the wall, and two (count them, *two*) Council portraits tossed to the wayside like yesterday's junk, he shrank five sizes.

If he could have, he probably would have melted into the floor completely.

But maybe there was something more to Sir Ichabod than the Tragicals assumed. Maybe he wasn't completely immune to the sound of their tears when they cried themselves to sleep at night. Maybe he wasn't entirely against them. Because with-out waiting for anyone to ask, he straightened up. He walked right up to Birdie and plucked her off Ralph's shoulders. He reached up toward the wall and coaxed the manor into releas-ing Cricket's drawing. He grabbed hold of Magician Slickabee's portrait, slung him back into place along the wall, and had very nearly dealt with Griselda, too, when terribly, awfully, tragically—

"AHHHH!" the real Griselda Peabody let loose a bloodcur-dling scream. She had turned the corner into the Dark Hallway!

Several of the Tragicals screamed right along with her.

A few others threw their hands over their eyes.

Little Amelia had finally lifted her sleepy head off the floor and began wailing at top volume.

Surely it was all over.

Except Griselda Peabody wasn't irate over her cast-off por-trait. Griselda Peabody had not even noticed her cast-off portrait; she was staring instead at the fat rat with the silver pompadour striding down the center of the room like it was a runway. Birdie blinked. She knew that rat. It was the very same rat that had merrily climbed into her lap in the dungeon. But what was a dungeon rat doing up here?

Griselda Peabody jabbed a shaking finger in the rat's direc-tion as if she had the power to stop it. But Triumphants, for all their happy endings, weren't trained in magic. According to the Chancellor, they didn't need magic because they already had everything they would ever need. Griselda Peabody, however, looked like she would have really appreciated a chair to stand upon right then.

As it was, her powder pink skirt was hiked over her wrinkly knees. Her silver-slippered feet shimmied to and fro as if she thought a perfectly executed waltz was the answer to every-thing. It wasn't, but it did give Sir Ichabod the perfect oppor-tunity to prop her portrait back on its hook and slink back into the shadows, like he hadn't just done several astonishing things.

Throughout all the commotion, the rat stayed his course. He had eyes for one person and one person only. And despite the evil, cursing glare of Mistress Octavia, despite the presence of the headmistress of the Triumphants, despite all the Council's portraits sneering down upon him, the rat continued along until he plopped on top of Cricket's shoe with a contented sigh, curled his long, fat tail beneath him, and promptly took a snooze as if all was right in the world.

What a day it was turning out to be for Cricket.

What a day it was turning out to be for Mistress Octavia, because Griselda Peabody's face had turned a bright tomato red. She began slashing her quill against her clipboard with deep, broad, furious strokes.

"What are you doing? What are you writing on that paper?" Mistress Octavia barked.

"This place is a nightmare! And I don't mean that in the complimentary way," Griselda Peabody said, holding up one finger. "It's too clean! It's too bright! These children look well-nourished! And pets? You have allowed them to have pets? Never mind that it's a rat; this child has developed a *relationship* with something!" Griselda Peabody paused. She lifted one distinguished eyebrow in Mistress Octavia's direction. "The Chancellor will have much to think about."

Mistress Octavia rolled back her shoulders and lifted her

head high. She set her gaze in Sir Ichabod's direction and said three seething words: "Get. That. Rat."

But Cricket had already scooped him up and was running about, like she actually believed a Tragical (and her illegal pet) could escape. Whether out of honest confusion or in an effort to assist Cricket, the other Tragicals began to run about too. Soon, the rat was being passed back and forth, as if in a festive game of hot potato, leaving Sir Ichabod to lunge uselessly after them because their billowing black gowns made it appear like *everyone* had something stuffed beneath their sleeves.

Amid the chaos, Birdie barely noticed the large gray moth that charged down the hallway from the direction of the dungeon and came to rest upon her shoulder. When it began to bat its wings noisily in her ear, she tried to shoo it away, but it got terribly huffy. Only then did Birdie realize she wasn't dealing with a moth at all, but a letter disguised as a moth. A letter from her witch! A letter Mistress Octavia definitely could not see, because surely the only thing more punishable than a magical letter would be a magical *friendly* letter (if, of course, Ms. Crunch had come to such a decision).

Birdie cupped her hands around the moth. She felt the little pile of ash fall into her palms, and without waiting for it to transform into a sheet of paper, she stuffed it deep into the cradle of her pocket and patted it once against her thigh.

She rejoined the commotion just in time for Mistress Octavia to bellow, "Caroline, give me that rat *now*!"

The Tragicals stopped running. Griselda Peabody fanned herself so briskly her mane of silver hair whooshed behind her. But Cricket was a very literal eight-year-old. No matter how many times Mistress Octavia called her "Caroline," the false name simply hadn't stuck. Not to mention how busy she was whispering soothing words over the rat snuggled in her arms.

"Caroline, I am talking to you!" Mistress Octavia insisted.

Birdie gulped. Someone was going to have to answer Mistress Octavia. Surely Mistress Octavia wouldn't take too kindly to it being someone other than Cricket, but with a new letter from Ms. Crunch simmering in Birdie's pocket, a trip down to the dungeon didn't sound so bad.

"R-right here, Mistress Octavia," Birdie blurted out.

Mistress Octavia threw her hands in the air. "You're not Caroline!"

"Who *is* Caroline?" Griselda Peabody asked with a sniff.

Mistress Octavia pointed at Cricket. "She's Caroline!" With nary a warning, Mistress Octavia lunged for the rat being held in Cricket's arms. Cricket shrieked. She shut her eyes, tossed her rat as far away from Mistress Octavia as she possibly could, and begged, "Run for your life, Sprinkles!"

"A name! That rodent has a name?!" Griselda Peabody said. She bent her head, scribbling fiercely on her clipboard.

Mistress Octavia shoved Sir Ichabod to the side and dove after Sprinkles herself. At last, seeming to realize the dire urgency of the situation, Sprinkles revved his little feet to full throttle. Much to the delighted squeals of the younger Tragicals, he bounded lithely across three pairs of shoulders, leaped spectacularly off a shrieking Francesca's hair, and finally disappeared beneath the wall upon which Mistress Octavia banged her head. Hard.

Mistress Octavia slowly stood up. She looked like she had been through a war instead of a surprise visit from the Council. Her voice was a terrifying whisper. "Sir Ichabod, you will set one hundred—no, two hundred; no, *three* hundred—rattraps on this eve! And with every sickening snap you children hear, you shall think about how it is all your fault. You are doomed! There is no way to escape it, and if you try, you shall only infect others with your own misery."

Cricket collapsed in a heap of black fabric. Her shoulders heaved beneath her gown.

Birdie's heart ached too. Almost as if Cricket's tears were her very own. Did such a thing happen between friends?

While the other Tragicals shuffled silently back into line, Griselda Peabody tucked her clipboard beneath her elbow. With her lips drawn tightly together, she said to Mistress Octavia, "Your nasty little speech along with that rat's death sentence was the first—I repeat *first*—sign that you're doing even one thing right. Be warned, Octavia: the way a kingdom handles its bad endings has everything to do with its happy endings. You slipped through this inspection by a brittle hangnail." With that, Griselda Peabody whirled her purple Council cloak around her and disappeared in a puff of smoke.[33]

The Tragicals needed no further instruction. They gathered the long hems of their gowns in their shaking hands, and—even in the absence of the audience they had been expecting—they trudged. They trudged as they had never trudged before. And almost every single one of them forgot about the drawing on the wall filled with hope.

Except Birdie.

Birdie hadn't forgotten. In fact, along with the letter in her pocket, it was all Birdie could think about. No one had ever chosen Birdie for anything before. And of all the things Cricket could have drawn, Cricket had chosen her. Birdie and Cricket, together. And that's why Birdie determined, on that night, she would save the life of Cricket's pet rat. That night, for once, Cricket wouldn't have to lose something.

Of course, a doomed child hadn't much business in saving the life of anything (even the life of a rat), but neither did a doomed child have any business dabbling in something as wonderful as friendship. But surely that's what was happening. Surely that's what it had to be.

---

33. Or rather she flapped the fabric of the cloak up and down a bit, as if she expected it might take flight like the wings of a bird. It was a bit embarrassing, but that was hardly her fault. As I mentioned before, Griselda Peabody was not magical. Still, every Council member was allowed the use of a magical cloak, because with an entire kingdom to boss around—er, manage—instantaneous travel was of utmost importance.

NINE

The Oldest Tragical of All

That night, the Winds of Wanderly wrapped around the manor. They rocked the manor back and forth like a babe and then, when it was time, rapped gently against the window of the Tragicals' dormitory.

Tap-tap-tap.

"Mmmmm," Birdie said, stirring sleepily. It had been quite a day. Certainly, the Tragicals had suffered many such days at the hand of Mistress Octavia, but the disastrous visit from Mistress Peabody seemed to raise Mistress Octavia's ire to new heights. Quite literally, because she ordered Sir Ichabod to bring forth every rickety ladder he had and prop them up in various locations around the manor. She then forced each Tragical to climb to the top rung, where they had to balance for the entire rest of the day.

Though it was Mistress Octavia's great hope one of them might topple down and incur a fantastic injury, no such thing happened. Mildred, whose cracked eyeglasses slipped clean off midafternoon, and young Amelia, who was still dreadfully sleepy, came closest to disaster, but even they survived, in part through the nonverbal signals of the other Tragicals, including a semicoordinated series of foot-banging, artificial sneezing, and throat-clearing guffaws.

Unfortunately for Birdie, ladder balancing was not the sort of activity that permitted letter reading; nor was Mistress Octavia's requirement that, at bedtime, Sir Ichabod weave about the dormitory whispering terrible endings into the Tragicals' ears until every one of them was fast asleep. Indeed, Birdie's last thought of the day had been nothing more comforting than "wandering alone in an overgrown jungle of child-eating plants."

Tap-tap-tap, the Winds insisted a bit more loudly. Birdie rolled over, and her rusty bedframe trilled, *Squeeeeak!*

Not unlike the squeak a mouse might make. Or maybe even a rat.

A rat! Birdie bolted upright. It wasn't just an ordinary night full of the usual nightmares, discomforts, and endless tossing and turning. It was the night upon which Cricket's rat must be saved. But first, Birdie had to take one moment to read the letter she'd waited all day long to read. If it turned out to be the friendly letter she hoped, it might even provide just the right boost for a night of heroism.[34]

Birdie set her bare feet on the cold floor and slipped against the window. All the windows in the dormitory were covered in the manor's customary thick black-out curtains and outfitted with four different sets of locks. But on the window closest to Birdie's bed, there was a small nick in the fabric that allowed for the teensiest sliver of moonlight to spill out onto the floor. On that night, the sliver was so bright Birdie could scarcely imagine how very full the moon must have looked hanging high above the manor. Full and lovely.

Lovely. Birdie wasn't at all used to thinking about lovely things. As a Tragical, there had been times when it was nearly impossible to imagine there existed anything lovely at all. But it was getting easier. It seemed one lovely thought led to another, and that it was even the sort of thing one could practice.

Birdie pulled Ms. Crunch's letter from her pocket while the Winds of Wanderly pressed tight against the glass. She read:

To Birdbrain:

Is that name better? If not, tough. As for you being all alone without any parents, I say, "Congratulations!" No matter how hard I've tried, I've never been able to make my mother disappear. Sure, she abandoned me in a pit of

---

34. Or even just a hair above tragical would do.

vipers when I was six, but I still bump into her from time to time. Every time I do, she manages to do something rotten like lob a bucket of slugs at my face or dump a fistful of beetles down my pants. She stinks like rotten fish eggs!

Speaking of stinks, there is simply no other word to describe that book you've got. First off, there's no way I'm reading that thing. Not that the idea made me faint in the corner—ha!—but it did make me want to throw up. Second, if you're still holding out a flicker of hope that I might actually want to be your ~~f f frie~~ BLECH! We've gotta come up with something better. That word is simply not meant to roll off my evil fingers. In fact, the best a witch could ever hope for in the witching community is a . . . barely foul foe. Ooh! That sounds about right. Barely Foul Foe. But just because I'm lazy, let's call it a "BFF" for short.

As I was saying, I DO NOT WANT TO BE YOUR BFF!

Lucky for you, I've also changed my mind about eating you. Okay, fine, I'm not actually that sort of witch, but I might have been planning to do you in. Are you scared? You should be. You should also be thanking your lucky stars, because if that Octavia lady wasn't so awful, I probably would have kept my sights set on you. That ought to teach you a thing or two about taking risks, because for crying out loud you're doomed! What'd ya expect???

So, back to Octavia.

First and foremost, Council people drive me batty. What do they know except what the Chancellor tells 'em, and he's a total nincompoop! Second, what business does she have hoarding mail, banishing little brats to the dungeon, and getting fussy over a bit o' magic? My stone-cold witchy heart's stirred up! There's nothing I love more than putting people in their places.

So, here's where you come in. I need all the info on Octavia. Everything! Tell me all her weaknesses. Tell me all her routines. Tell me every last thing you can think of, and don't leave a single thing out! Everyone's got a breaking point, and it's just a matter of time before we figure out hers.

Now, it's possible you might be thinking this gets us a little closer to that BFF thing. Hint: it doesn't! Not even a smidge. Even though me doing Octavia in might be the best thing that's ever happened to you and all those other bad endings you live with, that's not why I'm doing it. In fact, if there was a way around helping you out, I'd take it. I'm doing this for me.

Because all of a sudden, wouldn't you know it, I'm not feeling so bored anymore.

Agnes Prunella Crunch is back.

Not Your BFF,
(You Know who)

PS: Since that cupcake thing made you all googly-eyed, you'll probably be glad to hear your last letter came as a—yuck—butterfly, and I almost smashed my nose trying to trip after it. If you feel bad about that, think how disappointed I was to hear my crow saved you from a scorpion.

PPS: I'm still waiting on your address. Even if the Winds of Wanderly are willing to deliver a wicked letter, I doubt they're up for delivering a whole witch. How can I do your headmistress in if I don't know how to find you?

The letter fell from Birdie's hands. She couldn't believe she'd waited all day long to read it. She couldn't believe she'd drawn even an ounce of comfort from feeling it rustle about in her pocket. A wicked witch openly admitted that she wanted to do Birdie in! Surely Birdie had never come so close to her Tragic End before. It felt like Ms. Crunch's hands might reach through the letter to snatch her up right that instant!

The worst part of all was Birdie had hoped upon hope that Ms. Crunch—a witch—might be the one thing she wanted more than anything else in the world. The best thing Birdie could imagine. Birdie thought Ms. Crunch was going to be her friend.

She felt so foolish.

It was an awful feeling; a feeling she couldn't remember ever having had, because in all her days past, she'd never felt responsible for any of the awfulness—it was just part of a Tragical's way of life. But this was different. Writing back to Ms. Crunch had been her idea. No one had forced her to do it.

Birdie sighed. She folded the letter up and slipped it beneath her pillowcase. If friendship was complicated, being a BFF—whatever that was exactly—promised to be a heap more complicated. Birdie couldn't imagine it would be a good idea to cooperate with Ms. Crunch, who couldn't even bring herself to *write* the word "friend," but neither could she deny Ms. Crunch had a point about doing Mistress Octavia in. If Mistress Octavia wasn't around to torment the Tragicals, wouldn't their lives—and maybe even their futures—simply *have* to improve? Birdie wished she could ask Cricket for advice, but she still hadn't breathed a word about Ms. Crunch's identity, and such an admission hardly seemed appropriate on a night of grave importance.

Birdie tiptoed four beds over to where Cricket lay shivering beneath a holey blanket with a pillow stuffed over her head. Birdie reached her hands out, placed them gently on Cricket's shoulders, and shook her ever so slightly. Cricket sat up with a great heaving gasp.

"Shhhhh!" Birdie whispered. "It's me. It's just me. It's Birdie."

Cricket's eyes glistened in the dim light. "You didn't hear anything, did you? I've been trying my hardest not to hear anything."

"Not a thing," Birdie promised. "But let's keep it that way. Let's go save Sprinkles!"

"Save him?" Cricket said, as if the thought never occurred to her. "But how would we do that?"

Birdie reached over and began rolling Cricket out of bed. "Simple. We'll just undo all the rattraps."

"But didn't Mistress Octavia say there would be three—"

"Hundred? Yeah, I know. I didn't say it was a genius plan, but well, it was the only thing I could think of."

"And so we—we have to go out there?" Cricket lifted one shaking hand toward the door leading out to the hallway. "In the dark? With Sir Ichabod creeping around?"

As if the word "creeping" had caught her attention, Francesca Prickleboo, five beds over, stirred. A single orange braid tumbled across the edge of the mattress. Birdie and Cricket waited with breath held tight, but Francesca must not have fully woken because a series of soft, wheezing snores escaped her lips.

"We'll simply have to try our best not to get caught," Birdie finally whispered.

Cricket nodded and placed her feet on the floor. Her black gown swooshed around her tiny frame, nearly swallowing her up. She turned to Birdie. "You could get in big trouble for this. And I never even told you I had a pet."

"I know," Birdie said.

"Do you like rats a bunch too?"

"No, not at all, really."

"So then, are you doing this because of that . . . book you've been reading?"

"Maybe," Birdie said softly.

"Hmph" was all Cricket said. But then she reached out and scooped Birdie's hand into her own. "Just so we don't get lost."

And together, the two girls pushed through the door of the dormitory[35] and slipped down the hallway. It was as dark as Birdie expected, but hanging a few feet away was the lantern Sir Ichabod Grim always kept burning. Birdie knew this because she often fell asleep to the flickering shadow it cast beneath

---

35. Quite curiously, the dormitory door was never locked. This was not a testament to Mistress Octavia's negligence, but rather a reflection of the Tragicals' keen logic. It makes little sense to traipse about a place in the dark when all one can expect to find is: (1) more creepy-crawlies, (2) even darker hallways, and (3) highly secured (i.e. Tragical-proof) kitchen pantries.

the dormitory door. And when she would awaken from a bad dream, with nothing but her own arms to hold her, the flicker would lull her back to sleep. The light was as constant as the darkness, and never overcome.

Birdie shone the lantern in all directions, hunting for traps. She gasped when she saw the first one. Its shiny metal jaws gleamed sharp in the lantern's light. Birdie gestured for Cricket to stay put while she scurried closer. She breathed a sigh of relief that the trap did not yet contain any unfortunate rodents and, most of all, not Sprinkles.

Being ever so careful not to snap her own finger, Birdie turned the trap this way and that. She looked at it from above, and she looked at it from underneath. She flipped the trap on its side and even nudged it with her toe. Birdie didn't have much experience with rattraps, but there could be no mistaking the one before her was already broken. Broken beyond repair, even. Birdie frowned. She wondered if Sir Ichabod had simply been too exhausted to set the traps correctly or if something else (or rather *someone* else) was at work?

Birdie's stomach flip-flopped.

What if Ms. Crunch had figured out where she lived? Or if Ms. Crunch really had convinced the Winds of Wanderly to deliver her whole witchy self, and she was sneaking around the manor right that instant?

Shuffle-shuffle. Shuffle-shuffle.

Birdie clamped her hand over her mouth so as not to holler

out loud. Behind her, Cricket bounced up and down. "What is it? What's wrong?"

"The trap's already broken!" Birdie managed to choke out.

"But—but—but . . . isn't that *good*?"

"And someone's coming!"

Shuffle-shuffle. Shuffle-shuffle.

This time Cricket heard the footsteps too. She stepped forward and tugged on Birdie's hand. "We've gotta get back to the dormitory! We've gotta go now!"

"We don't have time. We have to hide!" And though it pained Birdie to do so, she bent her head low and snuffed out the lantern's faithful little flame so as not to be detected.

"Oh!" Cricket said. "It's so dark! How can we hide if we can't see?"

And for the next few moments, the two girls bumped up and down the hallway, until the striking of a match on the wall caused them both to jump.

The bright orange spark cast an eerie glow on Sir Ichabod Grim's face.

"What do you two think you are doing?" he said. And he yanked the lantern right out of Birdie's hand. Judging by his tone, Birdie thought he might toss the lantern against the wall, but instead, he reached in toward the center and used the match to light it once more. The hallway was again filled with a dim, warm flicker.

Neither Birdie nor Cricket said a word.

"Was it you two who were responsible for this?" he asked.

"Um, responsible for what, sir?" Birdie finally managed to say.

"The traps! All of them broken! Every single one!"

"Every single one?" Birdie echoed at the same time that Cricket exclaimed, "Sprinkles is saved!"

Sir Ichabod frowned. "So you two didn't know about this?" When Birdie and Cricket shook their heads, he put his hands on his hips. "Well, then, why are you roaming about in the dark?"

Without answering his question, Cricket leaned forward. "How do you see so well in the dark? You came right up on us when it was pitch-black!"

"I suppose I've been fumbling about in the darkness for so many years I've simply grown used to it. Most times I don't even notice if the light is there or not."

Cricket shivered. "I don't think the dark is something I would want to get used to."

"No, I don't suppose it is." And then Sir Ichabod lifted one bushy eyebrow, still awaiting the answer to his last question.

While Birdie wondered what she could possibly say to avoid getting into trouble, Cricket took matters into her own hands. She crossed her short arms against her chest, tapped her foot, and said, "What are *you* doing out here?"

"Me?" Sir Ichabod said.

"Yes, because *we* were here doing the only thing that makes sense. *We* were trying to save my pet rat. But you were doing something terrible. You were trying to kill my pet." And every time Cricket said the word "we," she looked straight at Birdie with a fierce nod of her head, and Birdie was certain her heart would burst.

We.

Sir Ichabod, on the other hand, was wilting. Apparently, he didn't just cower beneath Mistress Octavia's tone, but even at the honest accusations of an eight-year-old Tragical. He shrunk back against the wall, his hair fell across his eyes, and he merely shrugged his shoulders while saying, "Mistress Octavia told me to."

Birdie's heart sank.

Sir Ichabod made it sound so simple.

But nothing that happened to the Tragicals ever felt simple. Wasn't the constant rattle of their broken hearts proof of that? Couldn't Sir Ichabod see that?

Birdie's voice trembled. "But you're a grown-up. Grown-ups don't have to do what people tell them. You could say no."

"I did say no. Once," Sir Ichabod whispered. "And because of that, I never say no to her again." Sir Ichabod sucked in a shallow breath. His fingers grazed across his bronze medallion. "I am cursed."

And outside the manor, the Winds of Wanderly howled.

"Cursed?" Birdie whispered.

"Yes, because I refused to sign my Oaths. My Tragical Oaths. And now I can never leave this mountain. I can never refuse her command. I don't pick blueberries because I like them."[36]

Birdie's hand flew against her mouth. "But Sir Ichabod, if you refused to sign your Oaths, that means—you are—"

"Just like us," Cricket finished.

And Sir Ichabod's eyes widened. But only for a moment. "No," he said, shaking his head. "I am not just like you. You are children. And for the time being that is far more important than being a Tragical."

So many thoughts were flying through Birdie's head. She was having difficulty pinning down even one of them. She tried to focus. She tucked her hair behind her ears. "But why did you choose not to sign your Oaths?"

Sir Ichabod Grim met Birdie's stare. "Because words matter."

And Birdie knew instantly that he was right. In a kingdom where lives unfolded precisely as they did in storybooks, words *did* matter. Very much even. And hadn't the single word "friendship" made everything different for Birdie? Were there other such words out there? Words that gave wings instead of chains?

"That was very brave of you," Birdie said.

The corners of Sir Ichabod's lips lifted up just a hint. If it was

---

36. Despite the gravity of Sir Ichabod's confession, it should be noted this statement wasn't entirely true. He liked the taste of blueberries just fine. But eating them and being cursed to fulfill a quota of picking *ten thousand* a day are two very different things. Not to mention the endless washing, boiling, and mashing. It should come as no surprise that if Sir Ichabod didn't see another blueberry for the rest of his life, he wouldn't raise a single complaint.

a smile, it was the saddest one Birdie had ever seen. "Or perhaps I am the most foolish of all."

Foolish. Birdie was surprised to hear the word again. And most especially in the context of being brave. Birdie didn't think the two words could have anything to do with each other, but maybe the line wasn't so clear. Maybe a person could appear both brave and foolish at the same time.

"Do you wish you had made a different choice?" Birdie said, breath held tight.

"I don't think so," he said. For a man in Sir Ichabod's position, Birdie supposed that was saying quite a lot.

"Sir Ichabod," Cricket began, "if you're a Tragical too, then how come sometimes you're bad to us even when Mistress Octavia doesn't tell you to be?"

"I don't think there's any good way to answer that question."

Cricket blinked. "Then how about you just say what's true?"

A shadow crossed Sir Ichabod's face. He leaned in close. He whispered hoarsely, "Sometimes I feel as if I have fallen fast asleep. And in my slumber, I haven't a clue who I am or if I am even anything at all."

"So we just need to find some way to keep you awake?" Cricket asked. "Like loud noises?"

"I don't suppose it's that easy."

"Oh," Cricket said. And then: "How come you didn't ever tell us any of this before?"

Sir Ichabod was quiet for a moment. He looked up and down

the hallway as if he were trying to remember something. But his expression was blank. "No one ever asked."

Birdie's heart squeezed tight. Sir Ichabod was right, of course. In fact, no one had ever asked him much of anything. The children had trudged past him day in and day out without ever once *wondering*. For all their looking, for all their probing around the manor for trinkets to treasure, they had continually failed to see one another. They had failed to see that stories didn't just exist in books; they existed in people too. Stories that, despite what the Chancellor decreed, were not yet finished.

Sir Ichabod straightened up and gestured at the broken rat-traps propped in the corners. "Mistress Octavia will not forget, you know. Tonight your rat is saved, but she will find another way. For now, you should go back to bed."

Cricket nodded solemnly. She linked her arm through Birdie's. But before she could wheel around with Birdie in tow, Sir Ichabod cried out, "Wait!" And he plunged his hand deep within his pocket and pulled forth the drawing of Cricket's that had hung temporarily in Griselda Peabody's place. "Does this belong to one of you?" he asked.

With flushed cheeks, Cricket took a step forward, but Sir Ichabod pulled the drawing just out of reach. "I know where this came from," he said. And Birdie began to wring her hands because it had come from the book she'd discovered in Sir Ichabod's kitchen cupboard! The one she suddenly felt terribly guilty about taking because Sir Ichabod was so much more than a shadowy figure with callused hands.

"I know," Sir Ichabod continued, "that this paper was torn out of a book. I only hope it was one of Mistress Octavia's worst. But regardless, you must promise to be careful. Something is afoot at this manor. I—I can't put my finger on it, but *something*. And whatever that something is, I have not yet decided if it is good or bad. Frankly, I don't know if I can tell the difference anymore."

With that, Sir Ichabod shuffled toward the wall. He dropped down to his knees, untied an empty sack from around his waist, and began shoveling the broken rattraps in. Lantern in hand, Cricket and Birdie turned in the direction of the dormitory, but they made it only a few feet when Birdie paused. She looked back at Sir Ichabod. A circle of darkness waited eagerly around him, and only promised to grow thicker still.

"Hold on," Birdie whispered to Cricket. She ran back to Sir Ichabod and plunked the lantern down beside him. "The light helps," she said. "Even if you don't think it will, and maybe especially then."

When Birdie returned to Cricket, Cricket gripped her hand fiercely. Birdie assumed it was a result of the darkness or perhaps their chance meeting with the oldest Tragical in all of Wanderly, but it was the sound of crinkled paper that accompanied Cricket's whisper.

"I should've told you about my drawing," she said. "I should've never used something like your book page for that. I-I'm sorry."

Birdie's heart thumped. She thought back to Cricket's drawing. The paper falling from the sky like magic. How Cricket had chosen to draw her. Birdie couldn't imagine there existed any words in the world to tell her more about friendship than that.

"Don't be sorry," Birdie said softly. "I told you that book was different. Maybe it was never meant to be finished in an ordinary way. Maybe this is what it's been waiting for."

Cricket gasped. "To be torn apart?"

"To come true."

And the two girls slipped through the doorway of the dormitory, for once buoyed by the hope that accompanies the miraculous rescue of a pet and the glimmer, however faint, that perhaps not everything in Wanderly was against them.

TEN

IMPOSSIBLE CUSTOMER SERVICE

*A*gnes Prunella Crunch crossed her arms.

She bore a most quizzical expression.

On five separate occasions, she had lifted her fingers toward her jar full of worms and zapped 'em good! But all they did was cackle devilishly at her. As unnerving as a jar full of diabolical worms can be, it was—for once—the exact opposite of the effect Agnes was aiming for.

"Bah!" Agnes exclaimed. She slumped against her cauldron and snatched up the corner of the Bird-Girl's latest letter in her glittery grip. Agnes wished for once the girl's letters would explode into something useful like gooey slime or even a nice lump of malleable mud—anything would be better than glitter. Not to mention how unnerving it was to know something egregiously adorable could sneak up on her at any moment.

That morning it had been a bunny. Not a hare. Not even a rabbit. A *baby* bunny. And it had nuzzled its way past Agnes's cabin door and snuggled up against every grimy thing, like it hadn't just strolled into a properly horrific witch's abode. The nerve!

But none of that was as frustrating as the letter itself. Agnes read it aloud one more time:

Dear Ms. Crunch,

I guess the first thing I ought to say is I'm real glad you changed your mind about wanting to do me in (and that you're not the child-eating sort of witch, of course). I'm also trying to get excited about you wanting to do Mistress Octavia in, but I have a few important questions.

First off, if we're going to work together on this, I need to know exactly what you mean by "doing her in." As much as I would love to have a break from Mistress Octavia, there's a real difference between sending someone off on an indefinitely long vacation (even if that happens to be on Snaggletooth Isles) and stirring them up whole in a boiling cauldron.

Second, I never meant to make you feel sick to your stomach with my book talk. And if it's that big of a deal, we don't have to use the F-word ever again. Especially since your "BFF" idea has a real nice ring to it. Almost like the letters were just meant to go together. It also makes me feel like we've got our own secret language, which is definitely a BFF-ish thing to do, don't you think?

I know you still don't actually want to be my BFF. I know you're a witch, and I'm a Tragical. I know you think that me knowing all of this and still wanting to be your BFF proves I have half a brain, but maybe being BFFs is about more than just the facts. Maybe that's why the Winds of Wanderly chose us. And I think it'd be a real shame if something big like the Winds was moving, and we didn't move along with it.

You asked me to give you all the info on Mistress Octavia. Honestly, I don't know much. When she's not smacking her broomstick handle against the blackboard, whispering horrible things into our ears during instruction time, or eating with her back turned toward us in the dining hall, she spends every other minute (except for the three hours she sleeps) in her Room of Sinister Plotting. Considering the blood-red door and three hissing cobra snakes that guard the knob, no one has ever tried to find out what she does in there. I know I'm a doomed kid talking, but to me, she seems just about invincible.

There is one thing though.

One small thing that seems sort of silly, but I figure I at least ought to mention it. I think Mistress Octavia is allergic to laughter. Not just any laughter, but genuine laughter. Maybe even as specific as genuine kid laughter. Because a week or so ago, it happened with an eight-year-old. She laughed. And Mistress Octavia collapsed! Mistress Octavia wriggled all over, broke into itchy red hives, and couldn't even talk she was sneezing so bad. I think if Sir Ichabod hadn't have been around, we almost could have gotten away with anything we wanted. So . . . I'm not sure how that helps, but you asked.

As for my address, I still feel sort of squeamish about handing it over. I know I've kept you waiting, and I am sorry about that, but maybe if you give me some more details about your plan (specifically the Mistress Octavia parts, so I'll know it's not still me you're after), that will help? In any event, I was real glad to find out your whole name. As soon as I saw it, I wanted to say how pretty it was (especially that Prunella part!), but I figured you'd appreciate it a whole lot more if I told you it was awful. So I will. It's the awfullest name I've ever heard.

Very truly yours,
Birdbrain (I'm not really a fan of this nickname, but it only seems fair considering you're not a fan of BFFs.)

PS: This will probably seem like a weird question, but you didn't happen to figure out a way into our manor and dismantle three hundred rattraps, did you? If so, it made Cricket's whole year (and maybe even her life).

Agnes tossed the Bird-Girl's letter in the air.

It sounded even worse than the first time she'd read it.

And to be honest, she was starting to understand why most witches avoided children at all costs. For goblin's sake, were they always so *stubborn*? Why couldn't the girl just let Agnes commit her wicked deed in peace? Why couldn't she give up the BFF thing? Why couldn't she get it through her doomed little head that witches didn't need anybody!

Much less the Winds of Wanderly. Bah! Agnes knew full well what she was made of. She knew the inky darkness of her stony heart, and frankly, if the Winds were recruiting the likes of her, that was reason enough not to put much stock in them.

But the cherry on top of the whole mucky mess was the laughter bit.

Of all things, Octavia's one known weakness *had* to be laughter.

Whatever instruction the Bird-Girl was receiving, she didn't know a thing about witches. Conjuring up laughter was out of the question! Of all the wonderfully horrific spells witches could cast, they couldn't squeeze out a drop of intentionally *good* magic.

And laughter—genuine laughter—was an expression of joy. Laughter—genuine laughter—sprang forth from (gulp) the heart. Agnes snarled. She wasn't used to dealing with such wishy-washy things as feelings. The thought alone left a terrible taste in her mouth, as if she had been chewing on too many icky-sticky jelly beans at once.

Still, there Agnes was.

Trying to make a jar of worms giggle.

All the while, they kept cackling at her. Like a heap of witches would cackle at her if they knew what she was up to. Agnes wondered if it would just be easier to accept Rudey Longtooth's ultimatum and attend the Annual Witches' Ball. To elbow a bunch of witches she couldn't stand, jaw off a mediocre curse, and maybe even waltz off with a fool's golden egg–laying chicken she could use to torment some commoners.[37] Maybe she didn't need to win the top prize, but just *a* prize. Maybe that would be enough to take the edge off her boredom.

But half-baked spells and mischief were a dime a dozen. Agnes had done all that before. Agnes wanted to experience something different; something important. Doing in an uppity Council member like Octavia felt *awfully* important. Maybe the most important—and most wicked—thing Agnes would ever accomplish. It was Agnes's chance to show everyone what witches could really do, and she'd be a fool to throw in the towel!

---

37. Despite their namesake, the commoners in Wanderly likely lived the most interesting lives of all. Whereas everyone knew precisely what lay ahead for a Triumphant or a Tragical, for commoners, a happy ending was just as likely as a bad ending. Consequently, they were always on the hunt for fairy godmothers, magical beans, wishing wells, and anything else that might tip the balance in their favor. Unfortunately for them, witches were more than happy to provide counterfeit substitutes that tended to range from the hilarious to the devious, but never failed to be 100 percent disappointing.

And so she wouldn't.

She would do whatever it took.

Even if that meant stooping to the level of purchasing pre-made magic. It was embarrassing; it was humiliating; it was what witches stuck in a never-ending loop of Wickedry 101 did, but surely the best-laid plans were not without sacrifice.

As such, Agnes Prunella Crunch, supremely wicked witch of Wanderly, swallowed her pride (which, if you haven't tried it—and Agnes never had—tastes like an awful combination of old fish sticks and sour grapes) and stomped toward the door with a gruesome scowl on her face. Without even being summoned, her trusty broomstick swept beneath her and scooped her right up. Her ever-ready cauldron flickered a cheery goodbye of hot-pink and purple flames.

For the first time in decades, Agnes Prunella Crunch was headed to town.

In a kingdom of Wanderly's size, there were very many towns.

But there was one that was the most famous.

It was called Pigglesticks.

Pigglesticks's town square wasn't really a square at all, but instead a whole network of narrow cobblestone streets, a few heart-pounding side passages, and even a tangle of underground tunnels (used by only the most sinister sorts). The bevy of stores were stacked one on top of the other, with those at the tippy-top being connected to foot traffic by the use of great sliding ladders the citizens of Wanderly scurried up and down like a colony of hardworking ants.

At the heart of it all, at the place that connected the self-proclaimed noble north side of Pigglesticks to the unapologetically seedy south side of Pigglesticks, was a store known, quite simply, as Wands and Broomsticks, Inc. Wands and Broomsticks, Inc., was the oldest magic-dealing establishment in all of Wanderly. It was also, not surprisingly, highly regulated by the Council.

It didn't always used to be that way.

Before the Council stepped in, Wands and Broomsticks, Inc., did a fairly booming business. It was the central hub for new and fantastical sorts of spells that magical folks were eager to sell and trade. Others would gather round just for the fun of it. But such was no longer the case. The Council had severely limited the potency of the type of magic that could be sold in Wands and Broomsticks, Inc., citing the tired maxim: "If you can't brew it, you likely don't know how to use it," and yada, yada, yada.

When Agnes Prunella Crunch breezed through the glass door with the annoying little chime, she was hardly surprised to find it empty, save for the on-the-clock magic dealer who had fallen asleep in his chair. His neck was bent at an awkward angle, and a glistening trail of drool dribbled down his chin.

Agnes turned up her nose. She hadn't a single intention of seeking his assistance, but the *clickety-clack* of her witchy boots must have woken him. He tipped all the way over in his chair, thumped hard against the ground, and made a most unbecoming snarfling noise.

"Can I help you?" he called out.

Agnes didn't bother answering.

A moment later, however, the stubborn little bugger shuffled to catch up with her and had the nerve to ask much more pointedly, "Can I *help* you?"

"NO," Agnes said with a gusty exhale. The man's face paled because, in addition to the scent of rotten quail eggs, you must remember how very many toothbrushes Agnes owned. (Hint: not one.) Nevertheless, he rushed to bob up and down alongside her *again*.

Agnes skidded to a halt. She turned full upon him. She thrummed up her most awful, horrible, terrifying smile—the one that showed every crooked tooth, and the bug legs stuck in between. Indeed, a witch's smile is a most fearsome weapon! Remarkably, the man barely flinched.

Instead, he pushed his wiry glasses up along the bridge of his sweaty nose and gazed into the gaping black abyss of Agnes's nostrils, because standing side by side with her, he barely reached the top of her well-rounded bosom.

"I'm afraid, ma'am, that in order to shop at our fine establishment, you must first request assistance. I see you are of . . . hmm." He paused and narrowed his eyes a bit, as if in doing so, he could actually see past Agnes's row of artfully stolen gold doubloon buttons; through the gnarled cage surrounding her stony, little heart; and into the twisted chambers of her heart itself. The magic dealer nodded with full certainty. "Yes, most definitely of the wicked variety. You will be shopping over there." He gestured toward the half of the store that led out to the seedy south. It was cloaked in darkness. It swarmed with squeaking vampire bats. Beetles skittered about on the floor; a thin green haze was wafting about; a rickety wooden sign hanging from the ceiling said in scrawling script "Wicked Witches and Dark Magicians Only"; and it smelled as stale as a loaf of moldy bread.

The magic dealer prattled on, "You will not be disappointed with our latest additions. Why, just today, we received two vials of frog croaks, a gallon of serpent venom, and"—he drew near, like he was sharing a delicious secret—"a dragon's toenail clipping!"

Agnes's blood began to boil. "A dragon's toenail clipping? Frog croaks? Serpent venom?" she screeched. "Do you even know who I am? I am AGNES PRUNELLA CRUNCH, and the day I need assistance procuring those beginner's trinkets is the day I die a slow and miserable death!"

The magic dealer stared at her. He adjusted the name tag on his wrinkled shirt that read "Bob." "Oh" was all he managed to say. And then, quite aggravatingly, he asked, "Are you sure you don't want to even take a look at the toenail clipping? I think there's a bit of fungus on it."

Agnes leered at him. She wrapped her long, curly fingernails around the collar of his shirt and pulled him closer. "Look, *Bob*—I once flew over to Snaggletooth Isles and trapped an entire full-grown dragon myself. Do you want to know what I did to it? I barbecued it! Limb by limb. So I'm not impressed by your toenail clipping. I came today for a laughing potion, and I bet my last eyeball it's sitting on one of those shelves over there."

Agnes jerked her head toward the noble north side of the store. It was full of light and sparkles. Glitter rained down periodically from the ceiling, and a kaleidoscope of colorful butterflies flitted in and out and sometimes even in the formation of hearts and rainbows. The delicate aroma of iced lemon cake abounded, a flowery sign posted along a white picket fence said in perfect penmanship "Wizards and Fairy Godmothers Are Welcome Here," and a chorus of sweetly chirping birds burst spontaneously into song every few minutes.

Bob gulped. He tucked his chin against his chest and refused to meet Agnes's gaze. Below his breath, he mumbled, "I'm smommy, dwat's gingossible."

"What did you say?" Agnes barked.

"*I said,*" he yelled out, but then grew terribly quiet again, "I'm smommy, dwat's gingossible."

Agnes stomped her foot. She stuck her hands on her hips. "I don't give a hoot about your mommy and whoever Gingossible is. I want you to take me over there and get me a laughing potion, NOW!"

Bob gasped. "How dare you! You leave my mother out of

this! I know your type! I know the sorts of awful things you do! Anyhow, I was only trying to be polite because you seem sort of clueless."

Agnes snapped her teeth in Bob's face. "I don't do polite," she said.

"Fine, then. You want to know the truth? You want to hear how it is? You can't go over to that side of the store. It's *impossible*." Bob straightened the rumpled collar of his shirt and said to himself, "Man alive, you try to do something nice for someone, and this is how they act. . . ."

But Agnes was stuck. Stuck on that word.

Impossible.

"What do you mean?" she cried out. "You don't have good magic here? It looks like there's plenty! Is there some sort of hefty price tag on it, because I've got oodles to trade. Name your price, and I know I can match it!"

Bob sighed. "There is no price. Even if I wanted to, I *can't* sell it to you. In fact, the Council's enchanted the place so you can't even set a wicked pinkie toe on that side of the store." Bob pushed his glasses up along the bridge of his nose again. "Look, Aggy Pruneface Munch, you seem like a real good wicked witch. Better than the bunch I see creeping in and out of here in the wee hours of the night. Maybe it's best not to stir up trouble."

"My name's *not* Aggy Pruneface Munch, it's—" But Agnes paused. Suddenly, it didn't seem all that important. Bob didn't care about her name; he didn't care who she was. He only cared *what* she was: an unmistakably wicked witch. A week or so ago, Agnes might have found that immensely satisfying, but right then, it was nothing more than an impediment.

"If it makes any difference to you, you're the first witch I've ever met to make such a request. Most of 'em grumble and snarl because they even have to be within ten feet of that side. But people will put up with most anything because, like I said before"—he threw his shoulders back and blared, like he was a walking advertisement—"this here is the finest magical establishment in all of Wanderly. It's where magical folks come when they want the best!"

Feeling terribly deflated, Agnes asked, "But how am I supposed to acquire good magic if I can't get it here?"

"That's just it. You don't. That kind of magic isn't meant for you, and it's best to forget you even asked. In fact, you and I can both forget about it. I'd be willing to do that for ya, you know?"

Agnes supposed he was trying to be helpful, but she wanted to crunch the bridge of his nose in between her teeth. "But I don't want to *be* good! I just want a good potion so I can do something *evil* with it."

Bob actually reached out and patted Agnes on the shoulder. "Sure, you do," he said.

Agnes smacked his hand so hard it flew up, crashed into his own forehead, and knocked him goofy for a spell. "It's the truth!" she screeched at him. "Somehow, someway, I've got to get my hands on a good potion so I can be *evil*!"

Agnes was thoroughly worked up.

She stomped her feet.

She clucked her tongue.

Agnes began to tantrum.

Bob sputtered. He tripped along after Agnes as she crashed through the store, knocking things left to right. He leaped through the air to catch a skeleton head Agnes tossed high, and he dove to the floor to swoop up a molted rainbow snake's skin Agnes whacked with the back of her hand. His cheeks began to flush a scarlet shade of panic.

"Stop!" Bob begged. "Please stop that! I'll tell you—I'll tell you everything I know if you just stop!"

Agnes froze. "So you do know something? Something that can be of help to me?"

Bob slumped against the wall with his chest heaving. He fanned himself with his hand. "Blue," he breathed out, "Dragon."

"Blue Dragon?" Agnes echoed. And then again, "Blue Dragon?" When Bob nodded, Agnes thrust her big nose centimeters from his forehead. Her voice was a low growl. "You think you're going to get rid of me with a made-up hokey story like the Blue Dragon?"

"But that's just it!" Bob said. "It's not made-up! It's true! The Blue Dragon has the power to change people, and you can find him in the Deepest, Darkest Bog. He waits there where the green fog is its thickest."

Agnes tried to ignore the shiver that rippled up and down her spine. It couldn't really be true. In a kingdom where everyone had their roles, everyone knew there was no way to get around that. The Council alone had the power to demote citizens through disciplinary action or, very rarely, to promote citizens as Triumphants. Though the agony of Agnes's recent boredom had driven her to do unthinkable things like write letters to a child, she hadn't once entertained the idea of being anything other than a witch. But the thought, the mere possibility of change—real change that didn't have a thing to do with the Council—made her skin tingle.

Agnes narrowed her eyes. "If a dragon as powerful as that is really in the bog, why hasn't the Council gotten rid of him yet?"

"Simple," Bob said with a shrug of his shoulders. "No one in Wanderly believes the Blue Dragon is real. If the Council acts as if he's a threat, people will probably get curious. So, for the past decade or so, the Council's ignored him, and so has everyone else. Also, considering your story about catching a dragon—"

"That wasn't just a story!" Agnes interrupted.

"Okay, *fine*, considering you've apparently caught and roasted your own dragon, you of all people should know dragons are sort of cumbersome. The Council's not going to go out of their way to deal with one—by the way, I've heard he's *enormous*—if they don't have to. But you could."

"Could what?"

"Go see him. But"—Bob jabbed a short, thick finger right beneath Agnes's nose—"if you do, you better not go alone."

"I do everything alone!"

"Well, then plan on getting charred! Everyone knows the good guys don't work alone, and if you want to be good, you're going to have to offer some solid proof."

Agnes rolled her eyes. "If this Blue Dragon's really real, and if *everyone* knows so much about him, then why hasn't there been a single success story, hmm? Anyhow, he sounds ridiculously picky. All I want is one measly potion; I don't want to be good forever!"

Bob shrugged again. "It's probably not worth the risk, then." He lifted his arms overhead and tried unsuccessfully to stifle a yawn. "Say, Maggie Droopface Munch, I've done just about all I can for you. If there's really nothing you want on your side of the store, do you mind if I escort you out now? I've got seven more hours until the next gal comes in to cover my shift, and frankly, you've exhausted me."

Agnes frowned. Even if the Blue Dragon *was* real, he sounded like a heap of trouble. Not to mention she'd already traveled miles away from her haunted abode, endured the supreme annoyance of Bob, and was anything but patient.

Agnes's gaze flickered over to the north side of the store. It was so close; everything she needed was right there! She nodded in Bob's direction. She tried her best to sound calm. "Yes, I suppose you're right. If I can't get the potion I need, it's pointless to stay even a moment longer. May you please show me the way out now?"

Despite the dead giveaway of witchy trickster words—such as "May you," "please," and (horror of all horrors) "you're right"— Bob breathed out a little sigh of relief. He turned on his heel and ambled toward the front of the store as quickly as his feet could propel him.

That was when Agnes struck.

She dug the heel of her boot into the shag carpet as if she were a charging bull. She revved up her arms. She sprang—she flew—toward the north side of the store. She flew at it with all her might and with all her small, stony heart, because surely the Council couldn't keep a witch of her stature out!

But Agnes was wrong.

Terribly wrong.

The Council's enchantment pushed right back. It pushed so hard her witchy hat was knocked clean off her head. It pushed so hard she was sent reeling and catapulting toward the south side of the store as if she were being spit out like a distasteful bug. Agnes's back smacked hard against the wall, and she landed— *splat!*—on her bottom. A can of green goo from a high-up shelf split open and oozed down, down, down, coating her purple hair in sticky gunk.

Near the front of the store, Bob stood with his mouth gaped open. He rubbed his eyes as if he couldn't believe what he was seeing.

Oh, what a pitiful sight Agnes was!

Hurriedly, she swiped the goo away from her eyes. She

gathered her black skirts in her trembling, gnarled hands. She brushed past Bob and that annoying door chime.

Agnes ran.

She ran away from Wands and Broomsticks, Inc.

She ran away from Pigglesticks.

She ran and she ran and she ran, but no matter how hard she huffed and puffed—no matter how loudly her stone heart rattled in her chest and her witchy boots *click-clack*ed against the cobblestones—it seemed nothing would make that awful word go away.

Impossible.

By the time her trusty broomstick caught up with her, Wands and Broomsticks, Inc., was awash with reporters from the Chancellor's favorite news press, the *Wanderly Whistle*, and Agnes was spent.

ELEVEN

EIGHT-LEGGED WONDERS

Birdie Bloom slipped out the door of Sir Ichabod's kitchen and breathed a sigh of relief. She had done it, and no one had seen her. Birdie was not in pursuit of more unauthorized storybooks or even looking to ask Sir Ichabod one of the dozens of questions sparked by his Tragical confession three nights prior. No, Birdie was busy protecting the life of a hero.

Surely only a house full of Tragicals would nominate a fugitive rat as their hero, but a hero was what Sprinkles had become for the sole fact that, despite Mistress Octavia's most extensive efforts, *she hadn't been able to do away with him (yet)*.

Fortunately or not, Sprinkles hadn't a clue of his peak position on Mistress Octavia's lengthy most wanted list. He insisted on sleeping cheek to cheek with Cricket; he demanded to ride atop the children's shoulders rather than be stowed safely away in a pocket; and his silvery plume had never looked quite so dapper. These sorts of antics, however, made the Tragicals' job of keeping him safe infinitely harder. Indeed, amid the constant shooing, stuffing, cooing, and squeeing, they were very nearly forgetting they weren't supposed to talk to one another. They were very nearly forgetting they weren't supposed to do things *together*.[38]

And perhaps that was what made Sprinkles the most heroic of all.

Even if his reward was being stuffed into a wholly undignified cage constructed of the Tragicals' formerly useless pencils and long threads unraveled from their gowns. They simply had no other choice—Sprinkles couldn't accompany them into the Instruction Room nor roam about the manor laden with booby traps.[39] And so, the children took turns tucking Sprinkles's cage away in a remote pocket of Sir Ichabod Grim's kitchen, because other than the dungeon, it was the one place Mistress Octavia

---

38. Or rather, together minus Francesca Prickleboo. The children had not excluded Francesca in any sort of malicious way, but as a matter of necessity. Over the years, Francesca Prickleboo had proven time and time again she simply could not be trusted. Her allegiance was to Mistress Octavia and any decree—no matter what it entailed—of the Council.

39. The ratty booby traps were perhaps better described as butlerish booby traps. In the span of three days, Sir Ichabod Grim had snapped three fingers, two toes, and even got his nose caught in a trap Mistress Octavia hung from the ceiling. Of course, despite Sprinkles's impressive opinion of himself, he could not (as was typically the case with rats) fly.

never ventured due to the overwhelming "stench" of blueberries.

Birdie cast one last glance in the direction of the kitchen and moved swiftly down the gloomy hallway. She was late for trudging and would need to catch up. Still, when she approached the door leading down to the dungeon, she skidded to an abrupt halt.

The dungeon door was cracked open.

Just a smidge, but still, unmistakably, unlatched.

Had Birdie not been the recent recipient of magical letters, well aware that a witch wanted desperately to know her whereabouts, and the recent victim of a rainy curse, she might not have thought anything of it. But she *was* aware of all those things. And the last time the dungeon door had been left cracked open, a curse had arrived. Certainly that didn't bode well for—

Birdie yelped when a shadow flittered toward the crack in the door and a shiny-fanged gray bat pushed its way out. Birdie stumbled backward, but the bat didn't waste any time. It dove after Birdie. It tangled up its wings in her already-tangled hair and trounced atop her head. Birdie tried to swat the bat away with her hands, but it kept right on coming. Birdie was certain it had to be one of Ms. Crunch's letters, but this one seemed particularly ornery. Finally, in one last hair-raising nosedive, the bat exploded in a bombastic firework of ash that rained down from the ceiling.

Birdie didn't stop to take a breath. She lunged toward the dungeon door and clicked it shut in case anything else was lurking about and looking to be set loose in the manor.

Meanwhile, the ash began to swirl together. It lifted up and transformed into a letter with familiar, stabby penmanship.

Birdie bit her lip. Ms. Crunch's last letter had been so frightening that part of her worried she might never hear from Ms. Crunch again and part of her worried that she would. Why *exactly* did Ms. Crunch keep writing back? Moreover, for someone who wasn't at all interested in being BFFs, Birdie hardly imagined she could find a more responsive one than Ms. Crunch.

Birdie took a deep breath and brought the letter near.

To Bird-Girl:

Your last letter was the worst yet. Your little tip about Octavia's kooky laughter allergy was worthless. And the whole thing ended up in me having the worst day ever. Is that BFF enough for you?

In all seriousness, we've got a problem. Because you seem to be totally clueless about the fundamentals of being a witch. For starters: we don't do good magic. In fact, we can't do good magic. And how many spooky, scary, terrifying stories have you read where someone is about to meet their doom and they . . . giggle? GENUINELY? Zero. Zilch. Zippo. Do you see my point?

So I went to some pokey old magic shop and tried to buy that dumb laughter potion. Get this: the blockhead at the front wouldn't sell it to me. Me! Agnes Prunella Crunch! And when I tried to take it with a little sweat and muscle, I got tossed out on my behind by the Council's enchantments. The whole thing was such a disaster the Wanderly Whistle wrote a report on it!

Lucky for me, the clueless store clerk remembered my name as Maggie Pruneface Punch. So far, no one's been able to put two and two together. If they had, I would have been hauled in for a detention by the Council faster than you could say "Poof!" If that happens, neither one of us is gonna get what we want.

Anyhoo, I didn't wind up with a drop of that laughing potion. I'm considering staking out some character called the Blue Dragon, but considering he (1) lives in the Deepest, Darkest Bog; (2) requires visitors to use the buddy system; and (3) supposedly works by changing people (ha! Good luck!), it seems like a long shot.

All right, two last things. You asked if I found a way into your manor. Believe me, if I found a way in, I'd stop wasting my time with these chitchatty letters! Also, three hundred rattraps? What in the world sort of rodent problem do you have at your place, and why is a cricket glad none of the rats bit the dust? Don't rats eat crickets? Finally, for the love of all that is wretched—SEND ME YOUR ADDRESS!!!! Can you tell I'm starting to lose my patience?

Totally disgruntled,
AP Crunch

PS: I'm not purposefully ignoring you on the definition of "doing Octavia in." But there's not really an answer for it either. It all depends on how I'm feeling at the moment. Given all she's done to you, you should focus your attention on throwing me a party.

PPS: I'm sorry not sorry if I somehow send another curse your way. I think something happened to my magic when I tried to steal that potion. Wicked spells have been flying off my fingertips left and right as if to drill into my head that's all I've got. This morning I got chased out of bed by a swarm of green wasps (the worst kind!), dunked my behind into a pond for protection, and was herded out of that by snapping crocodiles! By the time I finally crawled back into my cabin, the curtains turned into wolves and nearly snapped my favorite rocking chair in half! So, I guess what I'm trying to say is . . . heh, heh . . . good luck.

Birdie gulped.

Ms. Crunch wasn't exaggerating. Her day out to town sounded truly horrible. And with a morning full of wasps, crocodiles, and wolves, it didn't sound as if things had gotten better since. Birdie, of course, had never been allowed to peruse the *Wanderly Whistle*, but she'd caught Mistress Octavia reading it plenty of times. Sure, there were dozens of cheery celebratory reports about Triumphants claiming their latest (surprise, surprise) victories, but even those weren't featured on the front page. What *was* splashed across the front page were those citizens detained for Wanderly's most heinous crime: attempting to step outside of one's role.

Birdie could only guess that was right where Ms. Crunch's story landed. Ms. Crunch didn't seem too worried about it, but with publicity like that, wasn't it only a matter of time before someone figured out who Maggie Pruneface Punch *really* was?

And just like that, Birdie grew cold. She had always been told there would be consequences if she failed to accept her Tragic

End. That somewhere, someone else—someone better—would have to pay the price. But what if it was even worse than that? Hadn't Mistress Octavia alluded to as much when, on the day of Griselda Peabody's visit, she said the Tragicals could "infect" someone with misery? Surely since knowing Birdie, Ms. Crunch had never experienced such a string of bad luck. What if it was only going to get worse? What if Birdie's doom was contagious?

Birdie leaned hard against the wall.

Her chest felt tight.

Birdie would never have thought she'd have to protect a wicked witch from anything. But maybe in all of Wanderly, there really was nothing worse than a Tragical. Maybe there was nothing worse than . . . Birdie. Maybe the most friendly thing she could do for Ms. Crunch was to stop trying to be her BFF.

Birdie jolted at the sound of a scream.

And then another.

And another still.

The other Tragicals! Birdie hurriedly stuffed the letter beneath the collar of her gown—decidedly *not* in her pocket in case Mistress Octavia demanded they be emptied—and pounded down the hallway in the direction of the library. She rounded the corner with a screech of her shoes. The curtains rippled encouragingly as she whipped by, and even the ten spiders swinging from the overhead cobwebs seemed to pump their jointed legs in the air with extra panache.

Birdie froze.

Ten spiders? Because yes, the manor housed a fair amount of arachnids, but ten swinging all in a row? As Birdie had occasion to glance more carefully around, however, she noticed there were not actually ten spiders. Crawling along on the ground, scaling up and down the walls, and winding down from the ceiling, there looked instead to be at least *fifty* spiders.

And they were all trickling out from under the library door that lay just ahead of Birdie. Birdie gulped. Ms. Crunch warned her a curse might be on the way, but refreshing storm clouds and an army of spiders were two very different things!

"Help us!" came a muffled cry.

"Somebody, please!"

Birdie wrapped her suddenly sweaty hand around the doorknob. She gave a mighty tug. But it wouldn't budge! Birdie banged her hands on the door.

"I can't get in!" she shouted. "Is everyone okay in there?"

"There are so many of them!" Cricket's voice cried out.

"Long live . . . Wanderly" came Francesca's breathless voice.

"Keep pulling on the doorknob, Birdie!" Ralph shouted. "And when it budges, hang on to something!"

Hang on to something? Birdie thought. *That's an odd thing to say.*

Nevertheless, she did as Ralph suggested. And after several more epic tugs, when the door came barreling open, and the tidal wave of spiders came tumbling out, it all made sense. Birdie yelped as the spiders gushed past her. She dug her fingernails into the doorframe as her feet rose upon the spiderly swell.

Inside the library, the other Tragicals were perched along bookshelves and wrapped around marble columns. They swayed from chandeliers and even the scanty plumes of dusty, artificial plants. And lying beneath them, stretching from one end of the room to the next, were books. Hundreds of books. Not one single book remained on a shelf; they had all been tossed to the ground. Their front covers lay open in a gesture of surrender, and spilling forth from their spines were spiders. Spiders gleefully trouncing upon the very, many terrible words Mistress Octavia read to the children day in and day out. Spiders that kept right on coming.

Birdie attempted to wade through the spiderly tide to where Cricket clung to a column. On the way, the six-year-old boy who Mistress Octavia insisted on calling "Tom," but whose name was actually Benjamin, blew his nose on the sleeve of his gown and sobbed, "I always knew these books were gonna get us one day!"

"Hush!" Francesca chided. Unlike the other children, Francesca had *not* sought a safe, high-up spot. She instead sat in a reading chair, holding a book opened wide, while the spiders crawled all over her so that it looked like she was wearing a wriggly jumpsuit. "Any minute now, one of these spiders will get hungry. Their fangs will pierce my skin, and the venom will enter my bloodstream. I will have minutes, maybe even mere seconds. I don't want to miss it! With my last dying breath, I want to say something important for Wanderly!"

Ralph swung by from a chandelier. "I wouldn't wait around too long," he said. "These spiders don't even bite."

Francesca's left eye flew open and rolled in Ralph's direction. "What? What are you talking about?"

"I squished one by accident. You know what happened? It exploded—"

"Ewwwww!" a chorus of children cried.

"Not like with blood and guts and stuff. It exploded into powder because these spiders aren't ordinary," Ralph said. "These spiders are *magical*."

Whoosh! The Winds of Wanderly swept onto the scene. They swirled and whirled outside the library windows, but no one seemed to notice except Birdie.

Especially not Francesca. With wide eyes, she jabbed a shaking finger in Ralph's direction. She sputtered, "You—you—you shouldn't have said that word!"

And for once, Francesca may have been right. Because the largest mound of spiders—the one in the dead center of the room—suddenly shuddered and shook! It twisted and writhed! It looked as if it might swirl up in a gigantic spidery tornado, but what emerged instead was something much worse.

It was Mistress Octavia.

It was Mistress Octavia dripping with spiders. It was Mistress Octavia with spiders clinging to the strands of her hair, swinging from the threads of her black cardigan, and spilling down the folds of her skirt as if it were a playground slide.

Wheeee!

Except not.

"These are not magical spiders!" Mistress Octavia shrieked.

The spiders, however, did not seem to like that very much.

The spiders began to pour out of the books *faster*.

The youngest Tragicals began to whimper. The sixteen-year-old girl, Mildred, tossed her eyeglasses into the air because the sight was becoming too horrendous to watch. And Birdie bit her lip because, however delightful it was to see Mistress Octavia's terrible books taken down a notch or two, the fact remained that the children simply could not share the manor with an endless flood of spiders. At least not for very long.

But how to get rid of so many?

Sir Ichabod must have been thinking the same thing, because he sprang out of the shadows and into action. He sucked up a deep breath. He dove headfirst into the growing tide of spiders and attempted to wrangle the books' front covers shut. But every time he surfaced for a heaving gulp of air, the covers popped right back open and even more spiders gushed forth!

Outside the library, the Winds of Wanderly stirred faster. They *tap-tap-tapp*ed on the windows like a curious child who desperately wanted a peek inside. Some of the other children began to notice too. And though their eyes grew wide in fright, Birdie wasn't a bit worried. In fact, Birdie could barely contain herself because the Winds of Wanderly had given her a brilliant idea!

Birdie jumped down from the tabletop where she had taken

refuge. She pushed through the spiders with all her might, cupping her hands in front of her and scooping whole handfuls up and aside.

Mistress Octavia, who had since retrieved her broken broomstick handle, was so focused on walloping the spiders' bulbous bodies or, quite eerily, dipping her broomstick in and stirring them up as if she were positioned at a cauldron, that she wasn't paying a lick of attention to Birdie.

With her chest heaving, Birdie drew near to Sir Ichabod. "We need to let the Winds inside. We need to open up the windows. Sir Ichabod, I need your help!"

But Sir Ichabod wouldn't even look up at Birdie. His eyelids hung heavy; his shoulders were slumped; he was staring down at all the very many spiders as if he would never find his way out from beneath them all.

Birdie reached out and touched his arm. She kept her voice low so Mistress Octavia couldn't hear. "Sir Ichabod, the other night you told us that being a child was more important than being a Tragical. What if being a grown-up is more important too? Please, Sir Ichabod, I can't do it alone."

Sir Ichabod looked up. He blinked his eyes. Sir Ichabod was stirring *awake*. And ever so slowly, he nodded. With every child watching, with Birdie's heart soaring, and with Mistress Octavia's jaw gaping, Sir Ichabod strode to the window. He tossed open the thick black curtain, and a wave of stone-gray light tumbled into the room.

The children gasped. They held their hands up in front of their eyes.

Everything was so bright! Everything was so beautiful! How *different* everything looked when washed by the light!

The Tragicals looked upon the faces of one another. Benjamin stopped sobbing long enough to notice that beneath his tearstained sleeves, a small cluster of freckles on his arm formed the curious pattern of . . . a heart. A heart on a Tragical. He rolled his finger over it, wide-eyed, but it didn't disappear. Whether or not he could see it, it had always been there, and it always would be.

Sir Ichabod Grim wasn't finished yet. He reached for the window locks. He began to wriggle and jiggle them about. He turned to his right, wrenched a chair free from the swell of spiders, lifted it high overhead and—

"SIR ICH-A—" Mistress Octavia began, but a particularly hairy, particularly gruesome, spider slunk across her mouth and planted its fat body square atop her lips, rendering her to nothing more than a harmless "MWARGH! MMAWWW!"

Without a clear order from Mistress Octavia—and with beads of sweat rolling down his face, and his arms trembling from the weight of the chair—Sir Ichabod sucked up a breath and brought it crashing down against the glass.

The Winds of Wanderly met him there at that window.

The Winds of Wanderly took hold of the broken shards and cast them far off into the distance.

And then the Winds swept into the manor.

The Winds gleefully tossed the thick window curtains over Mistress Octavia's head and wrapped her up tight like a mummy, tickled the cheeks of the gawking Tragicals, and blew all the covers of the books gently closed. They ruffled toward the spiders and propelled each of their eight legs toward the window. And, in one great marching exodus, the spiders heartily obliged.

The spiders followed the Winds of Wanderly all the way up to the windowsill, leaped into the Winds' open arms, and were carried gently away. Every single one of them billowing and parachuting down along the Winds' invisible hem.

Except for a very disappointed Francesca, the Tragicals cheered aloud. They scrambled down from their high places. Wobbling atop a bookshelf, Amelia reached her short arms out to Birdie, and Birdie helped her jump to the ground. The Tragicals peered gratefully in Sir Ichabod's direction, but he was leaning heavily against the wall, and his face was a peculiar shade of gray. While Mistress Octavia continued to roll uselessly back and forth in her curtain, even the manor joined in the celebration, gulping in breath after breath after breath of fresh air.

In the midst of a feeling as unfamiliar as excitement, no one saw Ralph. No one noticed him leap off the swaying chandelier and line the toes of his shoes up against the open window. No one saw him bend low and jump *out* the window.

No one, that is, except for Mistress Octavia's ravenous pack of wolves waiting just below the windowsill.

Oh Ralph.

TWELVE

THE HEALING OF A BOY

Despite what you may think—despite how very many of them find their way onto our pages—most books, including myself, are not fond of so-called "cliff-hangers." And so I shall tell you immediately because I cannot keep it in a moment longer: *Ralph did not die! Ralph was alive!*

Please feel free to cheer a bit. Happy moments are meant to be celebrated, and I shall gladly wait for you.

It is no small thing to pick up a book about a house full of Tragicals—eighteen, no less—and be brave enough to read it. The fact that we have come this far without losing a single one, especially in the presence of such formidable foes as witches and wolves, is not to be taken for granted.

This isn't to say that Ralph didn't suffer any injuries. He

did. And Mistress Octavia had banished him to the infirmary the moment Sir Ichabod carried him back inside the manor.[40] To Mistress Octavia's utter disappointment, the bulk of Ralph's injuries occurred during his fall from the library window, i.e. her ferocious wolves had barely touched him. In fact, before Sir Ichabod had managed to distract the wolves by waving about a large piece of beef, Ralph had even coaxed two of them into *lying down*. As if wolves were the sort of creatures that could be tamed. As if he was the sort of boy who could do such a thing.

But how?

Birdie was still asking herself this question as she stirred a giant pot of blueberry mush alongside Cricket in Sir Ichabod's kitchen. Sprinkles, seated on Cricket's shoulder, tended to his silver plume while Cricket stared at the edge of the dish towels hanging along the oven rack. They were moving. Or rather, fluttering. It was just one of the many oddities the children had been stumbling across in the manor because—though Mistress Octavia had ordered Sir Ichabod to board up the library

---

40. The infirmary was not a warm fuzzy sort of place with snuggly teddy bears, extra blankets, and a bright window to cheer the spirits. No. Indeed, the infirmary was created solely for the purpose of keeping the children's germs contained to one place, because Mistress Octavia couldn't bear the thought of sharing a single thing with a Tragical. As such, the miniature room was filled with one lumpy bed, one dimly lit sconce, one painting of a three-headed snake with venom dripping from its fangs, three pencils, and of course, no paper.

window hours ago—little wisps and hints of the Winds still swirled throughout.

Sir Ichabod emerged from the pantry with a frown on his face. "We are lucky a Council meeting was scheduled for this evening. It's the only event Mistress Octavia would leave the manor for after an episode like today's."

Cricket's eyes lit up, and she bobbed up and down. "Lucky? But, Sir Ichabod, Tragicals are never lucky. Maybe this means we are getting *less* tragical!"

Sir Ichabod's expression, however, remained blank.

Birdie lifted the wooden spoon out of the mush and set it beside the pot. "Sir Ichabod, do you think it would be a good idea for us to visit Ralph? Even though Mistress Octavia ordered you to keep visitors away from the infirmary?"

Sir Ichabod thrust a tray of blueberry mush, bandages, and tape toward Birdie. "You two are not visitors. I am far too busy to attend to him myself, and so—as—as *punishment*, I am sending you to be his caretakers."

With a small smile on her face, Birdie nodded. She wrapped her fingers around the tray and stepped toward the door. But Cricket hesitated.

"Sir Ichabod," she began in a quiet voice. "How did it feel?"

Sir Ichabod froze. Birdie did too. An image of Sir Ichabod popped into her mind. Sir Ichabod, tall. Sir Ichabod lifting a chair high overhead. Sir Ichabod with the Winds of Wanderly swirling around him.

"I'm not sure I understand the question," Sir Ichabod whispered.

"How did it feel to be a grown-up?" Cricket said.

"I—I don't know exactly."

"Was it scary?"

"Yes," he answered immediately.

Cricket nodded. "It was scary being a child, too. Not a Tragical child, but a normal one. I know I'm not, of course. That's just how it felt when you broke the window. All that wind blew in, and we saw Wanderly, and it almost seemed like . . . Well, it almost seemed like Wanderly was happy to see us." Cricket drew near and whispered, "I think I forgot to breathe."

"So . . . you didn't like it?" Sir Ichabod asked, small.

"I *loved* it. I'm just saying I was scared. But maybe that's all right. Maybe being scared isn't what matters most. Maybe even the best things are scary sometimes." Cricket paused. "Sir Ichabod, may I look at your medallion?"

Sir Ichabod's eyebrows lifted in surprise. He stared at Cricket for a good long moment and finally leaned down to where she stood on tiptoes. Her small fingers brushed gently against the cold, hard metal, and then suddenly, without any warning at all, she yanked on it with all her might.

"Ouch!" Sir Ichabod cried, straightening up and rubbing his hands against his neck, which was already turning a bright, angry shade of red. "What did you do that for?"

Cricket frowned. "I had to try. I just thought maybe if some-one else tried to get it off, it might work."

"You think it's as easy as pulling it off?"

"I—I don't know. But I'm sure you do. I'm sure you must have tried everything already. I'm sorry, Sir Ichabod."

Cricket linked her arm through Birdie's and pulled them both in the direction of the door. But Birdie couldn't help notic-ing how Sir Ichabod hadn't moved; how he stood frozen, with his hand hovering atop the medallion, almost as if he were afraid to touch it, as if maybe he never had before.

Holding tight to Ralph's tray, Cricket and Birdie scurried down the hallway. When they reached the infirmary, they heard an ominous series of moaning sounds coming from behind the door. The girls exchanged glances, but Birdie, nevertheless, raised her hand to knock. No one answered. Birdie proceeded to knock again, but there was still no answer. Birdie raised her hand to knock one more time, and a muffled voice finally called out, "Go away."

"But it's not Sir Ichabod, it's us!" Cricket said, pressing her lips against the door.

It was quiet for a whole minute at least. Birdie began to tap her foot. Cricket twiddled her thumbs, and quite curiously, Ralph asked, "Is Sprinkles with you, too?"

As if Sprinkles understood, he threw back his ratty shoulders and rose up on his haunches like the distinguished gentleman he was. "Of course!" Cricket said, and couldn't have looked prouder of her rat, who was turning out to be not only a hero, but an astute diplomat.

"Come in, then," Ralph said.

The girls entered the dark room and tried not to gasp. Ralph had a thick bandage wrapped around his head. His left arm was wrapped from his wrist all the way up to his shoulder. His right leg was elevated on several pillows, and he had a series of angry scratches on his cheeks and one particularly nasty one across the bridge of his nose.

"It's, uh, not as bad as it looks, I'm sure," he said. But when he tried to point toward the foot of the bed, his face crinkled up with the effort, and his breathing grew heavy. Birdie and Cricket plunked down as quickly as they could so as not to cause him any more pain.

Ralph looked toward the tray. "Where's Grim? Did you steal that out of his kitchen?"

Birdie bit her lip. She wanted to tell Ralph who Sir Ichabod Grim really was—not just the oldest Tragical in all of Wanderly, but a grown-up who might be on their side. But it also seemed the sort of story that was Sir Ichabod's to share.

"Not exactly," Birdie said. "We asked him if we could visit you. We wanted to see if you were okay and . . . are you?"

Ralph's expression darkened. "As okay as I always am being stuck at the manor. I thought . . ." He pressed his eyes shut for a moment. "I thought it was different this time. I thought it was the perfect opportunity.[41] I thought . . ."

"What did you think, Ralph?" Birdie pressed gently.

Ralph's voice was tight. "I thought the Winds of Wanderly would carry me off the way they did for those spiders. But I don't know why I thought the Winds would do something like that for me."

"Maybe they will someday. Maybe they left you here for a reason that's more important." Birdie's voice trembled with urgency. "I don't think the Winds are the sort of thing you should give up on."

Ralph kept his head low. He was quiet for a full minute before Cricket leaned forward and plunked Sprinkles into his lap. "There," she said. "I don't know why, but he helps with stuff."

Right away, Ralph reached his good hand out to pet Sprinkles. He nodded and said, "That's why I stayed awake all night breaking rattraps. I never did think I'd track them all down, but it worked, didn't it?"

Birdie's mouth dropped, and Cricket's hands clasped tight against her chest. "That was *you*?" they both exclaimed in unison.

---

41. If anyone should be able to recognize such an opportunity, it was Ralph. Since his arrival at the manor, he had tried to escape on nine different occasions at least (including a death-defying shimmy up Sir Ichabod's chimney that very nearly worked!). For the fact remained that, however awful life at the manor was, it was infinitely worse for a child who had grown up in the Beyond and knew precisely what he was missing out on.

But Ralph's cheeks flu

me, I should tell you the o

you a favor."

Birdie frowned. "For w

"Well, do you rememl

on the wall?" Birdie and

breath, Ralph continue

pillow, climbed one of

portrait off the wall, and stuck Cricket's ...

Cricket's lower lip trembled. Her eyes glistened. "But I didn't mean for anyone else to see that. I . . . It's not any good."

"But I didn't hang it up because it's good; I hung it up because it's brilliant." Ralph paused while Cricket's jaw gaped and Birdie nodded in fierce agreement. "And I wanted everyone else to see, too. I just never imagined Griselda would, you know, show up at the manor. Do you . . . I mean . . ." Ralph took a deep breath. "I'm sorry?"

Cricket nodded and then echoed softly, "Brilliant?"

Birdie waited a moment and then asked Ralph the question that had been bubbling up ever since his dramatic leap from the window. "Ralph, how did you tame Mistress Octavia's wolves? Did you use *magic*?"

Ralph's eyes widened, but he shook his head. "If I had something like magic, I would have escaped from this place a long, long time ago."

"Wait, you want to have magic?" Cricket said, leaning in

thought magic was supposed to hurt us? I
could only make things worse?"

ped. If only she'd been honest with Cricket from
ing; if only she'd been brave enough to tell her about
runch's identity, then surely Cricket would be curious
out magic too. Surely she'd be thinking Ms. Crunch and her
magical plan to "do Mistress Octavia in" might even be the *best*
thing that could ever happen to the Tragicals.

Should I say it now? Birdie wondered.

But Ralph piped up, "That's what the Council wants us to
think. They don't want Tragicals anywhere near magic because
they know magic could change things. Maybe even make us not
Tragicals anymore, and then what would the Chancellor do?
Who could he convince to take on our roles?"

"Nobody," Cricket whispered.

Ralph nodded and continued, "Anyways, I didn't tame Mistress Octavia's wolves half as well as I thought I could. They've
been under her influence so long they've forgotten what it's like
to be anything else."

"And what were they before?" Birdie asked.

"Pups," Ralph said with a grin. "Even dark creatures have a
beginning. And most dark creatures end up the way they are
because of the people who take them in. It's just plain animal
sense."

"Animal sense," Birdie repeated. "Is that something you
learned when you were living in the . . . Beyond?"

Ralph was quiet for a moment. "Why are you asking?"

Remembering her conversation with Sir Ichabod, Birdie lowered her voice and said, "Because I never asked before. And I should have."

Ralph's eyes grew cloudy. His forehead crinkled. "It's been . . . a really long time."

"Will you try?" Birdie pressed. And then again, with Cricket nodding her head. "Please?"

Ralph took a deep breath. Slowly, he began to speak. "I used to live at Barnabus McNuttle's Pets for the Dastardly. Barnabus wasn't my . . . father, but he did find me. He found me curled under a bench at Pigglesticks Wharf. When he fished me out, he said I was so scruffy and coated in dirt, he thought *I* was some sort of creature. He took me back to his shop, planning to give me one meal and a decent night's sleep, but when he found me the next morning playing with the snakes in the snake pit, he decided to keep me. So we worked out a deal: I took care of the animals, and he gave me a place to stay."

"So why'd you end up here?" Cricket asked. "Did you get tired of taking care of the animals?"

"Of course not!" Ralph said. And then, with his head low, he continued, "Barnabus got tired of taking care of me. And now here I am."

"And now here we all are," Cricket said, shaking her head sadly. "And then one day soon we'll die, and no one will ever miss us."

Unless a witch saves us first, Birdie thought. And she knew she couldn't waste another moment. She had to say something. Maybe not *that* exactly, but something.

Birdie cleared her throat. "If it's possible that magic might help us instead of hurt us, maybe there's a way we could find some of our own."

"Even if we found magic, I doubt we'd know what to do with it," Ralph said. "Take that rainstorm and those spiders. Whatever Mistress Octavia says, that was definitely magic. But how did it get here? Why? What good did it do us?"

Cricket's hand flew against her mouth. Her eyes grew as wide as two full moons. "Birdie," she said breathlessly. "Your magical letter! You've been waiting so long on a response, so many strange things have been happening, that I almost forgot. But your letter came right before the rainstorm—do you think the two are connected?"

Ralph's head snapped up. "Magical letter? What magical letter? No offense, but who would write to you? To any of us?"

Birdie's heart thumped. This was it. She absolutely had to reveal Ms. Crunch's identity. If she didn't do it now, how could her actions be described as anything else but lying? Lying, even, to friends. Birdie couldn't imagine there was room for any such thing between friends.

With her head bowed low, Birdie finally laid her burden down. Her voice was soft. "I've been writing to a witch."

The infirmary was dead silent.

Cricket and Ralph were speechless.

So speechless Birdie wondered if she had merely made the confession in her head, so she went on and said it again, although this time a wee bit louder. "I've been writing to a . . . a witch."

It didn't sound any better the second time.

Even Sprinkles buried his head in his little tiny paws.

Ralph's voice was low. "Are you saying you got a letter from a witch, and the rain and spiders came from her? Those were . . . curses?"

Birdie's words tumbled out at an extraordinary speed. "Well, yes, the first one was a curse. But the second one she sent entirely by accident. Really the good news is that—"

"There is no good news with witches!" Ralph interrupted. "Haven't you read any of the storybooks? The witches in Wanderly are raised on those same stories. Those stories plant ideas in their heads. Wicked ideas they're supposed to use on *us*! And if the witch you're writing to seems different—if she seems like she might be good—then she's probably even worse because she's tricking you."

Birdie shook her head vehemently. "But that's just it. She's not trying to act good at all. She told me from the start she was a wicked witch."

Ralph raked his hands through his hair. "You knew she was a wicked witch when you wrote back to her?"

"Yes. I've written her, um, a few times now." Birdie tried to ignore the flicker of surprise in Cricket's eyes.

"But how? I mean, I get how she sends letters to you, but how do you send letters to her if you don't have magic?" Ralph asked.

"The Winds of Wanderly have been delivering our letters. Not just mine, but hers, too. Ralph, I—I think the Winds want to help us."

Ralph's shoulders slumped. "By introducing you to a witch? Birdie, what if this witch is your Tragic End?"

"But that's what I'm trying to tell you. She *can't* be my Tragic End because she wants to do Mistress Octavia in! And if she does, we all might have a real chance." With Ralph still shaking his head, and Cricket staring at her hands, Birdie's voice rose. "Don't you see? We're Tragicals. I know this is risky, but we're not going to have many options; in fact, this might be our only option forever. What happens if we miss it?"

Cricket finally broke her silence with a whisper. "Have you tried the friendship thing with her yet?"

"Friends? Friends with a *witch?*" Ralph shrieked.

But Birdie ignored him. "Yes," she said.

"And, um, how's it coming?" Cricket asked.

Birdie sighed. "Slow."

"Then you must keep trying. It takes a while with people who've . . ." Cricket paused. She finally met Birdie's eyes. "With people who've never had one before."

"I'm not supporting this," Ralph said, shaking his head. "I'm saying right here and right now this witch business is a terrible idea!"

Birdie reached into her pocket and pulled forth a few sheets of paper she had torn out of her book on her last trip to the dungeon. She had been saving them for Cricket, and pressed them now into her palm. It felt good not to have any more secrets, even if Ralph did look aghast.

"Paper? How did you . . . ? Where did you—" he began.

But Birdie interrupted him. "Maybe it would help if Cricket drew another picture?"

Cricket shook her head to and fro. "Oh, but I couldn't. That book is yours. You already gave me more than I ever hoped for, and I think you should be the one to finish it."

"No way," Birdie said. "A book like that is meant to be finished together. Anyhow, Ralph likes your drawings, and he's had a pretty rough day."

Ralph crossed his arms against his chest. It began as a grandiose gesture, but ended much more gingerly considering his bandages. "Nice of someone to remember," he muttered.

"Oh, I'm sorry." Birdie bit her lip. "Maybe it would be better if we let you rest. Or maybe just . . . me. I would understand if you just want me to leave."

Ralph looked straight at Birdie. "You really tore those blank pages out of a book?" Birdie nodded, and he continued, "What's your book about, exactly, and what business do you and Cricket have trying to finish it?"

"It's about friendship," Birdie said without hesitation. Lately, it was becoming easier to say out loud. Lately, it was becoming easier to believe in. "And we're trying to finish it because we think it wants to come true."

Ralph's eyes flickered. Soft, warm. Like candlelight. And then he pulled the covers up beneath his chin and shut his eyes.

Birdie wondered if that was her cue to go, but the moment she set her feet on the ground, Ralph said, with his eyes still closed, "If Cricket's going to draw, you might as well do something too. You know, like write a letter to your witch."

Birdie plopped back onto the bed. "Wow, really? You wouldn't mind? Because I do owe Ms. Crunch a letter!"

Ralph groaned. "Actually, I was trying to be funny, but now that you said her name, I don't know how I can forget it, because Crunch? Her name is actually *Crunch*?"

Cricket poked her head up. "That just gave me an idea for my drawing!"

"Please don't make a scary one," Ralph said.

And Cricket giggled. Much the way she did on the day Ralph grew a blueberry mustache. But this time she didn't look surprised by the sound. "Is this . . . fun?" she asked, looking eagerly back and forth between Birdie and Ralph.

"I don't know," Birdie said. "How would we know what fun is?"

Cricket leaned toward Ralph. "Ralph, you must know! Is this what fun was like in the Beyond?"

Ralph thought for a moment. And then he shook his head. "I didn't experience anything quite like *this* in the Beyond. But I don't think that means this isn't fun. And maybe, in some ways, it's even better."

Whether due to the flood of spiders, the treacherous fall, the ravenous wolves, the threat of a witch, or the barrage of questions posed by Birdie and Cricket, that was it for Ralph. Within moments, the sound of his soft, wheezy snores mingled with the imaginative scritch-scratching of Cricket's pencil. Birdie pressed all of it close and tried to still the anxious thump of her heart. She simply couldn't be wrong about Ms. Crunch. For once in her life, with Cricket and now Ralph by her side, Birdie had something no Tragical ever had: something to lose.

Birdie bent her head and wrote:

Dear Ms. Crunch,

I'm real sorry all this laughter talk has caused so much trouble. What happened to you at that magic store where you tried to get the laughing potion really did sound awful. So awful, in fact, I couldn't help noticing it sounded almost tragical.

Ms. Crunch, I'm going to ask you something I think you should think long and hard about. I'm asking you even though I don't want to, because the more I think about Mistress Octavia being done in, the more excited I get. But here it is: Do you think my tragical is contagious? Do you think maybe my doom is rubbing off on you? If so, what if there's not a single thing we can do to make this Mistress Octavia plan work?

If you haven't crumpled up my letter into a ball, I have something else to say I think you'll find equally surprising. You may even want to sit down in a chair for this one. You said witches can't do good magic, but how do you know for sure? So far you've sent two curses to our manor and several wicked letters to me. But here's the crazy thing: since knowing you, we've never felt less tragical.

So here's my idea. Maybe you don't have any reason to go looking for that Blue Dragon you mentioned. Maybe you're capable of brewing the potion yourself. Maybe you just need a little practice being good.

Please stop cackling. Or launching banana peels all the way from the Dead Tree Forest. This isn't as impossible as it sounds. I think it's as easy as getting a pet. Something you can have around day and night, because it's hard to be good if you don't have anything to practice on. But just remember, above all else, pets are not for eating.

You'd be amazed what a pet rat has done for Cricket (who's a girl and definitely not a bug). In fact, Sprinkles has grown on all of us. I think that's why Tragicals aren't supposed to have pets. Maybe pets bring about so much happy, it's easy to forget the unhappy. Maybe a pet will make you forget about the wicked.

I guess that just leaves me with one last question to answer. My address. You keep on asking for it, and I keep on finding ways not to send it. But I'm not going to do that anymore. I don't see how I can expect you to be my BFF if I'm not being one to you. At the heart of it, I think BFFs are all about trust.

If you happen to be tricking me, this is probably the moment you've been waiting for, but I hope not. Because I like you, Ms. Crunch. You maybe weren't exactly what I wanted, but maybe you're just what I need.

So if you want to address my next letter properly, here it is: 0000 Nothing Drive, Nowhere, Wanderly 00000.

Yours truly,
Bird-Girl (I like this name a lot better)

PS: If you are tricking me, and zooming off on your broomstick to come do me in right this instant, can you please not hurt any of the other Tragicals? Thanks.

THIRTEEN

A Bothersome Jar of Peanut Butter

Agnes Prunella Crunch bent down beside her bed and pressed her saggy cheek against the floor. Even she wrinkled her nose in disgust. The dust bunnies—or rather dust *dinosaurs* given their size—were staging a coup! They'd brandished every stray crumb, toenail clipping, and loose strand of purple hair Agnes thought she had shoved into oblivion. She had no idea she was feeding a pack of little monsters.

The dust dinosaurs tumbled closer to Agnes, and she snarled at them. This was, after all, her bed (even if she hadn't bothered to look beneath it in years), and she was sure it had to be there somewhere.

Of course, she hadn't opened the thing since it was first plopped into her chubby little hands during Wickedry 101. At the time, she thought it worked much better as a boomerang than for something as quiet and obedient as reading. But ever since the Chancellor took command, the reading of forbidden books—those books written *before* his reign—had become the naughtiest act one could do.

At the time of the round-up nearly forty years ago, all the witches Agnes's age had long since given up on reading and didn't have any books to contribute to the Chancellor's sky-high pile (let alone to hoard away for their own evil doing). And so, when the Chancellor's doltish security force, known as the Quill, came knocking on Agnes's door, all she had to do was toss her empty hands into the air and launch a spitball at them. No one batted an eye. They didn't even bother to conduct a cursory search. And so, Agnes was perhaps the only citizen in all of Wanderly who hadn't surrendered her unauthorized books.[42]

Or, rather, book.

She had only one.

Agnes pulled and pried and clawed after the book she was certain she'd kept. She tried not to think about how tired she was, considering the Bird-Girl's latest letter had begun cooing into her ear earlier that morning before the sun even contemplated rising. By the time Agnes had wrestled herself awake, she

---

42. As a book reader, this should give you pause. For you and I both know that readers, wherever they hail from, tend to be fiercely protective of books they have grown to love. As such, if imagining a few brave souls tenderly stowing their books away like buried treasure, or even conducting an entire underground secret library, should strike your fancy, who am I to stop you?

was so fed up with the dove's sweet little sounds, she determined to pluck its feathers out one by one before serving it up for dinner. But the thing had exploded into another glitter bomb before she could lay a finger on it.

Since knowing Birdie, Agnes had never been so sparkly in all her life.

It was disgusting.

But way worse had been the letter itself. The big-ticket items, of course, were a no-brainer. If Birdie thought she could scare Agnes away with a little threat like "contagious doom," she had another think coming. Second, every time Agnes thought about wrangling some creature, dragging it into her haunted cabin, and calling it a "pet," she burst into uncontrollable cackles.

But it was that one line that kept coming back to haunt Agnes.

That one line that wasn't like anything Agnes had ever heard in all her life: Because I like you, Ms. Crunch.

Agnes resumed her search with an extra vigor, tossing items over her shoulder left and right. Somewhere beneath all that dust and dirt and witchy odds and ends, it had to be—*yes!*

Agnes wrestled the book away from the dust dinosaurs and held it in front of her as if it were a prize.

But it really was ridiculous.

Of all the books for a wicked witch to stow away in her haunted cabin, of all the books to thumb her nose at the Council for, it *had* to be a picture book called *Georgie the Giant Dragon*.

Agnes opened the front cover. She squinted and held her breath, but it didn't help much. The illustrations were even cuter than she remembered. In fact, she had to imagine something suitably disgusting so as not to lose her wormy breakfast. The words were even worse. They *rhymed*. And Agnes's nosy cauldron was already peeking over her shoulder and trying to gurgle and burp to the beat!

"Silence!" Agnes chided. But her witchy toes were having their own difficulty staying planted firmly on the ground. Apparently, they remembered quite well what it was to be seven years old.

Agnes gritted her teeth and flipped a few more pages. Her knobby finger chased along after the words. She couldn't believe she was down to combing through a picture book for a tip or two, but if she was going to go after that Blue Dragon on her own, she didn't want to arrive completely empty-handed. After all, asking a dragon for help was a mite bit different than roasting him.

Agnes's finger drew to a skidding halt. There. Right there. That was exactly the sort of tidbit she was looking for! Agnes brought the book near. In a decidedly *non*-singsongy voice, she growled, *"Georgie is shy with all things new, but if you want him to follow you, just leave a trail of peanut butter, and he will like you more than any other."*

Agnes drummed her fingers together. Toting a jar full of

peanut butter was a heap easier than, as Bob suggested, trying to rope someone into coming along with her. Peanut butter didn't talk. Peanut butter wasn't annoying. Peanut butter would do exactly what she told it to. And, lucky for Agnes, she had one jar of peanut butter stuffed into the farthest corner of her pantry that she had purchased twenty-five years ago out of sheer necessity when a little girl—who obviously hadn't a clue she was in witch country—dared to knock upon Agnes's door for a school fund-raiser.

Agnes tossed the jar of peanut butter into her knapsack along with the other essentials she'd packed just that morning: two cans of pumpkin juice, a jar of snail slime, three twig bars, and a handful of toadstools. Most people who are about to set off all alone on a dragon hunt might see fit to pack a shield, a bit of armor, and maybe toss in a potion if they're lucky enough to have such a thing. Agnes merely packed a midmorning *snack*, because she was certain she'd have that dragon beneath her thumb with enough time to make it home for lunch.

Agnes snapped her fingers in the air for her trusty broomstick. She pointedly ignored her cauldron, which was still bubbling up rhymes and had flushed an annoying shade of tickled pink, and slammed the door in a way that caused all the Dead Tree Forest to stir.

Unfortunately, Agnes only made it about two miles from her haunted cabin when things went south. Two miles if you're a runner is a hearty warm-up; two miles if you're on a horse is a nice stretch; but two miles if you're on a broomstick is like blinking your eyes, because broomsticks are fast! So fast that if you aren't being careful—if your arms, legs, and feet aren't tucked close to your side, and if you don't secure all loose items before takeoff—it is really easy to lose something.

And that's what happened to Agnes.

She lost that blasted jar of peanut butter!

Considering the last thing she wanted to do was go traipsing into town for the second time in a week to purchase, of all things, a jar of peanut butter, she figured it would be far better to simply find the one she'd lost.[43] And so, instead of fiercely blasting through the atmosphere in hot pursuit of the Blue Dragon, she was schlepping about the Dead Tree Forest.

Pinpointing a single jar of peanut butter among miles of forest turned out to be no small task. Indeed, a full two hours later, Agnes's feet were dragging. She had already blown through her entire knapsack of goodies; her prune-y lips were feeling particularly parched; and her broomstick kept sighing. Agnes very nearly dozed off with her nose buried in a pile of shrubbery when a loud "RIBBIT!" rang out.

Agnes jerked her head up in time to see a fat, slimy toad

---

43. Worst of all, those busybodies from the *Wanderly Whistle* would be out in full force sniffing for clues. Of course, Agnes could always conjure up a disguise, but the moment she heard one spout off about "Maggie Pruneface Punch," there's no telling what she'd do. Self-control wasn't exactly Agnes's strong suit, and she'd likely blow her cover in an instant.

bound across her path. It even appeared to give her a buggy-eyed wink before leaping onto a nearby tree trunk. Without thinking, *Agnes followed it*. The toad continued to hop from tree to tree to tree. Curiously, Agnes forgot all about her missing jar of peanut butter. Even more curious, Agnes had the strangest notion that there was something about the toad she liked.

Agnes never liked anything.

The feeling was so astonishing it reminded her of what the Bird-Girl had written in her letter. Maybe she was experiencing the sort of feeling that convinced someone to do something ridiculous like acquire a pet. Of course, Agnes hadn't failed to notice the toad's scrumptiously long toes. She did so love a delicate platter of toad toes! But Birdie had been most adamant about not eating pets, and if Agnes was going to go to the trouble of trying it out, she supposed following one rule was not too much to ask. Regardless, at the moment, anything sounded better than a dead-end hunt for peanut butter.

Agnes slowed to a slink. The toad had stopped on a low-lying tree branch. It had its back to her and was less than five steps away; maybe four. She was nearly close enough to lunge and secure it in her witchy grasp. Agnes fought the urge to cackle, because a toad really was the perfect pet for her, wasn't it? It was appropriately ugly; it had loads of countable warts; it preferred much the same diet of bugs as Agnes; and she had plenty of windows she could toss the toad against to see how sticky its slime really was.

Agnes curled and uncurled her gnarled fingers. She ran her squiggly tongue across her lips. She bent low and—

"MEOOOOOWW!"

Agnes jumped at the pitiful sound that erupted from behind her. Her toad must have heard it too, because it turned and looked Agnes full in the face. It blinked its bulbous eyes at her; it launched forth its long, sticky tongue and caught a delicious fly in midair as if to prove its perfection; and then, most important of all, *it didn't run away.* It was almost like the toad wasn't opposed to Agnes. As if maybe it even wanted to go home with her. Agnes didn't waste a moment. She ran for the toad. She scrambled up the tree after the toad.

But the toad must have changed its mind.

Or it was merely taunting her the whole time. In any case, it bounded away with nary a backward glance, leaving Agnes with her arms wrapped around a very scratchy tree branch not at all designed to support the weight of a witch. The branch quivered. Agnes lost her grip, careened down the tree trunk, and splashed into a mud-filled ditch at the base of the tree.

"MEOOOOWW!"

The awful sound erupted *again.*

Agnes raked her fingernails through the mud and tried to stumble to her feet. But the mud was very, very slippery. Every time Agnes placed her witchy boots beneath her, they slid right out again. She splished and splashed and sploshed about. Even her eyelashes were coated in the gooey substance, not to mention the continuous meowing sound that grated against her nerves!

Agnes swallowed her witchy pride for the second time that week (a burden no witch should have to bear) and rolled onto her belly. She thrust her neck out like the worms she loved to slurp. With her eyelids still caked shut, she wrenched her head back and forth in the direction of the meager sunlight eking through the trees and slithered along in search of a patch of dry dirt to scramble onto. But her hands landed squarely on something else.

Something *furry*.

"MEEOOW!" came the anguished cry. Then, quite promptly, a row of little needle-sharp teeth sank into Agnes's outstretched hand.

Agnes yowled.

"You blasted little bugger!" she cried, grasping wildly about. But it is a terribly hard endeavor to grab ahold of something when you can't see a thing. And so, Agnes spun only to coat herself in even more mud.

"Where are you? Come here! Come—" Agnes coughed and sputtered. "Wh-what are you doing? Hey, hey stop that r-r-right now! Y-you hear me? St-st—"

At the barest hint of a warm, sandpaper-like tongue scraping against the tender skin of her eyelids, a sound slipped out of Agnes's mouth.

It was a sound Agnes had never made before.

It was a sound that caused the dry, brittle leaves of the Dead Tree Forest to rattle and stir.

It was a sound closely related to her highly practiced, wholly bone-chilling, and marvelously polished cackle, except without the edge. The sound was softer somehow, and it seemed to roll one right after the other like children turning somersaults in the grass.

Agnes's jaw dropped open. Her eyes popped open too, because the incessant licking had managed to wash all the mud away.

Agnes was staring face-to-face with a kitten.

"Did you . . . ? Could you . . . ? How did you . . . ?" Agnes paused. She took a deep breath. She summoned up her best, most intimidating bellow. "Did you make me GIGGLE?"

The kitten blinked its one big green eye at her. It attempted to fluff up its mangy coat with the haphazard network of scars stamped all along its skeletal frame. It wasn't a monstrous kitten (for then Agnes might have taken an immediate liking to it), but merely a miserable, scrappy thing who seemed to have had a rough go of it.

Agnes slapped the palm of her hand against the ground. "Do you even know who I am?" she asked the kitten.

"Who-who-whooooo?" an owl hooted cheerily from a nearby tree.

Agnes jerked her head up and scowled.

Since when did the Dead Tree Forest become so chatty and full of life? she wondered.

Amid her musing, the kitten leaped on top of her head. It began to groom itself. It kneaded its paws in Agnes's nest of ratty purple hair. Every so often the kitten dipped its tongue near enough to have another lick of Agnes's eyelid such that Agnes giggled *again*.

Agnes had enough. She plucked the kitten off her head. She plunked it on the mud beside her and turned on her heel, fully determined to put the nonsense business of pets behind her once and for all, because it was a toad or nothing.

But the kitten dashed in front of her.

It parked itself directly beneath Agnes's witchy boot such that if Agnes fully executed her step, the little bugger would be pierced straight through in the chest! The last thing Agnes wanted to deal with was the mess associated with a speared kitten, so she stepped aside. But Agnes's reflexes weren't quite what they used to be. And she got to teetering and bobbling about all over again until she toppled fully over into a *second* muddy ditch!

The kitten bounded back into Agnes's lap, and Agnes gave it her most wicked glare.

The kitten couldn't have cared less. It swiped its paw against Agnes's cheek; quick as a whip, and without even a warning!

Agnes touched her fingers to the place where her skin burned. She felt the four neat lines where the kitten's claws had dug in and the warm, ooze of blood.

If you can believe it, Agnes Prunella Crunch *smiled*.

"My, you are an especially rotten one, aren't you?" she said.

And she began to think. Maybe the kitten was nearly as rotten as she was. Maybe the sort of creature who would ruin a perfect plan was the only sort she could stomach. Maybe they could even try to outrotten each other for kicks. Of course, that seemed to completely contravene the Bird-Girl's hope of turning Agnes good, but that was never going to happen anyways, was it?

Agnes stuck the kitten beneath her smelly armpit. She snapped her fingers for her broomstick, which had forgotten all about being bored and was instead anxiously shedding entire bristles because, small or not, that kitten looked to be a heap of trouble it did not want to tangle with.

Agnes's broomstick pointed meekly in the direction of the Deepest, Darkest Bog, but Agnes pooh-poohed her hand in the air. "Goblin's goo!" she said. "That dragon's been there for a decade at least, and it'll still be there tomorrow. Anyways, our rotten quota's filled for the day because we're going to take this kitten home and ruin its life for good. Ha-ha!"

Nestling in closer to Agnes, the kitten vibrated.

Agnes thrust it out in front of her. "What's wrong with you?" she demanded. "Is that some sort of warning? Are you going to explode?"

But the kitten was as obedient as Agnes was (meaning not a hint) and persisted in its mysterious vibrating all the way home. It also managed to nip Agnes's earlobe three times and administer four new scratches on her craggy neck, which was impressive given the speed of broomstick travel. By the time a muddied, bloodied Agnes finally rolled through the doorway of her haunted cabin with the kitten in tow, Agnes's broomstick was trembling all over, her cauldron had paled to a wan shade of lime green, and the enchanted ceiling rumbled with round after round after round of thunder without any prompting from Agnes.

Because what place did a kitten have in the haunted cabin of a witch, i.e. *what had gotten into Agnes?*

FOURTEEN

A Terrible Choice

Birdie Bloom was trying not to worry about the fact that she had trusted a witch with her address and hadn't heard from her in two whole days. She hoped that meant Ms. Crunch was busy training a pet. She hoped that meant she was so busy getting "good" that the laughter potion was practically brewing itself.

Whatever the reason, Birdie desperately hoped she would hear from Ms. Crunch soon. Because lately Mistress Octavia was acting stranger than normal. Indeed, the night she arrived back from the Council meeting, instead of popping magically back into the manor with her usual jarring *BOOM*, it was more of an explosive *BOOM, THUD, THUD*! Moreover, Mistress Octavia was no longer retiring to her bedchamber at night, but remained holed up in her Room of Sinister Plotting only to emerge each morning with terribly bloodshot eyes. Most strange of all, on that morning, with the children seated at their desks in the Instruction Room, Mistress Octavia was *late*.

Birdie and her classmates were getting a bit restless.

A few weeks prior, they would have thought to do nothing other than lay their heads on their desks for a short snooze, or maybe silently count their fingers thirty times in a row, or simply stare at the thick black curtains without ever wondering what the world (if it even existed) looked like outside of Foulweather's Home for the Tragical.

But the Tragicals had grown used to so much more than that.

Even Francesca Prickleboo's aloneness had taken on a new and somewhat troubling dimension. Whereas before she simply failed to notice the other Tragicals, now she seemed to notice them a great deal. She seemed to notice their newfound togetherness, and she was going to great lengths to avoid them. On that morning, however, she hadn't needed to make the effort given her assignment of kitchen duty.

With the small slice of unexpected freedom, Cricket shyly pulled a piece of paper from her gown pocket. She unfolded it carefully. The other Tragicals made no attempt to hide their curiosity and gathered near. Benjamin, the six-year-old with the heart pattern beneath his sleeve, shuffled so close he came to lean upon the back of Cricket's chair. He peeked over her shoulder and began to nod his head.

"This one," he whispered. "This one for sure is my favorite."

Cricket took a deep breath and turned the drawing around so the rest of the children could see.

The Tragicals, seventeen of them, were gathered in what looked to be a library and were surrounded by—of all things—books. The ends of their hair, and the hems of their clothing, were lifted by an invisible wind. The pages of the books turned beneath the wind's hand, and on every page was an image so lovely some of the younger Tragicals began to cry.

Most remarkable of all, however, were the expressions Cricket had drawn on their faces. They were expressions of . . . joy. Small expressions, subtle expressions, but still, joy. Birdie knew it was joy because, lately, she had seen it on the faces of the other Tragicals. She nodded in recognition; the others did too. Though they might never have dared to believe it on their own, by the light of Cricket's drawing, they could not deny it. Joy. Real joy. Joy even among Tragicals.

Five-year-old Amelia twisted a lock of tangled hair around her finger. She pointed at a girl in Cricket's drawing and then pointed at Mildred. "Y-you do that. That thing where your eye crinkles. I—I've seen you do that when Sprinkles is being silly."

Mildred's face lit up. "Really?" she said. Birdie watched as Mildred slipped off her cracked eyeglasses and held them in the palm of her hand. Perhaps Mildred thought she could see far better through the eyes of a friend.

Still hovering near Cricket, Benjamin began to bounce up

and down. "What about me? What about me?" he asked. "Can anyone tell which one's me?"

Ralph stepped forward. "This one, of course." He pointed to the drawing of a boy whose sleeve was raised just enough to reveal a heart-shape pattern on his arm. Benjamin's eyes shone because, certainly, that *was* him. Certainly, it couldn't be anybody else.

Amid the Tragicals' excited whispering, Birdie was the first to notice Francesca slip through the doorway. Though Francesca's expression was initially smug, when she saw the other Tragicals all clustered together, she thrust her hands on her hips and scowled. And then she did what she hadn't done for over a week. She marched right up to them. She eyed the drawing in Cricket's hand while Cricket tried desperately to fold it shut and stick it back inside her gown pocket.

But Francesca was too quick. She snatched the paper away from Cricket. Francesca lifted high her bony elbows and pushed her way out from the older children, including a still-healing Ralph, who tried to stop her. A few feet away, she flattened the drawing with the palms of her hands and stared at it.

Birdie's stomach flip-flopped. Surely Francesca would conduct a head count and realize that in an obvious drawing of the Tragicals, one of them was missing. And of all the children who were included, not one of them had perfectly plaited braids and a smattering of equidistant freckles. Cricket had left Francesca out. But Cricket had only been trying to draw what she saw, and

Francesca had made her choice long ago, hadn't she?

Francesca's face grew unusually pale. Quite roughly, she folded the paper back up. She folded it up even smaller than it had been before, as if she wished she could make it disappear entirely. When the *click-clack* of Mistress Octavia's high-heeled boots could be heard just outside the Instruction Room door, Cricket cried, "Please! Please give it back to me!"

Francesca continued to stare at the folded-up piece of paper. As if she could still see what was inside. As if she might never be able to forget.

"Please!" Cricket said again. "It's special to me!"

The doorknob to the Instruction Room twisted to the left. The children all scrambled back to their desks. When Mistress Octavia entered the room, the only one not where she was supposed to be was Francesca Prickleboo.

Mistress Octavia's eyes flashed. "Excuse you," she said to Francesca, and whipped her hand through the air in the direction of Francesca's seat. Without making eye contact with any of the Tragicals, Francesca held her fist clenched around Cricket's drawing and shuffled to her desk.

Mistress Octavia prowled back and forth at the front of the room.

Then, quite abruptly, she began to laugh.

It is never ever a good thing when someone like Mistress Octavia laughs. Especially because she appeared to be laughing at the Tragicals.

When she finally paused to collect herself, Birdie's heart pounded. Mistress Octavia licked her lips and said, "We have a problem in this manor. A very, very serious problem. Would any one care to raise their hand and reveal what this problem is?" Mistress Octavia paused for less than a second before she began, "Frances—"

But she stopped.

Francesca wasn't raising her hand. Francesca wasn't even looking at Mistress Octavia, and Birdie wondered if Francesca had heard a single word Mistress Octavia said.

Mistress Octavia narrowed her eyes. She cleared her throat. "Anyone?" she repeated. But no one volunteered. "Well, then. Let me spell it out for you. You children don't know how to tell the difference between real and make-believe! For example, rain that falls inside and spiders that climb out of books are not real! But . . ." Mistress Octavia paused. She strode near the back of the classroom, toward the far-off, gloomy area, and brought forth a squeaking contraption draped in a thick black sheet. "Today, children, I shall help you come to terms with the fact that nothing in Wanderly is more real than your doom. And so, instead of flipping to Booby Traps and Other Dangerous Weaponry in your readers, we shall have a demonstration."

Mistress Octavia swept the thick black sheet away, and the children instinctively covered their eyes.

They peeked through the cracks between their fingers.

Situated at the front of the room was a spinning wheel. It was black and ominous-looking, but the worst part by far was the long, shiny needle. It glistened and gleamed and seemed to fill the quiet of the room with an eerie *HISSSSSSSSSSSSSS*.

"Can anyone tell me the origin of this lovely device I picked up while I was away from the manor?" Mistress Octavia asked, stroking the side of the machine as if it were one of her mangy wolves.

Though the spinning wheel seemed to have finally captured Francesca Prickleboo's attention, she still did not bother to raise her hand.

Mistress Octavia puffed in annoyance before continuing, "This is a spinning wheel. It holds special significance for you because it was originally intended, perish the thought, to prick the finger of a *Triumphant*. But thanks to the loyalty of an Oath-signing Tragical who took it upon himself to be pricked first, the Triumphant's life was spared. The Tragical, of course, fell into a deep and unwakeable sleep and eventually died. Now, this spinning wheel is *not* equipped with a sleeping potion." Mistress Octavia paused again, and the children breathed a small sigh of relief. "Instead, it is equipped with an electric shock. A shock that will help prepare you for pain. A shock that will help ensure you embrace your Tragic End so that someone better doesn't have to!"

Mistress Octavia rubbed her hands together. Her voice was low. "The steward at the Archive of Magical Objects informed me the shock is strong enough to give a *rat* a heart attack but not strong enough to lay up a child for more than three days. I promised you a demonstration, children, and I fully intend to keep my promises." Mistress Octavia tossed her head back and bellowed, "SIR ICH-A-BOD!! SIR ICH-A-BOD!!"

A few moments later, Sir Ichabod trudged through the doorway. His face was a sickly shade of green. The tip of his bulbous nose gleamed with beads of perspiration. His heavy medallion thumped against his neck, and his hands trembled. Hands that cradled a cage made of pencils and black thread. Racing around inside the cage, with his silver pompadour splayed in distress, was none other than Sprinkles.

The cry bubbled right out of Cricket's eight-year-old heart. A desperate cry. "Sprinkles!"

But Birdie couldn't take her eyes away from Sir Ichabod. Hadn't she and Cricket tried hard to keep him awake? Hadn't he been remembering that he was a grown-up? *How could he do this to them?* The answer was simple, but nearly too much to bear: despite Sir Ichabod's progress, he was still a Tragical. A cursed Tragical, nonetheless. And as long as Mistress Octavia was around, he could never be fully trusted.

"Sir Ichabod," Mistress Octavia purred. "Come show the children what I discovered just this morning in your kitchen. Come show the children the unlucky rat who avoided his first tragical ending in exchange for one much, much more painful."

"No! Please!" Cricket begged. "You mustn't!"

Mistress Octavia whirled toward Cricket. "Shut your mouth,

you miserable child! None of this would have happened if it hadn't been for you and your ridiculous idea that you could keep a rat a secret. Now you shall learn once and for all that you *are* nothing. You will always *have* nothing. And you are *destined* for nothing!"

Birdie's heart raced. For Cricket's sake, for the sake of all the Tragicals who had found a way to hope in the life of a heroic rat, she had to find a way to stop Mistress Octavia!

Creeeak! Mistress Octavia opened the door of Sprinkles's cage. She jabbed her fingernails inside and wrenched Sprinkles out by his tail. Both Sprinkles and Cricket screamed, and Birdie slammed her hands against her ears.

The room began to spin around her. She couldn't see. She couldn't feel. She felt like she was turning numb. She felt like she was becoming what Mistress Octavia said she was, what maybe she always had been.

Nothing. Mistress Octavia's words echoed dully in her ears. *Nothing . . .*

And then Birdie remembered. Regardless of what Mistress Octavia believed to be true about Birdie and the rest of the Tragicals, there remained at least one person's identity Mistress Octavia couldn't argue with. One person who everyone in Wanderly would agree was someone. One person who might frighten even Mistress Octavia.

The words exploded from Birdie's mouth like fireworks.

"I'm friends with a witch!" she said.

Boom!

At the word "friend," Sir Ichabod's drooping head snapped up. Mistress Octavia froze. She turned in an agonizingly slow circle while Sprinkles continued to lunge and wriggle and wrestle against her awful grip. "For a moment it almost sounded as if you said you're *friends* with a . . . witch."

Birdie gulped. She nodded. "It—it's true. She's the one who sent the rain and the spiders. And we never said any of it was make-believe; we called it what it is: *magic.*"

Mistress Octavia thrust her hands to her sides and shouted, "Magic is forbidden here!"

It was quiet for a moment. Even Sprinkles paused to catch a breath. And then Birdie whispered, "But just because you say so, doesn't make it true, ma'am."

"Her name," Mistress Octavia said, sharp.

Birdie's chest tightened. "W-what did you say?"

"Her name. If you're such good friends with this witch, prove it! Otherwise, we shall proceed with our demonstration," Mistress Octavia said.

"But why do you need her name?"

"Because witches are anything but friends to children, much less to Tragical children. Let's just say I'm *curious.* I think others shall be *curious* too. But you must give it quick! Right now! Before I change my mind!" Mistress Octavia slipped her hand across Sprinkles's neck like a noose.

The children's feet shuffled against the ground. As if they

were trying to run, as if they would give anything to run far, far away. Worst of all was Cricket. She held her hands clasped tight against her chest, begging Birdie to do as Mistress Octavia wished.

Birdie pressed her eyes shut. When she did, she saw herself in Cricket's drawings. Standing tall; standing beside Cricket; looking more real than she had ever felt. Would she still be real if she did nothing?

HISSSSSSSSS, the spinning wheel whirred.

"Squeak!" Sprinkles screamed.

"Now," Mistress Octavia commanded.

With tears rolling down her cheeks, Birdie whispered, "Agnes Prunella Crunch."

"I can't hear yoou," Mistress Octavia taunted in a singsongy voice.

"Agnes Prunella Crunch," Birdie said again softly.

"Say it loud or the rat dies!" Mistress Octavia said, thrusting Sprinkles's neck near the gleaming needle.

Birdie shot up. Her chair fell behind her with a loud clatter. She shouted at the top of her lungs, "AGNES PRUNELLA CRUNCH!!"

Outside the manor, the Winds of Wanderly rose up. The Winds of Wanderly sprinted up the steep sides of Tragic Mountain and pounded the windows with such ferocity it sounded like the glass might shatter into a million pieces.

In much the way Birdie's heart felt.

Everything, inside, broken.

And a faint beat rolling across the debris.

Worst. Friend. Ever.

And as Cricket opened up her trembling hands for the return of Sprinkles, as Sprinkles miraculously twitched and sank his bucky teeth into the fleshy part of Mistress Octavia's hand so that she inadvertently tossed him to freedom, all Birdie could think about was what would become of Ms. Crunch.

Birdie was so lost in thought, she very nearly missed it when Mistress Octavia smacked her broken broomstick against Birdie's desk and hissed in the cadence of the spinning wheel, "Now we shall see to *your* punishment for daring to engage with someone outside the manor!"

With her head hanging low, Birdie merely nodded. She didn't know how it could get much worse. She didn't think she could feel more tragical.

Unfortunately, she was very, very wrong.

FIFTEEN

Worse than Wild Hogs

Agnes Prunella Crunch slunk through the Dead Tree Forest for the third day in a row.

She had not managed to track down the Blue Dragon.

She had not located the missing jar of peanut butter.

She could not even lift her head to jot out a letter to the Bird-Girl.

But if she had, Agnes knew exactly what it would have said: *Send Help!*

Because of all the magicians Agnes had outsmarted, of all the witches she'd outcursed, of all the goblins and ogres and trolls she'd flummoxed, it turned out there was no greater opponent in all of Wanderly than a scrappy, one-eyed kitten.

Even naming the kitten had turned out to be an out-and-out battle, and Agnes was more than certain it wasn't her fault. She had come up with a slew of perfectly ferocious names: Bruiser (her hands-down favorite), Spike, Fang, Tank, Bones, Dagger, and Spooky. The kitten had turned its nose up at each and every name, except of course for the final name Agnes had haphazardly tossed out on a whim, Spooky. Which would have been arguably okay, except for one little problem. The kitten only answered to the name Spooky when Agnes said it fast enough that her letters slurred together and it sounded like . . . like . . . Pooky.

And so that's what Agnes was doing.

Agnes was calling her pet kitten *Pooky*. The last thread of dignity Agnes clung to was that if anyone ever asked how it was spelled (which, really, whoever would?), she would emphatically insist that it was spelled with a *y* instead of an *ie* because everybody knows the difference between "Pooky" and "Pookie" is the difference between possibly wicked and a total joke.[44]

Pooky trotted in front of Agnes like she owned the place. Of course, if Pooky hadn't been up half the night gnawing on Agnes's anklebones, Agnes might have been able to keep up with her. Agnes could have mounted her trusty broomstick and really smoked her, but you-know-who had entertained herself by pulling out every single one of the broomstick's bristles and

---

44. You and I both know this name is as cute as cute can be regardless of its spelling. You also know enough about Agnes never to mistake her for an effervescent Goody Two-Shoes. So, for Agnes's sake, let's all pretend that Pooky is a perfectly wicked name and not a bunch of hooey.

scattering them around Agnes's haunted cabin like confetti!

Agnes fumed.

For a fleeting moment, she wondered if the Bird-Girl had done all this on purpose. But if the Bird-Girl knew getting a pet would drive Agnes bananas, why would she go to the trouble of sending her address? Why would she keep insisting on being BFFs? Why would she have said those words, those strange words: Because I like you, Ms. Crunch?[45]

Agnes kicked a witchy toeful of dirt in Pooky's direction. If it wasn't for Pooky, Agnes would have made it to the Blue Dragon and probably be strutting around with a vial of laughter potion jingling in her pocket. But Pooky had an exhaustive list of needs. She demanded a warm place to sleep (her preference was Agnes's squishy stomach); she insisted on fresh water (apparently pond scum wasn't satisfying); she expected items to play with (another week with Pooky, and Agnes's cabin would be in shambles); and she could not make it more than two hours without a snack (she deemed Agnes's stockpile of worm jerky totally unacceptable).

And so there they were. The wicked witch and the tyrant

---

45. The question had become so bothersome Agnes found herself lying awake at night contemplating what precisely the girl could have liked. Her cunning plans? Her blunt words? Her chilling penmanship? *What?* Because no one had ever bothered to explain to Agnes it was possible to simply like someone just because they were them. Which was certainly a great travesty because of all the very many reasons to like someone, that was, without a doubt, the most grand of all.

kitten. Combing through the Dead Tree Forest in search of a few tasty morsels. Spying a rotting log, Agnes hobbled near and collapsed on top of it. She stretched her sore feet out in front of her. She rubbed at her drooping eyes, because when one is accustomed to living alone forever, there is no quantifying the added disturbance of simply hearing something else breathing and rustling and stirring unpredictably about. Agnes simply wasn't made for such a life!

Pooky looked over her shoulder and blinked her one eye in Agnes's direction.

"You go on ahead," Agnes said. "I'll catch up with you."

Pooky bristled. She even managed to drum up a hissing spit. Then she looked to Agnes for approval.

It was a perfectly rotten display of behavior, to be sure, but Agnes hadn't the energy to offer little more than a halfhearted grunt. Moreover, she was beginning to wonder if she would have been better off encouraging the kitten to have a few manners rather than be rotten like her. She was beginning to wonder if her haunted cabin only had room for one supremely rotten being.

After a moment of waiting, Pooky got bored and resumed the boastful little trot that comes easily to a creature—however puny—that is backed by a wicked witch. But Agnes wasn't right behind Pooky anymore. In fact, Agnes wasn't even slumped on the rotting log for a moment of respite. *Agnes was sneaking away.* Agnes was tiptoeing through the Dead Tree Forest with the full intention of being rid of Pooky, and everything getting back to normal.

Pooky trotted obliviously on. She turned past this tree trunk and that one. Her eye was closed in a merry display of pride, and she failed to see the two giant owls that had left their perch far behind and were tracking her. She *crunch-crunch-crunch*ed right atop the piles of dead leaves and drummed up such a racket that every foul creature in the Dead Tree Forest stirred. And drew near.

But it was the wild hog who found her first.

In Wanderly, wild hogs look nothing at all like the squishy, round, pink image that may come to mind when you think of their well-known cousin, the pig. Instead, wild hogs were massive, hairy, long-tusked creatures that delighted in tossing their meals up into the air before crunching them into little bits. The wild hog took one look at Pooky and snorted in delight.

Despite Agnes's gnawed-on ankles, she had picked up a fair amount of speed. She felt a teensy bit guilty she had left without saying goodbye, but the prospect of returning to her haunted cabin gloriously empty-handed and possibly even catching a snooze in her favorite rocking chair sounded delicious.

"MEOOOW!"

Agnes skidded to a halt. She bit her lip. That was Pooky all right, but was she merely pulling the same sort of stunt as the first time Agnes met her? Perhaps she always made such a sound when searching for a bit of attention, and just because someone throws a fit doesn't mean they should get what they want.

Agnes pushed herself forward. Surely this was a lesson Pooky needed to learn. Independence was a good thing, and if she was going to grow into a respectable cat, she couldn't be so impossibly needy. Agnes tried to recapture the image of sitting lazily in her rocking chair and warming her feet by the cauldron.

"MEOOOOOOOOWW!"

Agnes's lip twitched. The terribly inconvenient thought crossed her mind that perhaps Pooky had stumbled onto a bit of real trouble? She really was nothing more than a mere slip of a thing . . . so small and scrawny . . . and with that one eye, maybe something had snuck up on her without her even knowing? With all the trouble Pooky had caused Agnes, she hardly had a duty to attempt something good like—*ugh*—help her, and maybe it would even make Agnes a total sucker—

"SNORT!"

Agnes thrust her nose into the air and took a deep sniff. Her small, stony heart began to thump. Wildly. That rancid scent could belong to one thing and one thing only: a wild hog! A wild hog that would tear Pooky to shreds!

Agnes forgot all about her ankles. She forgot all about how tired she was, how miserable she was, and maybe even how wicked she was. She ran through the Dead Tree Forest. She ran like she hadn't run since she was a witch in her teenage years. She sailed over knobby roots and leaped over giant boulders as if they were skipping stones. With her chest heaving, she gulped in breath after breath of crisp air. It flooded inside; it stirred up all that was old; it blew through every crowded nook and cranny, and when Agnes exhaled, even the tree trunks shimmied and shook beneath the mighty gust.

Agnes had never felt so necessary.

When she tore onto the scene and caught sight of the wild hog staring Pooky down with its long tusks dripping with sticky saliva, her witchy boots didn't waste any time. They sidestepped, skip to my Lou'ed, and sashayed near for a series of swift kicks in the belly, because dancing witches were the absolute worst!

The wild hog couldn't get away fast enough. It squealed like a piglet. It drummed its hooves beneath its body so fast and so furiously it flipped on top of itself. In fact, it stumbled three separate times trying to dart away from Agnes, and by the time it finally leaped through the surrounding brush and scuttled away, it was a big, weepy, blubbering mess. No doubt that wild hog would spend the rest of its days squawking about the time it almost tango'ed with a witch.

Agnes watched after the wild hog for a moment or two, snarled at the owls overhead that had the good sense to turn their tail feathers and flee, and then finally knelt down beside Pooky. Pooky was rolled up tight into a little ball. When Agnes tapped her on the shoulder, she sprang into the air, as if she'd been electrocuted, and then, seeing Agnes, she dove into her arms.

Agnes growled. She tried to pry Pooky off, but every time

Agnes yanked on her, the blasted kitten dug those needle-sharp claws even deeper into Agnes's skin!

"Oh, you're rotten! You are so, so rotten!" Agnes hissed.

Nevertheless, Agnes looked over shoulder. She made certain not a single soul was watching. And then, because it was just easier, she bent her chin toward Pooky and gave her a rough, unpracticed pat. The kitten vibrated. Absent a sudden craving for bacon, Agnes felt almost content.

Twenty-seven minutes later, Agnes's surprising feeling vanished. But not because of anything Pooky did.

It was, instead, the person waiting on the doorstep of Agnes's haunted cabin who ruined absolutely everything.

Rudey Longtooth fluffed out her obnoxious purple Council cloak. She adjusted her ridiculous badge and gnashed her black tooth in Pooky's direction. She executed one looooong, rolling sniff of her horrid nose.

"Ew," Rudey exclaimed. "That thing smells as wretched as it looks. Times must be tough, eh, Agnes?"

Agnes tried to stuff Pooky in the bell of her sleeve and then behind her back. Finally, she rolled her into a little ball and dropped her down the front of her pinafore where Pooky, for once, didn't make a peep.

"Oh, poor, poor Agnes," Rudey cooed. "You don't have to be ashamed in front of me. Indeed, we are old enemies, aren't we? If this is all you are capable of catching for your meal; if you have stooped so low as to eat *cuddly* things . . . Well, it's no surprise you've gone soft."

"What are you doing here, Rudey?" Agnes said.

"Not feeling very chatty today, are we? Well, if you must know, the *Council* sent me."

"What does the Council want with me?"

"Funny you should ask. It seems someone's been breaking the rules. Someone's been talking with a child. No, no, wait. It's much, much worse than that. Someone's become *friends* with a child. A Tragical child named Birdie Bloom."

Agnes's creaky knees buckled. Nestled against her bosom, Pooky mewed softly.

Friends? Agnes wondered. *Did the Bird-Girl really say they were friends?*

Rudey lunged at her. "Have you forgotten Witches' Manifesto Rule Number Nine? The one that says any and all contact with children is forbidden *unless* for the purpose of evildoing? Not to mention—ugh—*friends*. What in all of witchery do you think you are doing?"

Agnes swallowed back the knot in her throat. She knew the answer to that question. She did. She never intended to help a child. It was merely an unfortunate byproduct of her evil (and, by the way, *very* witchy) plot to do in Octavia Foulweather. Of course, what made that so deeply satisfying was the exact reason why Agnes couldn't tell Rudey. If Rudey caught even a whiff of Agnes's desire to do in a Council member, Agnes would get deported to Council headquarters for sure! The whole evil plot would be off. Both she and Birdie would remain hopelessly, endlessly, stuck.

"I'm tricking her," Agnes said hoarsely. "I sought the child out and have very nearly gained her trust. It's taken a disgustingly long time, but it's almost finished now. So don't you"—Agnes swallowed again and narrowed her eyes—"don't you dare get in my way!"

Rudey stuck her hands in the pockets of her cloak. She kicked her witchy boots up in the dust and began to walk around Agnes in a slow, lazy circle. "And how, dear Agnes, do I know you're not lying to me?"

"You said it, didn't you? I'm down to eating cute, cuddly things for dinner. I've never been to a Witches' Ball. Not until this year anyways. And so long as I'm going, I figured I ought to do something outrageous."

Rudey's tongue flicked across her long tooth. "I was told you have been sending good magic to assist the children against my Council sister, Octavia."

Agnes tried not to retch at the mention of Octavia's name on Rudey's lips. "Sister, is it? Witches aren't supposed to honor such a thing as family. Doesn't that go against the rules?"

"The interest of the Council rises above all," Rudey said quickly. "Anyhow, is it true? Have you been sending good magic?"

Agnes's eyes drifted down toward Rudey's shiny badge.

Despite what Rudey claimed, she was hardly anyone's witchy representative. The Council members lived to serve the Chancellor. And the Chancellor wasn't on anyone's side except his own.

Agnes snorted. "You of all witches should know wicked witches can't produce good magic. It's impossible! Has the dumbing down of the Council made you forget even the basics?"

Rudey swept in over Agnes's shoulder. She pressed her pointer finger into the base of Agnes's throat as if ready to toss off a curse. "Watch your tongue! You have no idea how fine a line you are walking. In fact, if it wasn't for that recent scandal involving Maggie Pruneface Punch, you would probably be seated in the Council's detention room for questioning right this instant."

"Oh, lucky me. Instead, I get this lovely visit from you?" Agnes said, twisting away from Rudey's grasp. "Anyhow, as I was saying, the only curse I am aware of sending was a bevy of rain clouds meant to flood the place silly. And spiders enough to bury the children up to their ears and squeeze the breath out of their lungs. You tell me how that's called *good* magic?"

Rudey frowned. She tapped her fingernail against her tooth. "Hmmm, I see your point. Maybe. Really, I'm just sick of you, and I want to get back to work. I've got a hot lead on Maggie Pruneface Punch, and she's on the Chancellor's top ten list. That makes her way more important than you. But before I go,

I'll leave you with this: you better be at the Witches' Ball, and it better be worth all this nonsense! The Council's feeling restless, and without some hard proof of your wickedness, there's no way they'll listen to your word over my sister, Octavia's."

"She's not your sister," Agnes hissed through gritted teeth.

But Rudey just patted her on the shoulder. "There, there, don't be jealous. The Chancellor made room for just one wicked witch on the Council, and of course, he chose the best."

With that, Rudey Longtooth whipped her Council cloak around and disappeared in a puff of purple smoke.

Agnes sighed a long, deep sigh.

She plopped down on the steps of her haunted cabin and almost planted her hand on an especially fat worm crawling her way. If Agnes had any appetite at all, she might have slurped it right up except, upon closer inspection, the worm was hopelessly covered in glitter. Pooky stuck her head out from Agnes's pinafore just in time to see the worm explode in a sparkling burst that felt about as celebratory as Agnes's last birthday party. The glitter whipped itself up into a letter, and Agnes drew it near.

> Dear Ms. Crunch,
>   I know you haven't had a chance to respond to my last letter, and I'm pretty certain you already hear from me more often than you'd like, but something's happened. Something terrible.

Or, rather, I did something terrible.

I imagine you're probably smirking right now, but this is real serious. It turns out even nonwitches can do wicked things. Worst of all, the wicked thing I did involves you.

Ms. Crunch, I told Mistress Octavia your name. Your whole name.

I didn't want to, and I never meant to get you into trouble. I did it to save Sprinkles. You may remember that Sprinkles is Cricket's pet rat and sort of a hero to the rest of us. Considering you likely eat rats from time to time, this probably sounds like the worst reason in the whole entire world, but if you took the advice in my last letter, if you're a pet owner too, maybe there is a teeny, tiny chance you understand.

Of course, it doesn't make it right. And I'm sorry. I am SO sorry.

I'm not sure if there is such a thing as forgiveness among witches, but I hope there is such a thing as forgiveness between BFFs. It would make what's gonna happen to me tomorrow a whole lot better.

And I guess that's the last bit I have to share. Depending where you stand on the forgiveness thing (and how hard I've made your life by disclosing your identity), you'll either be blowing up balloons or maybe a little bit sad to hear Mistress Octavia has sentenced me to the Drowning Bucket. This means I'm going to die. But considering I'm a Tragical, I guess this really shouldn't be a surprise to anybody. That's just how things go in Wanderly.

So . . . I guess this is goodbye. I sort of always hoped we might meet face-to-face, but it looks like we won't. Even still, I wouldn't give these letters back for anything. Because of you, I think I've fit more living into the past few weeks than I did in my whole entire life.

If you have a chance to write back before I drown, I'd really like that. If only just to tell me about your pet so I know, even if I've scared you away from letter writing forever, you won't be alone.

Yours truly,
Birdbrain
(considering what I did, this name feels most appropriate)

PS: I don't have anything else to say, really. I just sort of like how we usually include a PS or two. Maybe I just have a thing about "The End."

Agnes lowered the letter from beneath her warty nose. She dashed off the steps, and she ran ahead several feet with her fist raised in the air because what was she supposed to do with any of that?

She was breathing so heavy, the edges of the letter rippled to and fro.

Or maybe that was the Winds of Wanderly.

Because the Winds were gusting back and forth around Agnes's cabin. They dipped their fingers low through the dirt and rustled the scant leaves high in the trees; they swished around Agnes's ankles like Pooky tended to do and finally came to perch on her shoulder.

Go, the Winds whispered. *Go . . .*

Agnes stomped her foot on the ground. "Go and do what?" she demanded. "I'm nowhere near close to brewing that laughing potion. I've got nothing!"

Just go, the Winds insisted.

"Witches don't just go!" Agnes hollered.

The answer came immediately. Not from the Winds. But from Agnes. From somewhere deep inside Agnes's small, stony heart. It rose up, almost as if it flew on the wings of a bird.

"Friends do," Agnes croaked. "Witches don't just go, but friends do."

Agnes shut tight her eyes for a moment. She recalled the line of Birdie's last letter, the one she'd been repeating over and over in her mind since the first moment she saw it. The most unforgettable line Agnes would ever read: Because I like you, Ms. Crunch.

But why? How could anyone like a witch?

Especially when no one had ever liked her before.

Agnes didn't think she ever wanted anyone to like her. But then again, neither did she ever imagine she would keep a pet.

But there she was. Holding a letter from an orphan with a kitten cradled against her bosom.

Who was she exactly?

What did witches really do?

"Meow," Pooky mused.

Agnes's beady eyes lit up. *Sometimes witches protect.*

Agnes had certainly been good at showing that awful hog a thing or two. Maybe she would be just as good at snatching Birdie away from Octavia. Maybe only someone as terrible as a witch would risk brushing up against such formidable opponents. Maybe this was the mission Agnes had been looking for all along.

The Winds continued to whip through the tangled strands of Agnes's purple hair. The folds of her black skirts billowed all about. Agnes set her jaw. Agnes looked full upon the face of the Winds of Wanderly as the setting sun blazed across the horizon.

"Yes," she answered, and she dashed toward her cabin to complete the thoroughly annoying yet necessary task of rebristling her broomstick.

Unfortunately for Agnes, she didn't give a moment's thought to what day it was. And it just so happened to be October 4. For those dear readers who pay close and careful attention to details, I am sorry. For you are likely wringing your hands right now because, yes, Agnes did just do what you feared she did. Agnes just vowed to rescue a Tragical on the very same night the skies would be flooded with witches all headed to the Annual Witches' Ball.

SIXTEEN

A Rotten Twist

On the same day Agnes came to the decision to do something utterly astonishing, tucked into a quiet corner of Foulweather's Home for the Tragical, and way up high on Tragic Mountain, Ralph and Cricket huddled around Birdie.

Tomorrow Birdie would die. Unless, of course, she was "saved" by a witch.

More than likely Birdie's death would already have happened had Mistress Octavia not extended an invitation to the Chancellor in hopes he would attend. Though Birdie knew she was lucky to have one last night with her friends, and time to receive a letter back from Ms. Crunch, all she kept thinking about was how year after year, she had traipsed alongside Cricket and Ralph without once realizing what she was missing out on. And now—just now that they were friends—the Tragic End she had been dreading was upon her.

Why had she wasted so much time?

Cricket nudged Birdie gently. "Why don't you read Ms. Crunch's letter again," she whispered.

Despite the fact that she'd already read it twice, Birdie nodded. This letter wasn't like any of Ms. Crunch's other letters. It was different. Monumental, even. The sort of letter that could change everything.

Birdie cleared her throat and read aloud:

To Birdie,

I'm gonna make this short and wicked.

Tonight I'm gonna kidnap you. If that sounds scary, don't worry. Kidnapping is part of every witch's training, and I was top in my class.

But here's my condition: you've gotta find a way out of your manor. You've gotta be waiting for me outside, someplace where it'll be really easy for me to scoop you up on my broomstick. Because I am not—I repeat not—prepared for a full tangle with Octavia tonight.

I blame this entirely on you. If you hadn't tossed out your terrible pet idea, I would have made it to the Blue Dragon and been back with that laughing potion days ago. Instead, I've been toying around with a kitten. So far, she's ruined everything, and considering I've yelled more in three days than three years combined, I doubt she's doing much for my so-called "goodness."

Anyways, if you try to pull anything funny midair—like bringing up that BFF stuff in person. Blech!—I'll sic her on you. If you're wondering how bad a kitten can be, just know my entire cabin (which is properly haunted) is terrified of her.

See you at the witching hour (that's midnight, for beginners).

You're not off the hook yet,
AP Crunch

PS: Be prepared to swing by the Deepest, Darkest Bog for a little visit to the Blue Dragon. Though it's amusing to think how steamed Octavia will be when you've "disappeared," I still want MORE! And for that, we're gonna need the laughing potion.

Birdie laid the letter gently down in her lap and looked at Ralph and Cricket. "So . . . what do you think?"

"A kidnapping," Cricket said, shaking her head. "I'm scared for you, Birdie. Aren't you scared too?"

"Yes," Birdie said. And then: "Quite a lot scared, actually.

But didn't you tell Sir Ichabod that being scared isn't what's most important?"

Cricket frowned. "I don't think he listened though. Maybe I didn't either. Oh Birdie, when Mistress Octavia brought Sprinkles near that spinning wheel, I got scared! I got so scared I wasn't thinking what Mistress Octavia might do to *you*—"

"But you didn't make me do anything. I was the one who brought up Ms. Crunch, and I was the one who gave away her name," Birdie said.

Cricket laid her hand on top of Birdie's. "And now Ms. Crunch is gonna save you."

Ralph shook his head. "Maybe," he said. "But have you both forgotten what Ms. Crunch is? Have you forgotten what we are? Has anything good ever come out of a kidnapping? This has Tragical stamped all over it."

"Maybe," Birdie agreed. "But my only other choice is the Drowning Bucket. That's a for sure Tragic End. At least with Ms. Crunch, I have a chance."

"Getting kidnapped by a witch shouldn't be your best option!" Ralph said.

"I guess that depends on your thinking. If we believe what the Chancellor says, this will be a disaster. But if we think of Ms. Crunch as more than a witch—if we think of her as a friend—then maybe she really will be the one to rescue me," Birdie said.

"But how do you know she's telling the truth?" Ralph said.

"I think I'm supposed to trust her. I think that's what friends do."

Ralph didn't answer. Instead, he pushed up off the cold stone floor. He walked off with the shadows chasing after him, and Cricket nestled in tight against Birdie's side.

"Can we stay like this for just a little while longer?" Cricket asked.

"As long as we possibly can," Birdie said.

"Do you think maybe that could be forever?" Cricket asked.

"Forever and a day," Birdie said.

And the words settled soft and warm around them as if maybe, somehow, it could possibly be true.

Later that night, when the other children were asleep, Birdie tiptoed away from the dormitory and stood at the foot of the ladder leading up to the Plank. It was a place no child wanted to be, and it was the place Birdie would be the very next day if her kidnapping wasn't successful. The only thing waiting at the end of the Plank was the Drowning Bucket.

Birdie had never stood on the Plank before. Birdie didn't know if any Tragical had ever stood on the Plank before. But with Mistress Octavia's wolf pack prowling about the perimeter of the manor, it was the only outside place she could think to go where she could safely await Ms. Crunch's arrival. At least as safe as it was to teeter three hundred feet above the Black Sea while suspended from a narrow walkway.

Birdie began to climb up the ladder. A little wisp of the Winds still bounding about the manor from the day Sir Ichabod broke the library window surged beneath her feet,[46] urging her onward. At the top of the ladder, Birdie lifted her hands to push on the trapdoor, but it was stuck. She pressed her shoulder against it. She pushed with all her might, and when it finally burst open, her breath was swept clean away.

Birdie stood with her head poking out from the hole as if she were a field mouse. She eyeballed the great expanse of black night sky and the glorious presence of stars that burned with light; she drank in the death-defying heights from which she teetered atop a crooked mountain nearly ready to tumble into the sea, and then she ducked. With her chest heaving, she ducked right back *into* the manor. Because she was small. So very, very small. And what place could she possibly have in a world as grand as that?

Maybe she really was nothing more than a Tragical.

Maybe it was safer to think so.

Beneath her hand, the wisp of the Winds rose up. It wrapped around Birdie's fingers and began to pull. Gently.

---

46. For as much as Birdie loved hearing the Winds swirl outside the manor, it was absolutely nothing compared to having them live *within* the manor. Since their arrival, they had already accomplished a mighty work in redecorating. Namely, the Council portraits hanging in the Dark Hallway were in a ridiculously crooked state of disarray, and Mistress Octavia's thick black-out curtains simply could not keep from whipping about and letting in oodles of light.

Birdie shook her head. "No," she whispered.

Come, the Winds urged.

"I can't."

Come, friend.

Birdie's chest tightened. Was it true? The Winds had been the first to find her; they had never forgotten her; and they had connected her with a witch unlike any other. Without the Winds of Wanderly, would Birdie even have anything at all?

Birdie stopped pulling against the little wisp. She allowed it to lead her slowly through the trapdoor. She swallowed hard at the gleam of the Drowning Bucket's chain as it waited at the end of the Plank. She crawled along the narrow wooden walkway on her knees because there was no railway, no safety net, not one single thing to prevent Birdie from plummeting off the side. The wisp shut the trapdoor behind her and eased her into a cross-legged position. It swept softly against her cheek and then slowly tumbled away, rolling off into the unending black.

"No!" Birdie cried. "Please don't go! I'm scared!"

Shhhh, the Winds said. *Shhhh . . .*

Birdie whipped her head to and fro. Her heart banged like a drum, and everything inside her felt hollow. She fought off a terrible wave of dizziness that made it feel as if she were falling. She wanted to go back in; she needed to get back inside the manor!

"Birdie?"

Birdie froze at the sound of her name. When she spun

carefully around, however, she didn't see a pointy witch hat or the fastidiously smooth hairdo of Mistress Octavia. Ralph was climbing through the trapdoor. And Birdie's pulse raced because surely only one thing could have brought Ralph near the spot of a potential witch sighting.

"Oh no!" she cried. "Cricket—the others— Has something happened to them? What has happened?"

Ralph quickly shook his head. "No, no. Nothing has happened. They're all asleep." Ralph peeked over the edge of the Plank and shivered. "Wow, this is nice and creepy, isn't it?"

Birdie frowned. "Ralph, you shouldn't be out here. You need to get back inside. I don't want Mistress Octavia to punish you, too."

Ralph lifted his bandaged arm in the air. "What's the worst she can do? Throw me to the wolves?"[47]

"No. But she could sentence you to the Drowning Bucket. Like me."

"Nah, not happening—"

"But she—"

"Please let me stay. I—I couldn't sleep with the Winds of

---

47. Not only had Ralph already endured such a traumatic event, but Mistress Octavia wasn't likely to repeat it any time soon. Indeed, she was so disappointed in her entire wolf pack for not making mincemeat out of Ralph when they had the chance that she punished them with a diet consisting solely of blueberry mush. Curiously, instead of howling up a raging storm, the wolves had never seemed so content.

Wanderly blowing. And all I kept thinking about was how I didn't want a witch to turn out to be a better friend than me."

"Then you think I *am* doing the right thing?"

Ralph lowered his head. "Not really, no. But friends don't have to agree about everything, do they?"

Birdie paused. She thought back to her storybook. She couldn't remember any specifics about such a thing, but she knew how it felt to see Ralph. And maybe even especially so, considering his contrary feelings. "I'm glad you're here," she finally said.

And the two of them sat down together along the Plank. They swung their feet, back and forth, as if they were somewhere far, far away. Maybe even somewhere wonderful. Though Birdie was certain the Winds were long gone, she couldn't keep from whispering, "Thank you," because—however mysterious they were—the Winds seemed to be behind every good thing.

WHOOOOOOOSH!

The Winds of Wanderly were closer than Birdie thought.

SWOOOOOOSH!

The Winds of Wanderly swirled all about.

With the Plank trembling beneath the Winds' mighty force, Birdie and Ralph grabbed tight to each other's hands.

They watched in stunned silence as the Winds of Wanderly swept clean from the ground and all the way up to the heavens. The Winds billowed across the horizon, dipping fingers into the sea and snuffing a wave with one mere puff. The Winds ruffled the fur on the backs of Mistress Octavia's wolf pack and caused the light of the stars to ripple. They tapped softly along the windows of Foulweather's Home for the Tragical as if it were a xylophone, and all the world was its symphony.

Ralph's eyes were wide. "Wow," he whispered.

And finally, Birdie understood.

Perhaps more important than how small she was, was how big the Winds of Wanderly were. Uncountable. Unfathomable. Most astonishingly, their *friend*.

"What do you think about the Winds of Wanderly now?" she asked Ralph.

Ralph swallowed. "I think that if you're right about the Winds of Wanderly—if they really do want to help us—then maybe we've never needed to be afraid of anything at all."

As the Winds lulled to a soft breeze, Birdie resumed swinging her feet. "You know, I always figured when my Tragic End was getting close I would sense it somehow. But right now, it almost feels as if things are as right as they've ever been. Do you think that's a good sign, Ralph?"

Ralph opened his mouth to reply, but he froze at the sight of a dense cloud of fog tumbling across the horizon. The Winds stilled, and Birdie straightened up. She squinted, but the fog was too thick and soupy to see through. An odd smell wafted near. A smell not unlike that of dirty socks. Every so often the cloud of fog erupted with a jarring flash of light.[48]

Cruuunch! An ominous wail rolled toward Birdie and Ralph. And again: *Cruuunch!*

Birdie tried to control the tremble in her voice. "That must be Ms. Crunch. She, uh, must be announcing her arrival."

Birdie swallowed hard. She placed her shaking hands on the Plank and stumbled to her feet.

"What are you doing, Birdie?" Ralph asked. "I think we ought to wait a minute. We need to see what's going on."

"But Ms. Crunch told me to be ready. She said she needed to get me quick. I-it was part of our plan."

Ralph's voice rose. "Were the dark cloud and scary noises part of the plan, too?"

"No, but she *is* a witch. Maybe we should have expected that? Anyhow, I think it'd probably be safer if you went back into the manor."

"You want me to leave you right now?"

But Birdie didn't answer. She was trying to be brave. She set her jaw. She raised her arms over her head. "Ms. Crunch!" she called out. "Ms. Crunch, I'm over here!"

---

48. At the beginning of our journey, I warned you about the scary parts. THIS IS ONE OF THEM. But fear not, because there are still many pages after this one. And that is something to note about endings: sometimes a bad ending is simply the product of ending a story *too soon*. On the flip side, a reader must be prepared for things to get bad (sometimes really, really bad) before they can become good. Hold on, dear reader.

And then, like magic, the witch appeared.

She burst forth from the cloud, the fog continuing to fan out around her. It magnified her, making her appear at least three times her normal size. Tendrils of fog flicked and swished through her purple hair as if she were sporting a headful of snakes! She sat in a plump pile of gauzy black fabric, and her pointy hat was tilted to a jaunty degree. Her eyes gleamed dark as coal, and her nose was as warty as a cucumber.

Still clinging to the Plank, Ralph gasped.

Cruuunch! Cruuunch! The ominous moan came again.

"Why does she keep doing that?" Ralph asked.

Birdie shrank just a bit. "I don't know. I thought she didn't want to alert Mistress Octavia. . . ."

"Unless she's not the one making the noise."

"Who else could it be?"

"Look," Ralph croaked. "Just look."

Birdie followed Ralph's gaze past Ms. Crunch and into the thick cloud of fog. Her heart caught in her throat. Among the sporadic flashes of light, she could see the terrifying silhouette of . . . broomsticks. Lots of broomsticks. And sitting on those broomsticks, *witches.*

Birdie's breath came out in great, heaving gulps. "I don't understand. Why wouldn't she come alone? She didn't say anything about other witches."

But what Birdie really wanted to say was: *she's supposed to be my friend.*

Despite all Birdie had read about witches, despite all she had read about her certain doom as a Tragical, the letters between her and Ms. Crunch seemed more real than any of the Chancellor's authorized storybooks put together. But maybe the Chancellor was never the enemy. Maybe the Chancellor was nothing more than a messenger. Maybe the hope Birdie had was never real to begin with. Had she been wrong about everything?

Ralph sprang up from the Plank and grabbed hold of Birdie's hand. "Come on, we're going inside. *Both* of us."

At the sight of Ralph rising alongside Birdie, Ms. Crunch slowed up. But only for a moment. She sped forward with a shiny glint in her eye.

"Ralph, she's seen you!" Birdie cried. And Birdie was more afraid than ever.

A terrible wave of cackling rolled toward Birdie and Ralph. The air crackled and popped as if it were filled with electricity. The witches broke free of the foggy cloud and began executing an impressive series of loop the loops, dive-bombs, and curlicues. One witch whooshed so close to Birdie she was forced to drop to her knees lest she be knocked clean off the Plank.

Ralph helped Birdie back up. "Come on!" he shouted. "We can still make it if we hurry!"

But Birdie's feet were stuck. She swallowed back the knot in her throat. "Tomorrow I'll die in the Drowning Bucket for sure, but tonight there's a . . . slim chance that maybe this will still turn out okay."

Ralph's face was aghast. He looked at the witches streaking past. "But you can't— There's no way that— Birdie, you have to change your mind! It doesn't count as turning your back on a friend if she was never a friend in the first place."

But why did she write all those letters?

Birdie felt too foolish to say it out loud though. She knew it didn't make any sense. But neither could she leave without always wondering if she had made a grave mistake.

With tears streaming down her face, Birdie pushed Ralph in the direction of the trapdoor. "Please, Ralph," she said. "You have to go. You must go! *Now!*"

And when he had taken a few stumbling steps away, Birdie turned her attention to Ms. Crunch. Ms. Crunch was very nearly there. She was almost upon the Plank, and then she would scoop Birdie up. She would tell Birdie that everything was going according to plan; that there was never anything to fear because they were friends. *They had to be.*

Ms. Crunch lifted high her crooked, gnarly hands. Ms. Crunch swept ever so slightly to the left of Birdie. Birdie, confused, tried to dodge into Ms. Crunch's arms opened wide, but stumbled against someone and fell backward. It was Ralph! Ralph was still on the Plank! Ralph had come back to Birdie's side. And when Ms. Crunch swooped in, she wrapped her fingers around the scruff of Ralph's collar and plucked him up and into the air.

An awful noise ripped free of Ralph's mouth. His feet

wriggled helplessly as he swung from Ms. Crunch's grip like a rag doll against the vast night sky. Ms. Crunch never said a word to Birdie. She spun so fast upon her broomstick its bristles glowed an angry shade of red. She twirled her free hand through the air, and the other witches flying about willy-nilly hustled to line up behind her.

Ms. Crunch was leading them.

As they zipped off across the horizon, a witch with scraggly green hair flew by and yanked on Birdie's curls.

"Sorry, dear!" she hissed. "Maybe next time it will be your turn to go to the Annual Witches' Ball!" She erupted into a fit of wild cackling and flicked her tongue across the surface of her long black tooth.

Nobody cared that Birdie was screaming.

Nobody cared that Birdie was jumping and bouncing and pummeling her fists into the air.

Nobody cared because Birdie was nothing. Birdie was a Tragical. And maybe the most tragic of all.

A MAGICAL CLOAK AND A FOUL SECRET

The Annual Witches' Ball?" Cricket echoed in the quiet of the dormitory. "What's that?"

Birdie was still out of breath from sliding down the ladder, sprinting through the hallway, and tumbling toward Cricket's bedside, where Birdie had shaken her awake. "I haven't a clue. But that's where Ralph is. That's where the witches . . ." Birdie paused. "Where *Ms. Crunch* has taken him."

Cricket's eyes were wide. "But she didn't say any of that in her letter, did she?"

"No!" Birdie burst out. And then: "I—I guess I should have listened to Ralph. I guess he was right about Ms. Crunch all along. And now, because of me, he's gone."

"But why was Ralph outside with you?" Cricket asked.

Birdie's voice cracked. The weight of each word fell heavy on her heart. "He was being a friend. And that's why I have to save him."

"But didn't you say he's with a bunch of witches?" Cricket said, clutching her ratty sheet just below the tip of her nose.

Birdie gulped. "I'm scheduled to die tomorrow; what could I possibly have to lose?"

"But—but—how will you even get there? Ms. Crunch and her broomstick are gone. Even if you found a way past Mistress Octavia's wolves, how would you climb down Tragic Mountain and through Beastly Valley? Wouldn't it take an . . . awful long time?"

"Yes," Birdie said. "Too long. And that's why I'll need Mistress Octavia's Council cloak. It's the only thing that will work. The Council cloak can go anywhere. The Council cloak can fly. And the Council cloak is lightning fast!"

Cricket shook her head vigorously to and fro. "But the Council cloak is magic. You don't know how to use magic. Even worse, it's in Mistress Octavia's Room of Sinister Plotting! The door handle is inside a box full of snakes! Birdie, you *can't*!"

A flash of white and a sudden flurry of movement five beds over caused Birdie and Cricket to jump. It wasn't, however, a ghost, but merely an extraordinarily perturbed Francesca Prickleboo. She tossed her sheets aside and stomped near. A few of the other children began to rustle and stir and scratch sleepily at their mussed-up hair.

"Please go back to bed, Francesca. We'll try to be more quiet," Birdie said.

"Go back to bed? Go back to bed!?" Francesca said with her voice rising.

Birdie and Cricket exchanged worried glances. Amelia poked her sleepy head up and sprang from her bed and into Mildred's, where two other girls were already huddled. The boys weren't far behind. A trio of them, led by Benjamin—who had taken to wearing his sleeves proudly rolled up—bounded from mattress to mattress until they plopped atop the still-sleeping form of a teenage boy. The impromptu round of musical beds continued until not a single Tragical was left alone except for Francesca.

Francesca glowered at them all. "Ha! Because of all of you, I haven't had a good night's sleep for over a week! I used to sleep like a baby. I used to like shining my shoes and braiding my hair and impressing Mistress Octavia. I *liked* being a Tragical! But ever since your whispering and your secrets, ever since that stupid drawing showing everybody else together, you've been ruining it for me! You've been making me think. And it's just so much easier . . . not to." Francesca's lower lip began to quiver. She crossed her arms against her black gown, like she had suddenly grown very cold. "Do you know that Mistress Octavia hates me? I always used to think I was her favorite. But she sees me the exact same way she sees all of you: as nothing! And I don't think I want to be a Tragical anymore, but I don't have a clue what I'm supposed to do about that now!"

Cricket was the only one brave enough to speak.

"I could make a new drawing," she said. "I—I've still got some more paper, and this time I can put you in there, too."

Francesca thrust her lower lip out. "How's a drawing supposed to change anything?"

"Like you said, it helps us think. It helps us see. See that we're more than what Mistress Octavia says."

"But I want to *do* something," Francesca said. "I want to prove it!"

Birdie took a small step forward. "I think there's something you can do. But only if you're one hundred percent certain you want to help and one hundred percent certain you're tired of being a Tragical. If you help me, it's very, very likely that you'll get into trouble."

Francesca bristled. "What sort of trouble?"

"I don't know for sure."

"Like being sent to the dungeon or like . . . Drowning Bucket trouble?"

"It's Mistress Octavia, and who can ever tell what she's going to do?" Birdie said.

"Well, all right. Wh-what did you have in mind?"

"I need you to get Mistress Octavia's attention. I need you to scream as loudly as you can, and as many times as you need to, in order to get her out of her Room of Sinister Plotting and into the dormitory."

"Oh Birdie, you can't still be thinking about—" Cricket began.

"Thinking about what?" Francesca interjected. "If I get Mistress Octavia in here, where are you going to be?"

Birdie took a deep breath. "I'm going to be in her Room of Sinister Plotting. I'm going to snatch her Council cloak and use it to leave the manor. I'm going to the Annual Witches' Ball so that I can save Ralph, because he's been kidnapped. By witches. By . . . my witch."

The Tragicals in the room gasped. Mildred wrapped her arms tightly around the younger girls. Benjamin's jaw dropped. Wasn't this the precise sort of event they had been raised to fear? Wasn't it even worse considering most Tragic Ends happened *after* the Tragical Oaths were signed? Not to mention with first Birdie's—and now Ralph's—life threatened, had the Tragicals finally begun to notice one another merely to have something much more painful to lose?

Francesca trembled. "But wh-why do you think Mistress Octavia will come when I call her?"

"Because you're the best at tattling. And that makes you . . . the person we need more than ever. Will you help us? Will you help us save Ralph?"

"I—I never did like him much," Francesca mumbled. "And this plan sounds like it's doomed to fail. I mean, did you even hear yourself talking about witches? Multiple witches? A whole ball full of witches? And even if I call for Mistress Octavia, it's not like you can just slip inside her room. It's guarded by cobras trained to allow just two people to enter: Mistress Octavia and Sir Ichabod."[49]

Birdie's face lit up. "Sir Ichabod!" she cried.

But Cricket shook her head. "I don't know, Birdie. I don't think it's even fair to ask him for help. Did you see his face when Mistress Octavia ordered him to bring in Sprinkles? If the same thing happens again—if this time, he's dragging you to Mistress Octavia—I think it might crush him forever."

Birdie squeezed Cricket's hand. "I know, but I wasn't going to ask him for help. I was thinking instead of what he smells like."

"Smells like?" Cricket echoed. And then, with a quizzical expression: "Blueberries?"

"Yes! Blueberries! Quick, did anybody save some mush from dinnertime?" Birdie asked.

The Tragicals all began to dip into the pockets of their gowns; several of them emerged with whole handfuls of the sticky goo that they liked to snack on in the wee hours of the night. They hopped off their beds and shuffled toward Birdie, who began grabbing the mush and rubbing it all over her hands; smashing and smearing and smooshing it along her wrists, up to her

---

49. Considering Sir Ichabod was Wanderly's oldest Tragical, he may seem an odd choice to be permitted entrance to Mistress Octavia's secret room. Alas, even secret rooms need to be dusted, mopped, and tidied from time to time, and Mistress Octavia had vowed long ago never to engage in such "dirty" work.

elbows, and even beneath her fingernails.

"Ugh," Francesca said, wrinkling her nose. "That is disgusting!"

"Nope, it's genius," Birdie said, wriggling her blue fingers. "Those snakes are trained to recognize Mistress Octavia and Sir Ichabod by the way they *smell*. Sir Ichabod spends all day long picking blueberries, boiling blueberries, and mashing blueberries. Those snakes will think I'm him for sure!"

The Tragicals began to buzz and stir. They nodded and grabbed hold of Birdie's excitement, like it was a life preserver. Only Cricket remained quiet. She stepped toward Birdie and looked up into her eyes.

"Promise you won't come back," she said. Birdie opened her mouth to protest, but Cricket repeated more forcefully, "If you get Mistress Octavia's cloak, if you fly out of the manor, you have to promise not to come back!"

"But friends are meant to be together," Birdie said.

"No! If you come back, Mistress Octavia will still put you in the Drowning Bucket. Please, Birdie. If this works, you won't have to die."

Birdie hesitated. She hadn't wanted Ralph to help her on the Plank. She had wanted to protect him, but now she was risking everything to do the very thing she asked him not to do. Although Birdie couldn't remember reading anything about sacrifice in her storybook, she was watching it unfold right in front of her. Friends put one another first. And it wouldn't be fair to expect anything less.

Birdie threw her arms around Cricket. "Let's just wait and see," she whispered. "Let's just wait and see."

The two friends held on to each other.

Tight.

Finally, with a nod from Birdie in Francesca's direction, Francesca arched her head back in that oh-so-familiar position. She dug deep, and she bellowed loud and strong, "MISTRESS OC-TAV-I-A! MISTRESS OC-TAV-I-A!" the way she always did. The way she loved to do. Except this time Wanderly's #1 Tragical and world-class tattletale was on their side.

Birdie lifted up the long hem of her black gown and ran as quickly as her feet would carry her. The floor of the manor seemed to run along with her, shortening the distance as she turned down one corridor and the next until the door of the Room of Sinister Plotting loomed out of the darkness. Unlike the rest of the manor's gloomy interior, the door was painted a garish shade of red. And even from where Birdie stood, she could hear the three snakes—*hissssss*—as they writhed over and around the doorknob, held captive in a glass box.

Birdie jumped when another of Francesca's great and mighty screams barreled down the hallway. "MISTRESS OC-TAV-I-A! MISTRESS OC-TAV-I-A!!" Birdie barely had time to duck beneath the thick drape of a black-out curtain when the door to the Room of Sinister Plotting creaked open.

"MISTRESS OC-TAV-I-A! MISTRESS OC-TAV-I-A!!"

came Francesca's cry again.

"Oh, confound it!" Mistress Octavia said with a huff. "This better be worth my trouble."

She slammed the door shut and swept within inches of Birdie. Birdie tucked her feet as close to the wall as she possibly could and tried to still her breathing so as not to make the curtain rise and fall. She waited until the sound of Mistress Octavia's footsteps disappeared down the hallway, and then she scurried toward the door.

Birdie eyeballed the snakes. She pressed her hands into her pockets one last time for a fresh coating of blueberry mush. With her heart pounding, Birdie slid the small door to the left and stuck her hand inside the glass box.

The snakes froze. But only for a moment. Then they began to slither. They slithered *close*. One began to entwine itself around and around and around Birdie's small, bony wrist. Birdie gasped at the feel of its cold scales and the ripple of its muscles as it began to tighten around her.

Birdie tried not to look at the snakes' forked tongues as they flickered in and out. Slow at first, and then faster!

HISSSSSSS. The snakes sang as they tasted her skin.

Birdie's knees clattered in time to the wild drum of her heart.

HISSSSS. The snakes sang merrily along. *HISSSSS.* They wriggled about.

And then, just like that, they released her.

The rhythm of their tongues slowed. Birdie was free to move

her fingers and twist open the door to the Room of Sinister Plotting. With the glass box shut tight, Birdie bent down and met the snakes' cool gaze. Whether due entirely to the blueberries, or if the snakes were feeling particularly amicable that night, she whispered softly, "Thank you."

Birdie stepped into the Room of Sinister Plotting. It was much larger than she imagined. Or perhaps the better word was "taller." For it was an extraordinarily skinny room, and it's ceiling did not stop at floor three or even floor three and one-half, but extended all the way up to the roof of Foulweather's Home for the Tragical, where it was crowned with a spectacular glass window. Birdie arched her head backward. The stars winked at her. What a peculiar place for Mistress Octavia to spend her time.

But as Birdie's gaze fell back down, her eyes landed on an oversize painting of the Chancellor. Birdie cringed at the familiar sight of his ever-toothy grin. She reached her fingers out to brush lightly against the tarnished bronze plaque sitting just beneath the painting, covered in dust.[50] She supposed it would say something like all the rest of the plaques, such as "The Wise Chancellor," or "The One and Only Chancellor," or "Chancellor the Great," but it didn't.

---

50. Considering Sir Ichabod's servitude as a butler, this particular abundance of dust did not render him inept. It merely hinted at the Chancellor's dastardly nature considering Sir Ichabod refused to even draw near to his *likeness*.

Instead, quite astonishingly, the plaque said "Uncle Rupert."

Now, the name Rupert alone may have given you reason to pause. Indeed, when one has spent a lifetime referring to someone in such lofty terms as "the Chancellor," it is a bit disconcerting to find out they also possess a name as hopelessly ordinary as the rest of us. And certainly, "Rupert" was no exception. But far, far, far more astonishing was that other word. The one in front of it. The one that said "*uncle.*"

Was it really possible? Could it really be true that the Chancellor was not just Mistress Octavia's supervisor, but her family member?

Birdie stumbled backward. She toppled against a shelf full of books with broken spines. Breathing heavy, she turned her head sideways to glance at the titles. *A Life Without Magic. The Art of Being Common. Witchy No More.* Birdie's eyes widened at the title of the last book on the shelf: *A Nonmagical Guide to Waking the Dead.*

Birdie swallowed hard. Who would Mistress Octavia want to wake up? Who had Mistress Octavia lost? Who had she ever had? And then for the first time, Birdie realized it wasn't just the Tragicals who received no visitors, no letters, and not a single inquiry other than the Council—it was Mistress Octavia too. Mistress Octavia was all alone, just like the Tragicals.

Except, of course, for her uncle. For the Chancellor. But perhaps the fact that he utterly and completely ignored her—that he didn't even bother to keep his appointments with her—was even worse than having nobody at all.

Birdie did not want to feel sorry for Mistress Octavia. Mistress Octavia was plotting to kill her via the Drowning Bucket no sooner than tomorrow and had spent a lifetime telling her she was nothing! Birdie had a job to do—a job the other children were risking everything for. She was Ralph's only hope, and she had to stay focused.

Birdie eyes roved across the room, looking intently for any hint of the Council cloak's brilliant purple fabric. Other than the overhead light coming from the stars, the room was lit only by the waning puddle of three or four nubby candles. Birdie crept forward and nearly crashed into a pile of broomsticks that came as high as her waist. They looked identical to the one Mistress Octavia toted from room to room, swatting mercilessly at the children and smacking hard against the blackboard. Every single one of them, snapped in two.

Birdie bent down and picked up one of the broomstick halves. It crackled in her hand, and she was so startled she nearly dropped it. The broomstick, it seemed, still contained magic. But what would Mistress Octavia be doing with something that held even a hint of magic? She *hated* magic. Magic was forbidden! Instead of breaking the broomsticks in half, why didn't she just toss them out and be rid of them once and for all?

Click-clack, click-clack.

It was Mistress Octavia! Mistress Octavia was returning!

Birdie felt her way toward Mistress Octavia's desk. She felt along the back of the chair and threw open the top drawer. She gasped when a stack of papers gusted forth, grazing so close to her cheek she was forced to jump out of the way as the papers soared upward. Birdie watched as the papers scaled the walls and clustered against the window beneath the stars. They beat their edges against the window to no avail and then began to tumble back down in helpless chaotic waves. Birdie looked at the paper that fell into the palm of her hand. It was a letter. They were all letters. Letters that Mistress Octavia had presumably never sent. Birdie read one as quickly as she dared:

Dear Uncle,

I think I need more of the potion. I think my magic is brewing again.

Last night I fashioned another broomstick. I didn't mean to. But when I woke up in the morning, it was there. In my hands. And it crackled. I snapped it in half and added it to the pile, but the pile is getting so big.

Uncle, you must help me. I am too much like Mother!

I hate her.

Because of her, I grew up all alone in this wretched place! It was you who rescued me from a life of certain doom. You who offered me a seat at your table. The Council table. Your requirement that I drink my magic away was an easy one to swallow. But magic, it seems, is resilient.

Why did Mother have to be a witch?? Why was Father so easily tricked? Why did they both have to die? If only you would have always been the Chancellor—if only citizens had been taught from the beginning to stick to their roles—then everything would be different.

Please send me more of the potion, Uncle. I am weak; the temptation is strong; and magic is a hard habit to break.

In your debt,
Octavia

Birdie was shaking all over. Mistress Octavia was already awful, but Mistress Octavia as a *witch*—reformed or not—was horrific. And what of the potion she mentioned? Were there days that magic very well *could* have flung forth from a swish of Mistress Octavia's hand? Magic to bring about a Tragic End? Most puzzling of all, however, was the desperate tone of her letter. Mistress Octavia didn't seem to want her magic. Mistress Octavia seemed to think that if she kept her magic, she would revert to being doomed. She would revert to being what all orphans in Wanderly were: *Tragical*.

Birdie's heart sank. If Mistress Octavia couldn't escape a life of doom, if a real live witch couldn't undo the status of Tragical without the help of the Chancellor, what hope did an ordinary girl like Birdie have? In short, what in all of Wanderly did she think she was doing?

Click-clack. Click-clack.

Birdie stared at the toes of her shoes. Tears began to prick at the corners of her eyes. But Mistress Octavia wasn't there yet. Birdie's Tragic End, however close it loomed, hadn't officially occurred yet. Why should she act as if it already had? Why should she waste the one thing that, for a Tragical, was especially precious?

Time. Regardless of what the Chancellor guaranteed about Birdie's end, for now, she still had time. And maybe even a small bit used wisely could make a world of difference. Not just for her, but for Ralph.

Birdie leaped into motion. She kicked over a wastebasket full of paper scraps. She sent a coatrack wheeling wildly about, and she even managed to overturn a bookcase. As the heap of books crashed against the floor, they kicked up a swirling cloud of dust. A cloud of dust that swept through the room. A cloud of dust that reached into every nook and cranny and fluttered a piece of bright purple fabric.

The Council cloak. It was caught in the door of Mistress Octavia's file cabinet! Birdie sprinted near and tore the cloak free at the precise moment Mistress Octavia crashed into the Room of Sinister Plotting.

In the dim flicker of candlelight, Mistress Octavia's shadow loomed large. She gasped at the sight of Birdie smack-dab in the center of her letters still wafting about the room and whispering her secrets. And then her face turned a horrible, ominous shade of red.

But she was a hair too late. For Birdie had already swung the Council cloak around her shoulders, and she had already whispered for it to take her to the Annual Witches' Ball, and in less than a blink of an eye, Birdie became the second Tragical in one night to vanish from the manor completely.

EIGHTEEN

COME ONE, COME ALL TO THE ANNUAL WITCHES' BALL!

On the eve of her ill-fated trip to the Drowning Bucket, Birdie never imagined she'd be attending an event like the Annual Witches' Ball, but there she was. And her arrival via Council cloak was anything but pretty.

One moment she was caught up in a wild, swirling vortex of sights and sounds, and the very next she was rolling her way through a crowd of witches like a human bowling ball.

Fortunately, witches pride themselves on disregarding any and all manners, and not one of them seemed to pay a bit of attention to Birdie. This also, however, meant Birdie could hardly complain about the number of times she was inadvertently poked, prodded, and pushed as she stumbled toward the castle looming before them all.[51]

Birdie was certain it had to be Castle Matilda. Castle Matilda was Wanderly's oldest and most haunted abode and an infamous witchy hangout. Mistress Octavia loved to whisper about it in the dead of night. It was a place most people in Wanderly liked to pretend wasn't as bad as it sounded but that a Tragical knew was probably worse. Even the likes of Castle Matilda, however, couldn't compare to what Birdie saw all around her.

There wasn't just a little pocket of witches slinking alongside Birdie. There wasn't even a terrifying four or five dozen witches. There were witches as far as Birdie could see.

One hundred, two hundred, maybe even three hundred witches flooding the skies and streaming in from north, south, east, and west. Some traveled by boot; most careened wildly through the air mounted on fiery broomsticks; a handful skipped from witchy shoulder to witchy shoulder as if they were in a hopscotch tournament; and a few lone witches floated eerily back and forth above Castle Matilda's swampy moat.

Birdie tried to breathe. Birdie tried to remember why this had seemed like such a good idea. And then Birdie remembered

---

51. Of course, the specifics are stowed safely away in my memory. What is a book, really, if it doesn't pay attention to detail? So, for those interested, Birdie was kicked in the shins twice, elbowed in the side once, knocked down to her knees three times, stepped on (oooh, the pinkie finger!) once, and had at least three separate pairs of curly fingernails caught within her hair (*shudder*).

Ralph caught in Ms. Crunch's grip, with his feet swinging in the night sky. The way he had screamed and—

Birdie felt her heart breaking all over again. Was there anything worse in the world than losing two friends at the same time? Still, if Birdie could pull herself together, perhaps one of those friendships could be saved.

Birdie hurried to rejoin the crowd. She discreetly flipped the Council cloak inside out so that only the black lining could be seen, leaving the brilliant purple fabric hidden. She leaned heavily on her years of trudging and was certain she was close to mastering the witchy slink when a nearby witch skidded to a sudden halt.

The witch lifted her nose high and let loose a mighty sniff. Birdie froze. Despite the cover of night, and despite the tangled clump of witches of various heights and sizes all dressed similarly in black, there was nothing so astute as the concentrated sniff of a witch.

"What is it, Bernadette?" another witch hacked in a raspy voice.

"Call me crazy, but I coulda swore I caught a big ol' whiff of girl-child," the sniffing witch, Bernadette, said.

The other witch cackled wildly. "You ninny! Don't you pay any attention to invites? There'll be plenty o' young witches here tonight too. You better get that sniffer of yours checked out!"

Bernadette put her hands on her hips. "I ought to know the difference between a wee witch and one of them ordinary runts!

And there's not a blasted thing wrong with my sniffer! You're always telling me I'm wrong, and I'm plumb sick of it!"

Birdie instinctively took a few steps backward. Her hand hovered near the Council cloak. Before Birdie could use it, Bernadette reached out and snatched the other witch's hat right off the top of her head. It went whizzing through the air and floated down, of all places, at Birdie's feet.

Birdie waited for them to see her; for them to screech that there was an imposter at the ball—a child, no less—and then surely they would turn on her at once! Instead, the hatless witch grabbed two handfuls of Bernadette's frizzy blue hair and yanked hard enough to make her howl. Right away, the witches around them formed a little semicircle. They lurked with eyes that gleamed in the darkness, drumming their fingers together, licking their lips and hissing out venom like "Smoke her!" and "Make her pay!" and "Teach her a lesson!"

Birdie didn't waste a moment. She swept the witch's hat off the toe of her shoes and plunked it on top of her own head. With her new disguise, she scurried away as quickly as she dared. But she only made it a few strides when the arrival of a team of witches flying in a perfect V-shape formation caused everyone to stir.

Birdie looked up and gasped.

It was Ms. Crunch! And Ralph! And the rest of the awful gang of witches that had swarmed about Tragic Mountain earlier that very night. The witches around Birdie began to whoop and hoot and holler. They threw their hands into the air. They raked their nails through the night as if they could tear it to shreds. They jumped up and down with such vigor the tall grass beneath their witchy boots was mashed into a soggy pulp. High in the air, the witch with scraggly green hair and a horribly long tooth stood on her broomstick. The thick folds of her purple Council cloak swirled around her.

"SILENCE!" she bellowed.

But, of course, witches don't listen one bit. And these witches continued to chatter and snort, bumping elbows with one another and cackling up a storm.

The witch in the Council cloak, however, wouldn't have it. She jumped three times atop her broomstick, and every time her witchy boots came crashing down, a great thundering erupted from the sky—*BOOM!* A thundering so loud the ground trembled, and the orange candle flames in Castle Matilda's windows flickered violently.

The witches on the ground fell silent.

"Aha!" the witch in the Council cloak exclaimed triumphantly. "And now, wicked witches, I am tickled green to welcome you to this extraordinary event—THE ANNUAL WITCHES' BALL! You have gathered here tonight, from near and far, to let Wanderly know what it means to be *wicked*!" The witch paused to allow for another raucous wave of cackling. Birdie shivered, wondering if the other Tragicals could hear them all the way on top of Tragic Mountain. "Surely you are wondering why I have allowed a witch as inconsequential as this one"—the witch raised her hand and jabbed in the direction of Ms. Crunch—"to join me on an occasion as special as this."

As if on cue, the witches on the ground sent up a scurry of curses. Rotten banana peels, a few swarms of hornets, and a shower of smelly skunk spray pelted Ms. Crunch. Birdie could see Ralph had wisely curled up into a little ball with his hands thrown over his neck for protection, but not Ms. Crunch. Through it all, Ms. Crunch sat stoically. Her old, crooked shoulders were rigid. The only thing that moved even a smidge was her wild purple hair as the hornets buzzed by and made a mess of it. Ms. Crunch didn't even bother to wipe away the banana goo smeared across her cheek.

Birdie shifted uncomfortably. Witches, it seemed, weren't just generally awful; they were even awful to one another. Birdie thought back to all the times in her letters when she brought up friendship. No wonder Ms. Crunch didn't have any friends. No wonder she didn't want any friends. No wonder . . .

The witch with the long tooth snickered. "All right now, that's quite enough. I'm certain you shall find the answer to this little riddle quite ful*filling*. But until then, let us proceed. Let every citizen of Wanderly lock their doors tight and tremble beneath their sheets! For tonight the witches of Wanderly will be WITCHES!"

A deafening roar arose from the crowd. A shower of fireworks pop-boom-banged in the air, and with a brusque tap of her broomstick, the witch in the Council cloak—along with the others accompanying her—whipped through the air and soared through the open castle windows, leaving nothing behind but a cloud of smoke.

The witches on the ground stampeded for the door. They bumped and banged and bustled. They punched and pummeled and pounced. Witches were left flat on their backs, splayed on their faces, and some were even tossed up into the air and out of the way. It was utter madness! But the swiftly moving current of witches afforded Birdie a one-way ticket through the giant, creaking doors of Castle Matilda.

Once inside, Birdie tugged the edges of her witchy hat low against her ears and slipped off into the crowd. She hadn't a clue where to begin looking for Ralph, but she figured the best place to start was by finding Ms. Crunch and maybe that awful long-toothed witch. Birdie peeked toward a table where a trio of witches was hissing at one another over a game of Go Snitch.[52] Without spying a hint of purple or green hair, she shuffled toward the center of the room where a heap of witches was stomping their witchy boots on a rectangular wooden floor.

---

52. You are likely more familiar with this game than you realize. It is much the same as the ever-popular Go Fish, except the whole purpose is to catch your opponent in a lie. As you can imagine, given how adept witches are at lying, this game is almost as never-ending as that other popular and extraordinarily lengthy card game War.

Birdie nearly got caught up in the midst of a knuckle-cracking line dance, but she ducked out in the nick of time.

Birdie gulped. As far as she could tell, Ralph wasn't anywhere to be found in the main room, which meant she would have to go exploring. *Exploring in Castle Matilda.* Could she do it? Was it unthinkable for a Tragical to even attempt such a task? Of course none of those questions had anything to do with Ralph. . . . Ralph with his feet swinging against the night sky; Ralph being ripped away from her side; Ralph in the clutches of a witch who Birdie had trusted.

Birdie set her jaw. *I'm coming, Ralph,* she reaffirmed.

But she rounded the corner only to barrel nose-first into the paunchy stomach of another witch! A witch who smelled, curiously, of peppermint. And gumdrops. And . . . chocolate.

The witch grabbed hold of Birdie's wrist. "Off in such a hurry?" she cooed.

Birdie tried very hard not to wonder if standing before her was one of those witches who made gingerbread houses to try to trap children for funsies. Just in case, she kept her eyes low and hoped the brim of her witchy hat was enough to thwart her—gulp—delectable smell.

"Whatsa matter, dearie? Can't you talk? How you gonna cast hexes and curses if you don't got a tongue for talking?"

Birdie's heart pounded. If she turned and ran, surely the witch would get suspicious. If she said something, surely she'd say the wrong thing. If the witch happened to get a real good look at her, surely she'd know Birdie wasn't a witch at all, but merely a child. A Tragical child. A Tragical child about to meet her Tragic End.

Ding-dong, ding-dong, a bell chimed in the distance.

The witch in front of Birdie squealed. Her hands balled up into little fists at her sides, and her pointy-toed boots swept off the ground as she hopped to and fro.

"Oh my! It's nearly time!" the witch exclaimed. "By now you've must have heard what we're having for dinner? I almost punched through a wall when I heard it. Not that I was surprised the witchy community was coming around, but it hasn't ever really been a mainstream choice. And tonight . . ." The witch paused and clasped her hands against her chest. "Oh, tonight we eat child! I think I can already smell it now! Yes, that obnoxious 'ding-dong' means the child is about to be put into the pot. Soon, all of Castle Matilda will be filled with the scent of roasted arms and legs. Watch out, dearie! I'm gonna grab my seat."

The witch knocked Birdie out of the way and slunk out toward the main room. Birdie leaned hard against the wall and begged her heart to slow down.

Child.

They were going to eat *child.*

No doubt, the child they were going to eat was Ralph.

And soon. Very, very soon!

Birdie took off down the hallway. She streaked past several

groups of witches, but all of them had their noses tilted toward the main room and were pushing one another out of the way to get there. Birdie ran so fast the long flames of the candle sconces on the wall jumped out after her. She ran past open doors with rooms full of bubbling cauldrons brewing themselves, and dark and shadowy boxes with mysterious labels such as "Host of Eyes" and "Heap of Bones." She sailed past rooms full of cobwebs, broomsticks, and even a crystal ball with a ghostly head stuck inside. Birdie would have material for at least seventeen years of nightmares, but for the moment, all she needed to find was Ralph. And that meant she needed to find . . . the kitchen.

"Moooooooo!" a cow bellowed after her.

Birdie skidded to a halt.

She hadn't a clue what business a cow had at a frightening place like Castle Matilda..

Not a moment later, she heard the distinctive sound of a snake's rattle. But it was at least one hundred times louder than the awful knapsack Sir Ichabod shook at the Tragicals to wake them each morning. It was hard to imagine what sort of snake a rattle as loud as that could belong to.

The sounds all seemed to be coming from behind the door closest to Birdie. Beneath the lip of the door, shadows moved back and forth and a hefty spew of dust was sporadically expelled. Other than toting Sprinkles about and being terrified of Mistress Octavia's wolves, Birdie hadn't much experience with four-legged sorts. Things with teeth typically made her nervous.

Still, she had to have some sort of plan. She couldn't just stroll into a kitchen full of frenzied witches and demand that Ralph be removed from the chopping block.

Maybe the answer was behind that door.

Birdie took a deep breath. She put her hand on the doorknob and twisted it open.

Birdie gasped.

She found herself in a room so large it appeared to be *another* ballroom, though it certainly didn't smell like one. So overwhelming was the odor of hay and animal droppings, it was all Birdie could do not to pinch her nostrils shut. It could hardly be blamed on the animals themselves, however, for their quarters were less than ideal. Cage upon cage upon cage was stacked one on top of another and lined the room on both sides. The dimly lit candle propped up in the faraway window, coupled with the inconvenient haze of shedding fur and loose feathers, made it nearly impossible to see the animals in their shadowy abodes, but that was likely for the best. Indeed, just a few glimpses of several pairs of glowing eyes were enough to make Birdie's knees buckle.

Birdie swallowed back the lump in her throat and drew near to the cage closest to her. Unlike the other cages where animals were bumping and rustling up against the metal bars and making a fine sort of racket, the cage in front of her was very, very quiet.

Birdie peered into its dark, shadowy interior.

She tried to remember the way Cricket spoke to Sprinkles.

Cricket spoke gently and calmly; she sometimes even made kissing noises. Could such a thing work in the belly of a hopelessly wicked castle? Birdie figured it couldn't hurt. She pursed her lips and tentatively kissed the air once, twice—

A great ball of red fire exploded out of the dark and rammed itself against the bars of the cage. Birdie stumbled backward, tripping and teetering and crashing into the cage behind her, where a hairy moth the size of a fox blinked its bulging eyes at her and fanned out its wings. Birdie jumped forward and found herself face-to-face with the red fireball that, upon closer inspection, was not a fireball at all, but a parrot.

"You're disgusting! You're disgusting!" the parrot taunted in a singsongy voice.

"Hey, that's not a very nice thing for a parrot to say," Birdie said. And she began to scoot sideways. She eyed the door leading out to the hallway she had just come from. She was beginning to wonder if this was a good idea after all.

The bird, however, had fallen into another round of near hysterics. It catapulted from metal bar to metal bar and lost at least ten feathers in the process.

"Not a parrot! Not a parrot!" it shrieked.

"Oh, a-all right, then," Birdie said, though she tilted her head a bit to the side because the bird certainly looked like the sort she'd seen riding around the shoulders of scallywag pirates in storybooks. "But if you're not a parrot, what are you?"

The bird spread wide its wings and hovered in midair. It

turned its head this way and that, so Birdie could see every one of its brilliant colors. The bird was wondrous.

"Scarlet macaw! Scarlet macaw!" The bird let the message sink in a moment before whirling about and jabbing its wing in Birdie's direction. "Not a witch! Not a witch!"

Upon the scarlet macaw's proclamation, the whole ballroom full of animals began to twitter and stir. Deep groans and rustlings could be heard, and way down at the very wee end, Birdie was certain she saw a real lick of fire erupt from a baby dragon.

"SHHH!" Birdie begged. "I can explain, but first, you must tell me why you are all trapped here."

The scarlet macaw let out a haughty sniff. "Not trapped! Special prize! Special prize!"

Birdie frowned. "Is that what the witches told you?" The scarlet macaw's eyes gleamed, and Birdie continued, "And you think you would really like to go home with a witch and do her bidding forever? Because that's what will happen. You will belong to whomever wins you. I can't imagine most witches are very good caretakers. But if you want . . ." Birdie paused and licked her lips. Birdie couldn't believe what she was about to suggest, but it was perhaps something not even a ball full of wicked witches would expect. "If you prefer, maybe I can set you free. All of you."

The bird's eyes narrowed. "Stranger danger! Stranger danger!" it chanted.

"But I'm not a complete stranger. You said yourself I'm not a witch. Maybe that's reason enough to trust me. Do you want to be free or not?"

The bird held up its brilliant scarlet wings. It flicked the tips gently back and forth against the bars. It looked down at the little pile of feathers on the ground and then up toward the dimly lit candle in the window. Finally, it bobbed its head and sang gently, "Free."

Hearing that terrible *ding-dong* in the background, Birdie knew she didn't have a moment to spare. The sooner the animals were loosed upon Castle Matilda, the sooner she could make her way to the kitchen and whisk Ralph to safety. She lunged toward the scarlet macaw's cage and unlatched the door.

The scarlet macaw shot past her. It soared to the upper rafters of the ballroom and executed several brilliant and daring dives. Its feathers ruffled through the breeze and the animals remaining in their cages stomped, snorted, and whinnied with approval. Birdie's heart thumped. She never imagined she would find anything to be glad about in the depths of Castle Matilda, but she was glad about this.

"Come on, Scarlet!" Birdie shouted out. "Help me with the others!"

The scarlet macaw swept toward the cages on the upper levels. It used its beak to lift each latch and herded the freed animals toward the massive double doors at the other end of the ballroom. Birdie held her breath tight while setting loose such creatures as a midnight black tiger, a massive python, an oversize owl with its razor-sharp beak, and the fox-size moth she met when she first arrived. Creature after creature galloped, flew, slunk, or slithered past her and toward the scarlet macaw. The ground rumbled; the columns of Castle Matilda trembled and shook; the animals pressed hard against the double doors until they burst wide open. At least one hundred or more jubilantly free wild animals were ready to gallivant about Castle Matilda and astonish a crowd of unsuspecting witches.

Birdie couldn't imagine a more perfect distraction.

She waited one—two—three seconds, and when she heard a resounding peal of witchy screams, shrieks, and cackles erupt, she resumed her mad dash toward the kitchen.

On her way, Birdie leaped over a small mutiny of hissing cockroaches. She barreled around a corner and bounced off a witch performing a frantic two-step while a trio of baby dragons flambéed her heels. Birdie's heart soared. She had done it! Castle Matilda was in a complete state of chaos! Most important of all, no one was paying a lick of attention to how suspiciously unwitchy she appeared to be.

As Birdie pressed on down the hallway, the smell of burned rubber stopped her dead in her tracks. Now, both you and I would likely never think to follow the scent of burned rubber to a kitchen, and may have even turned back in the opposite direction, but Birdie was a very clever child. If Ralph was being boiled feetfirst (or rather *shoe*first), the smell of burned rubber made all the sense in the world.

Birdie burst through the kitchen door. A small cry escaped her lips.

She had found Ralph.

His head hung low against his chest. His eyes were shut, and a small dribble of drool rolled down his chin. He floated in midair above a cauldron with bubbles that snapped and popped like an anxious crocodile. Every so often, one fiery flame licked against his shoe and caused the black rubber to drip-drop into the pot.

Standing directly beside Ralph, with her crooked hands raised in the air, and her nose crinkled in fierce concentration, was none other than Agnes Prunella Crunch.

"Ms. Crunch?" Birdie choked out.

Ms. Crunch's eyes widened. Ms. Crunch shook her head in disbelief. "How did you— When did you— Why would you come *here*?" she hissed. And then, with her hands still carefully controlling Ralph's position above the cauldron, she jerked her head toward the right and said, "Quick! Scurry over there and hide under that table! Perhaps you can still be saved!"

Birdie glanced toward the little table covered in a dancing skeleton tablecloth. Its edges jitterbugged up, beckoning her to *Come, come and hide!* Ms. Crunch's mangy, one-eyed kitten peeked out at Birdie and meowed softly in agreement.

Birdie straightened up. "I'm not going anywhere without Ralph! That is so long as he isn't already . . ." Her voice trailed off as she eyed Ralph's terribly limp posture.

Ms. Crunch stomped her foot. "Of course he's not dead! Why else do you think my hair's lost its frizz? This night's been a disaster! Keeping this bugger alive has been the most exhausting thing I've ever done, and frankly, I don't know why he's worth the trouble—"

"Oh my warts! He's got me! He's got me! HE'S GOOOOOOTTTTT MMMMEEEE!" a raspy voice shrieked outside the kitchen door. Birdie and Ms. Crunch listened to the awful *thud-thud-clump* as a witch presumably went down. A moment later, a monkey's wild laughter erupted, and from the teeny-tiny window crowning the kitchen door, Birdie could see the silhouette of a monkey perched on a witch's head! The witch had been roped with a feathered boa and was being taken for a joyride that didn't look to end anytime soon.

Ms. Crunch shook the stunned look off her face. "That'll only keep 'em away for so long. Any minute now, Rudey-Poodey is going to be marching her black tooth back in here, and then our real trouble begins."

"It seemed like our real trouble began when you showed up with a whole gang of witches and kidnapped Ralph! Ms. Crunch, I trusted you." Birdie paused. She took a deep breath. She set free the words that had haunted her ever since she watched Ms. Crunch carry Ralph away. "I thought you were my . . . friend."

Ms. Crunch stared at Birdie. Even the warts at the end of her nose seemed to quiver. To Birdie's astonishment, Ms. Crunch nodded and croaked, "I am."

Birdie thrust her hand in Ralph's direction and cried, "Then why is *he* hanging over a cauldron?"

"Because I can't get him off it! Rudey's enchanted it so that only she can get him down. I snuck back in here to try to keep him out of the flames."

As if to prove her point, a long bead of perspiration rolled down Ms. Crunch's sooty cheek and splashed against the toe of her witchy boot. Could it be true? Despite how it looked—despite how everything looked—was Ms. Crunch actually trying to help Ralph?

Birdie shook her head. "Wait, this is all Rudey's fault? Is Rudey the green—"

"The green-haired gal with the nasty tooth? Yep, you guessed it, and she's a nightmare!"

"Oh," Birdie said. And her heart sank. She wrapped her arms around her stomach—which was busy executing somersaults, cartwheels, and even a backflip or two—because how was she supposed to save Ralph from a witch even Ms. Crunch found formidable?

That's when she saw it.

A little flash of purple.

Because Birdie was still wearing Mistress Octavia's Council cloak—the most powerful form of travel in all of Wanderly!

"Ms. Crunch!" Birdie cried. "Is Council magic more powerful than witch magic?"

Ms. Crunch scowled. "That's a question I don't like to think about."

"But is it? Please! I have to know!"

"Eh . . . maybe," Ms. Crunch said through the side of her teeth.

"Oh, Aaaaagnes!" a voice cried out.

Birdie and Ms. Crunch exchanged glances. The flames in the cauldron leaped with extra vigor. Pooky dove back under the skeleton tablecloth. "It's her!" Ms. Crunch hissed. "Rudey is coming!"

"Quick, put me over the fire, too!" Birdie cried.

Ms. Crunch's jaw dropped. Birdie could see every one of her crooked teeth. "WHAT?!" Ms. Crunch shrieked. "Have you gone bonkers? Is this a symptom of being a Tragical, or did you eat something off the hors d'oeuvres tray because, let me tell you, you should never EVER taste anything at a witch event."

"No! Please! Just listen, it's the only chance Ralph's got—"

"Yeah, well, this whole fiasco was about saving *your* life, and you're not gonna roast it on my watch!"

Birdie reached around her shoulders and flipped the Council cloak right side out. "But I've got this! And if Ralph can't get out of those flames, I have to go to him. But I need your help. I need you to—to put me in there and keep me out of the flames too."

Ms. Crunch licked her prune-y lips. "They'll think I'm doubly wicked. They'll think I've pulled you out of my sleeve for dessert."

Dessert. Birdie gulped. Why would Ms. Crunch even think such a thing? Had she really meant what she said earlier about being friends, or was Birdie walking into yet another trap? Another trap that could mean the end for both her and Ralph?

"Aaaaaggggnnneeesss!" Rudey shrieked again, and this time, much, much louder.

Ms. Crunch stomped her foot on the ground. "Gah! There's got to be another way!"

"There's not time! Put me up there! Do it!" Birdie begged.

Ms. Crunch leaned forward and pricked her finger against Birdie's cheek. "Only if you take me with you."

"What? Why?"

"Because we can still do Octavia in! We can still get to that blasted dragon."

"But wasn't all this wicked enough for you?"

"I told you already. None of this was *my* plan! Now promise me!" Ms. Crunch hissed.

Birdie glanced at Ralph. His black shoes had almost dripped entirely off his rosy-looking toes. His cheeks were flushed an awful shade of danger red, and his breath was coming in shallow bursts. "All right," Birdie said weakly.

And before she could close her eyes and gather in a deep (and possibly final) breath, the door to the kitchen burst open.

Rudey Longtooth skidded to a halt.

She looked from Ms. Crunch to Birdie and back to Ms. Crunch again.

Ms. Crunch quickly curled her fingers in the air and shot them straight at Birdie. "ALAKAZAM!" she shrieked.

A long, twisting snake of smoke shot out of the cauldron and wrapped clean around Birdie's ankles. It wrenched her to the side. She whirred upside down through the air at a dizzying speed. The air crackled and popped.

But she was with Ralph. She was right beside Ralph. In much

the same way he had been right beside her earlier that evening.

Birdie looked out past the shimmering wave of heat. Rudey slapped Ms. Crunch on the back in a gesture of hearty congratulations while Ms. Crunch subtly gestured for Birdie to wait for her.

But Birdie hadn't specifically uttered the words, "I promise."

And it wasn't just Birdie's life at stake.

She had trusted Ms. Crunch once, and whether it was Ms. Crunch's plan or not, Birdie had put Ralph's life in dangerous peril. She couldn't take that chance again, not when she'd worked so hard to rescue him.

Before Ms. Crunch could take a flying leap for the cauldron, Birdie held tight to one end of the Council cloak and flung the other corner around Ralph's shoulders. Birdie tried to ignore the panicked flicker in Ms. Crunch's eyes and the resounding ache in her own heart. Birdie whispered the words that would take her and Ralph far, far away from Castle Matilda and far, far away from Ms. Crunch.

"To the Deepest, Darkest Bog!"

The world around Birdie went black.

NINETEEN

DOWN IN THE BOG

irdie awoke in a pile of muck.

Gooey, sticky mud clung to her skin, her hair, and had even squished its way through the cracks in the soles of her shoes, making her toes feel slimy.

At first glance, the supposed home of the Blue Dragon hardly seemed a hospitable place, but it did offer one very important feature: Birdie couldn't see a hint of a pointy hat or a pair of witchy boots. The witches were all gone. And, most important of all, she and Ralph were alive.

Birdie looked over at Ralph lying in a mud puddle beside her. His face was streaked with grease and black soot. His eyelids fluttered every now and again, and he began to sputter and cough. Birdie could only imagine how many cooking fumes he'd inhaled and was worrying over how he was going to trek about the Deepest, Darkest Bog with his toes poking out from his half-melted shoes, when his eyes popped open.

"Oh no!" he cried out. "No, no, no!"

Birdie frowned. It was hardly the reaction she was expecting, but maybe Ralph wasn't fully awake yet. She placed her hand on his shoulder and shook him softly. "Ralph, it's just me. It's Birdie."

But Ralph merely rolled up into a little ball and groaned. "I didn't want it to be your Tragic End too! I really, really didn't."

"But that's just it, Ralph. It's not our Tragic Ends. We are . . . alive. Both of us!"

Ralph lifted up his head. "We're—we're not *dead*?"

"Not in the slightest!" Birdie said.

"But I was—the witch, she had me." Ralph paused and took a deep breath. "The very last thing I can remember is being held over a boiling cauldron that made my feet itch." Ralph glanced down at his feet and gasped aloud when he saw that a portion of his shoes had indeed vanished. He wriggled his soot-covered toes at Birdie. "See! Look! I'm not making it up! I bet I was already cooked to medium rare by the time I conked out."

"I know," Birdie said. "That's where I found you."

"Found me? But that's impossible. Your witch flew me all the way to Castle Matilda. *The* Castle Matilda. It was even worse than Mistress Octavia said. And there were witches everywhere—"

"Ralph," Birdie said gently. "I was there too."

Birdie reached down beneath her. She pulled the Council

cloak free. As she held it up, long sheets of mud rolled off, and the brilliant purple fabric gleamed. Ralph's jaw gaped open.

"How did you get *that*?" he asked.

"It was where Mistress Octavia always keeps it. In her Room of Sinister Plotting. I—I covered my arm in blueberry mush, got past the cobras, and found it inside her file cabinet. It isn't at all hard to work. You just slip it on, give it some directions, and well, *whoosh*!"

"Directions?" Ralph whispered.

"Well, not *directions* directions. I actually didn't even know I was headed to Castle Matilda. I just told it to go to the Annual Witches' Ball."

Ralph swallowed. Hard. He reached out for the cloak, and Birdie pushed it closer to him.

"Would you like to touch it? Despite the fact that it's had to drape across Mistress Octavia's shoulders, the fabric's actually really lovely."

Ralph touched the cloak ever so gently. When he spoke, his voice was thick. "With this, you could have gone anywhere in all of Wanderly—you could have escaped the Drowning Bucket—and you . . . and you asked the cloak to take you to a witches' ball? Why?"

"Because that's where you were. And it's the place where I would have been if you weren't out on the Plank with me. And . . . Oh, Ralph, I'm sorry. I'm so sorry that because of me you were kidnapped and nearly roasted!"

Birdie buried her head in her hands.

A few moments passed before Ralph said softly, "I don't think you were entirely wrong to trust her. Ms. Crunch is still a witch, of course—and she doesn't have any warm, fuzzy feelings for me, I'll tell you that—but I don't think she was lying about wanting to help you. I think those other witches set her up. And I think the only reason she kidnapped me was so she could save you. Where . . . where is your witch now?"

Birdie's voice was hollow and empty. "I left her. She wanted to come with us. It was because of her that I was able to get you off the cauldron. But I was . . . afraid. I couldn't put you in danger a second time."

Ralph met Birdie's gaze. "You rescued me," he said.

"We rescued each other."

"And now, after all these years, after so many close calls, it's really happened. Finally, we're free!"

As if on cue, an awful, melancholy moan ripped through the bog. "MWAAAAAAAAAAAAAAAAAAR!"[53]

Ralph's face fell. "Oh no," he said. And for the first time, he took a good, long look around. He looked up and down the trunks of the dense, swampy trees that called the Deepest,

---

53. If I am right in assuming there are no dragons where you live, it is a bit hard to put into words precisely how loud such a large creature can be. But perhaps it will help to imagine the sound of your mother vacuuming next to your head while you are trying to read a book. And then multiply that noise by 2,500. That ought to do just fine.

Darkest Bog home. He looked all around at the mysterious layer of smelly green fog winding about. "Was that sound what I think it was?"

Birdie smiled nervously. "Weren't you always kind of hoping to meet a dragon one day?"

"Possibly," Ralph said. "But definitely not on the first day I was freed from the manor after being trapped for four awful years."

"Oh," Birdie said. And then, seeing the hard look on Ralph's face, she settled back down into the mud. "Oh," she repeated.

"Don't look at me like that," Ralph said.

"I'm not looking at you like anything."

"Well, then stop *thinking* things."

"But it's good to think. Thinking is what led Francesca to—"

"Then think about it from my perspective, all right? I know what the sky looks like when the sun's setting. I know what it feels like to step into a stream and have the cold water rush across my toes. I've rolled down hills and ran through grass so tall it came up to my waist. Birdie, I don't want to go back there! I don't ever want to wind up at Foulweather's Home for the Tragical again!"

Birdie felt a pricking at the corners of her eyes. This wasn't what it was supposed to be like. All along she'd been worrying about whether she could possibly survive an attempted rescue of Ralph from among a gang of witches. What happened afterward was supposed to be the easy part. Because what else could they possibly do but try to find a way to rescue the others? How could they leave them all behind?

Birdie's voice was low. "I didn't rescue you by myself. If it weren't for the others—for Cricket, for Francesca of all people—I never would have gotten Mistress Octavia's cloak." Birdie paused. "Ralph, we know what it's like to be forgotten. How can we do the very same thing to them?"

"I don't know. But I also don't know how I can go back," Ralph said. "Birdie, you're asking too much! And if you're mad about that, I'm sorry. Maybe . . . maybe you saved the wrong person."

"What are you talking about?"

"Maybe you would have been better off saving your witch, so she could go with you to see that dragon. Birdie, out there on the Plank, everything happened so fast. I don't . . ." Ralph paused again and took a breath. "I don't really know if I meant to be some sort of hero. What if it was just a fluke?"

"But don't you see?" Birdie said. "You didn't have to be a hero. I didn't need a hero because I already had a friend. Only a friend would have been standing beside me. Only a friend would have put himself in that position. Ralph, you can make that choice again."

Ralph didn't say a word. Ralph stared hard at his bare toes, now caked in mud. And it gave Birdie a chance to notice the green fog ripple and twirl. Because the Winds of Wanderly were tumbling across it. The Winds of Wanderly were billowing about the horizon. And flapping vehemently toward Birdie was a bright orange bird with the pointiest beak Birdie had ever seen. The bird barreled toward Birdie at full speed before it exploded into a pile of tart orange zest, with a scent sour enough to make Birdie's lips pucker. Within seconds, the zest spun itself into a letter, and Birdie plucked it out of the air.

Ralph sucked up a little breath. "So that's what it looks like when the Winds of Wanderly delivers letters?"

Birdie shook her head. "Ms. Crunch's letters usually arrive like dark and spooky things. You know, bats, giant moths, and—oh, yes—the first one was a hairy hornet." Ralph's jaw gaped, but Birdie continued, "This letter is too bright and plucky. I think it must be from . . . someone else."

With shaking fingers, Birdie drew the letter near and read it aloud:

To Birdie:

 I never thought I'd write a letter to you. I never thought I'd need to write a letter to anyone. Even worse, I never imagined I'd have a thing to do with the Winds of Wanderly (which, if you ask me, seem very anti-Council), but that's how bad things have become around here.

 Mistress Octavia has gone berserk. After you made it out of the manor, she roused Sir Ichabod, marched into our dormitory, and did a head count.

After about ten tries, she finally realized not one but two Tragicals were missing, and she screamed loud enough I bet you could hear her at the Witches' Ball.

She couldn't figure out who the second missing Tragical was, so she's blaming you for everything. I guess she remembered that Cricket's your favorite, because she pulled Cricket up by the ear, and told her that unless you get back to the manor as soon as possible, Cricket will be the one to take your place in the Drowning Bucket.

Look, I don't know if you've found Ralph. I don't know if this letter arrived too late and you're busy boiling in a cauldron somewhere, but it just seemed like telling you was the right thing to do. It seems funny to wish a Tragical good luck, so I won't, but I guess I'm thinking it all the same.

Cordially,

Francesca Prickleboo

PS: Considering our ship's sinking fast, you may be wondering if I regret my decision to help. But I don't. Being a loser is not as hard as I thought it would be, and maybe some things aren't worth winning after all.

Birdie stared hard at the letter. But no matter how many times she blinked, no matter how many tears clouded her eyes, the words didn't change. They wouldn't change, until Birdie found her way back to the manor. Birdie tossed the letter into the mud and sprang to her feet.

She grabbed hold of the Council cloak. She shook out the wrinkles and prepared to toss it over her shoulders when Ralph cried, "Wait! Birdie, wait!"

"I know what you're going to say, Ralph. But if friends are friends because they show up, how can I do anything else?"

"But this isn't just about not needing to be a hero; this is about you walking into something that's guaranteed to be your Tragic End. And what about the Blue Dragon? We're so close! He's right here! We have to at least try!"

Birdie's head lifted up. "'We'? You mean, you do want to help?"

"Maybe," Ralph said.

"I knew it!" Birdie said, with her eyes shining. "I knew it."

"MWAAAAAAAAAAAAAAAAR!" the Blue Dragon roared from somewhere off in the Deepest, Darkest Bog.

"I'm going to act like that's his can't-wait-to-see-us sound, especially since Francesca's letter makes it pretty clear we've got to get a move on," Ralph said.

But Birdie shook her head. "I can't come with you, Ralph. If I arrive too late, nothing we do here will matter. I have to leave now. And that means you have to go see the Blue Dragon on your own."

"By myself? But I don't even know what I'm supposed to ask for. I thought the plan was for the Blue Dragon to make your witch good enough to brew a laughing potion. What's he supposed to do for me?"

Birdie tried to smile, but her expression was wan. "Turn you into a Triumphant, maybe?" Ralph lifted his eyebrow, and Birdie continued, "Honestly, I don't know. But I do know we're going to need *something*. Something probably only a Blue Dragon can do. And you grew up in a pet shop full of dark creatures. If anybody can convince the Blue Dragon to help us, it's you."

"I . . . well . . ." Ralph paused. He nodded. "Maybe you're right."

"You just have to promise that if it's looking bad, if the Blue Dragon's not willing to cooperate or if he's just plain nasty, you'll get out before you get hurt."

"That sounds like an awful lot of ifs," Ralph said.

"Yes, but did you ever imagine we'd be where we are right now? If we've made it this far, we have to find a way to believe we'll make it one step farther."

"I believe in you," Ralph said.

"Because that's what good friends do," Birdie said. "And that's who you are."

With that, Birdie swirled the purple Council cloak around her shoulders and shouted out, "Foulweather's Home for the Tragical!" while Ralph took off through the Deepest, Darkest Bog as fast as his feet could carry him.

Birdie should have, apparently, used a more specific term, such as "the children's dormitory in Foulweather's Home for the Tragical" or "Sir Ichabod's kitchen in Foulweather's Home for the Tragical," because the Council cloak sent her tumbling straight into the *dungeon* of Foulweather's Home for the Tragical. Birdie crashed against the brick wall of her familiar locked cell with an "oomph," "umph," and an "ugh!"

Birdie blinked her eyes. As murky as it was in the bog, it was infinitely darker in the dungeon. She rubbed her head where a red bump was busy swelling, and she stumbled to her feet. She shook out the long folds of the Council cloak, and she tried again.

She was careful to enunciate her words. "The children's *dormitory* in Foulweather's Home for the Tragical!"

There was no puff of purple smoke. There was no impressive *boom*. In fact, other than a meager bit of dust that rose into the air, not a single thing happened. Birdie hip-hopped a bit. She secured the Council cloak more tightly around her shoulders because what was wrong with it? Had she broken it? Was it angry at her for flipping it inside out at the Witches' Ball? Or was it much worse than that—had Mistress Octavia alerted the Council about Birdie, and had the Council somehow suspended the cloak's magic?

Birdie swallowed the knot in the back of her throat. She tried one final time. "The children's dormitory in Foulweather's Home for the Tragical, *please!*"

But the only answer she received was from the Drowning Bucket, groaning and jerking about on its metal chain outside the dungeon as if it were simply famished.

Birdie slid down to the floor. She had been in the dungeon enough times to know that no matter how loudly she screamed, whooped, or bellowed, no one would hear her. It could be days—maybe even a whole week—before Sir Ichabod happened to poke his head in and find her. By then it would be hopelessly too late.

Birdie laid her head in her hands.

She was tired.

And her heart was weary.

So weary that when the loose brick in the wall began to shift, she did not hear it. She did not hear it until it had wriggled free and fallen onto the floor of her cell with a dull thud.

Birdie didn't dare to breathe. Birdie didn't dare to hope. Birdie drew up against the hole in the wall and saw—

Not Cricket.

"Sir Ichabod?" Birdie said. "What are you doing in there? Has Mistress Octavia punished you again?"

But Sir Ichabod's eyes were wild. He waved his hands through the air. His medallion thumped heavily against his chest. "Go! Go, you must go!" he nearly shouted.

"I know," Birdie said, lifting up the folds of the Council cloak. "I never meant for it to take me into the dungeon, but every time I ask to go to the dormitory, it doesn't work."

"No, you must leave this place entirely! Leave it while you still can, before she finds you!"

Birdie frowned. "I'm afraid the Council cloak is broken. But even if I could, I wouldn't leave. I've come back for Cricket. To take my place in the Drowning Bucket so she won't have to be my substitute. Sir Ichabod, how is that you have ended up in the dungeon?"

"Isn't it obvious? Mistress Octavia found you in her Room of Sinister Plotting."

"But that doesn't have anything at all to do with you."

"Only two people are authorized to enter that room. She assumed it was I who let you in."

"But it wasn't you! It was me! I used blueberries to disguise myself as you, and the snakes simply chose to let me in!"

"Yes, but Mistress Octavia would never believe that. She has convinced herself you children are capable of nothing. And so . . ." Sir Ichabod paused. He lifted up his hand, and Birdie could see the ring of dungeon keys gleaming upon his wrist. "Here I am."

"Sir Ichabod!" Birdie exclaimed. "You have the keys! You have the keys right there! Oh, I nearly forgot that Mistress Octavia never locks us in herself. She loathes this place! She would never set foot in this place. Oh, this wonderful, wonderful dungeon!"

The dungeon walls, for once, straightened up a bit, for no one ever thinks to praise a dark and dreary sort of place.

"Now," Birdie said, jutting her hand through the hole in the wall and wriggling her fingers about, "please pass the keys so that I can unlock my cell and save Cricket."

Sir Ichabod sighed. He stuck his hands into his pockets. He lifted his chin the smallest bit, and with a great deal of effort, he whispered, "No."

Birdie's heart sank. "*No?* But, Sir Ichabod, why? You can help me. You can help Cricket. I won't ask you to do a single other thing, but please, please, just let me have the keys!"

"You said you have come to take Cricket's place, but that isn't what will happen. Mistress Octavia will not merely switch the two of you out like a Sunday hat. Don't you see? You won't be able to save Cricket. Instead, she will insist on drowning you *both*."

"But, Sir Ichabod, I have made it through a kidnapping, poisonous snakes, a castle full of witches, and a swampy bog! It cannot be that after all this, you would be the one to stop me. Please, Sir Ichabod, you must at least let me try."

"Tragicals don't try—Tragicals die."

"But remember, you yourself told me, I am more than just a Tragical. I'm a child—"

"I was wrong to plant such an idea in your head! Look what madness it's led to!"

Birdie's mind raced. She simply had to get to Cricket. Even if Sir Ichabod was right, even if Birdie couldn't save her, Cricket at least needed to know that Birdie came back. Because they were friends.

Friends.

Yes! If Sir Ichabod didn't understand, Birdie could show him. Out of all the nothingness in the dungeon, it did hold the one something that was perhaps the only thing any of them had ever needed: a book that was different.

Birdie jumped to her feet. She scurried over to the corner where she'd hidden her secret storybook. She flipped over the loose stone, pulled it free, and pressed the book tight against her chest. Since falling into Birdie's hands, the book had been through quite a transformation. Its spine was bent, and its binding sagged in remembrance of its missing pages, but inside, the words had never rung more true. Words that did not bear heavy on her, but laid themselves down before her—stepping-stones to a way out. She only hoped Sir Ichabod would see it, too.

"What are you doing?" Sir Ichabod asked from inside his cell. "What is that you've got there?"

Birdie took a deep breath and slid the book through the hole.

It fell into Sir Ichabod's open hands, and he began to shake all over.

"Sir Ichabod, it's not just you. You're not the only one who's told me I'm more than a Tragical. This book has changed everything. This book has changed *me*. Books, it turns out, are not all terrible."

"But how did you find this?" Sir Ichabod whispered.

Birdie gulped. "I found it in your kitchen. I—I know you don't read, so I—"

A sob escaped Sir Ichabod's throat. He pressed his knuckles

against his teeth. His eyes filled with tears. "You think I don't . . . read?"

"I—I've never seen you read, sir."

"That is because there is nothing *to* read!" he exclaimed.

Birdie gestured at the book. "You ought to give this one a try. It's like nothing I ever imagined."

Sir Ichabod lifted the front cover. His fingers hovered over the pages. He flipped through them and gasped. "What has happened to the ending?"

"It didn't have an ending," Birdie said.

"But it had pages. Where have the pages gone?" Sir Ichabod looked hard at Birdie. "Did you tear them out?"

"I—I had to."

"But I should have been the one to finish it! I wrote this book, and I should have finished it! This book cost me everything, and now I cannot finish it!"

"You wrote this book?" Birdie whispered. "But only scribes write books in Wanderly. And you are a . . . Tragical, aren't you?"

Sir Ichabod's whole body was trembling. "I didn't begin as a Tragical. I—I had promise. That's what the Council said, anyways. They poured through my collection of scrap paper; every sliver I could find, since the time I was a wee lad, filled end to end with fantastic snippets of *story*. Stories that lived and breathed inside of me. And so it came to be. At fifteen years old, I was promoted to the position of apprentice scribe."

"But, sir, I don't understand. You are here, at Foulweather's Home for the Tragical. How could you go from being as high up as an apprentice scribe to being doomed?"

"Simple: I didn't want to write their words. I wanted to write my own. I was a writer! And writers write. But it wasn't what they wanted, and what would I have without my words? If I gave my words away, what would be left? And so I refused, and after a lengthy Council detention, I was . . . sent here. They made an example out of me, and I'm quite certain no scribe has attempted such a thing since." Sir Ichabod lifted his head ever so slightly in Birdie's direction. His voice was thick. "Why did you have to go and tear *all* the pages out?"

"Because I thought the story wanted to come true. I . . . I wanted so desperately for the story to be true. True even for a Tragical. So I used the blank pages to write letters to a witch, and Cricket used them to draw pictures."[54]

Sir Ichabod leaned forward. His eyes glistened. His voice was stretched thin as if it were held together by a single, frayed string. "And what did the two of you find out? Did you find the story was, after all, true? True even for a Tragical?"

The dungeon groaned. It shifted and it settled, and its dust glittered in the air. Like magic. Long-legged spiders skittered

---

54. Regardless of our fancy covers or our elegant script, every book knows it is little more than a vessel. Our real value lies in the bits and pieces of truth buried within. Far less important than how that truth is displayed is that it is simply received (torn-out pages and all). Indeed, this is what it means to read a book.

forth from the shadows, and furry dog-size rats ambled away from the walls. Everything drawing near. Everything coming to light. Everything waiting and hoping and *wondering*.

"YES," Birdie breathed.

A small cry escaped Sir Ichabod's lips. And tears rolled down his dirt-stained cheeks.

"After all these years, I suppose it was never the ending that was missing. It turns out a story is not yet a story until it has found a reader. And you, Birdie, are a very, very good one."

"I only hope," Birdie said with a tremble in her voice, "that you won't change the story now."

"Change it? But how could I do that? You said yourself there are no more pages to write upon—"

"I'm talking about the story that's become a part of me. The one that says I am not just a Tragical, but a friend."

"And so it is. And so you've said. I'm afraid I don't understand what you are asking of me."

Birdie's voice was quiet. And clear. "I'm asking you to let me out of this dungeon cell. I am asking you to let me be the friend I know I've become. Please don't let me be just a Tragical anymore."

"But you're asking me to let you die!"

"Please, Sir Ichabod. I believed in your storybook. Now you must believe in what it has done for me. You couldn't have written those words if you didn't think they were true, could you?"

"Wanting something to be true and believing it is true are two very different things."

"Believe, Sir Ichabod. *Please*."

Sir Ichabod licked his lips. "You are far, far braver than I," he whispered.

"Bravery looks different on all of us," Birdie said. "And don't forget: Mistress Octavia may have ordered you to lock yourself in, but I bet she never said anything about how long you are required to stay."

Sir Ichabod nodded. He heaved a great and heavy sigh.

And then he slipped the keys through the hole in the wall and into Birdie's wide-open hand.

Free.

TWENTY

WHEN EVERYTHING FALLS APART AT THE BRISTLES

*A*gnes Prunella Crunch had crushed beetle wings in her hair. Her taffeta skirt had a big fat rip in it; she'd lost one of the hooks off her witchy boots, so the tongue of her shoe flopped about and made a slurping sound every time she stomped; three of her sharp, pointy nails were filed down to nubs (an injury incurred when they scraped against Rudey's gnarly tooth—bleh!); and her broomstick hadn't stopped trembling since she'd ditched Castle Matilda.

"Aiiiiiiiii!" Agnes screeched from atop her broomstick as the morning sun peeked over the horizon of Wanderly.

Pooky dove back beneath Agnes's pinafore, winding her way around Agnes's stomach so that Agnes looked to have some sort of monstrous growth or had eaten a meal inconveniently coming back to life.

"Oh, stop it," Agnes said. "I've been through enough trouble, and I don't need you adding to it. I'm a witch—a witch I tell you! I'm noisy and I'm stinky and I'm crude and I'm . . . evil through and through."

But Agnes drew up a bit slower on her broomstick. She looked over her shoulder, back in the direction of Castle Matilda.

Rudey Longtooth hadn't said any of those things.

Tabitha Toad, Peggy Goober, and Hildegarde Sniffer hadn't either.

When Birdie and Ralph disappeared, they told Agnes she was a dimwit. They said she was a joke. They said she was a miserable excuse for a witch.

And they were right about one thing.

Agnes *was* miserable.

She felt lower than the crumbs she loved to smash into the ground so the overeager squirrels crowding the Dead Tree Forest wouldn't get their hopes up.

But she wasn't miserable about ruining the Annual Witches' Ball. She wasn't miserable about being chased down the halls of Castle Matilda with a mob of angry, shrieking, and (worst of all) *starving* witches breathing down her neck so that she was forced to slink around in the rafters until she could locate her broomstick.

Agnes was miserable for a much, much more puzzling reason.

Agnes was miserable because Birdie left her behind.

She supposed she should have been glad about it all—glad

to be rid of messy things like children and do-gooding and friendship—but that didn't help the ache of her small, stony heart.

The Winds of Wanderly swept alongside Agnes on her broomstick. They dipped near and breathed softly into her ear.

Because I like you.

"Stop it!" Agnes said.

But the Winds of Wanderly weren't lying. Birdie had said it. Once upon a time.

Granted, since receiving that letter, Agnes had suggested a kidnapping, shown up with an entire gang of nasty witches, snatched Ralph instead, and held him suspended over a pot of boiling water as Castle Matilda's main course, but she had an explanation for all that! If Birdie would have given her even a few moments, she could have set the record straight.

And that was why, after making a break for it in the wee hours of the morning, Agnes had commanded her broomstick to head for the Deepest, Darkest Bog. She was going to spill every last detail of being hijacked by Rudey and her gang of nasty witches to the Bird-Girl, and if she still didn't want a thing to do with Agnes, fine. But at least Birdie would know the truth. And maybe then Agnes could get on with her life, and the Winds of Wanderly would stop stooping down to whisper bits of nonsense in her ear.

Agnes lowered her broomstick into the bog and sunk her witchy boots into the stinking heaps of mud. Pooky poked her head out from the cuff of Agnes's bell sleeve, and cast her one eyeball on Agnes.

"Mwargh," Pooky muttered.

"Yeah, yeah, I know. But what did you expect from a place called the Deepest, Darkest Bog?"

Slurp-slurp-slurp. Agnes lifted her boot with the flapping tongue up and out of the mud. She stooped down to grab a squishy handful in case Pooky got unruly and required a mud hat, but froze midway. From somewhere beyond the thick trunks of the mopey trees, a wave of green, smelly fog rolled near.

It caused Agnes's wart hairs to prickle.

Agnes's wart hairs *always* prickled when something was amiss. It was their best feature, really, and the only reason why she didn't pluck 'em out because, despite what you may think, even witches have a *few* aesthetic standards.

"I don't like this, Pooky," Agnes said, low. "I don't—"

"MWAAAAAAAAAGH!" The great, big, booming roar sent Pooky into near hysterics. She yowled; she howled; she clawed all the way up Agnes, exploded off the top of her purple frizzy hair and landed in the bough of a nearby tree.

Agnes stomped her foot on the ground. "Look at what you've done, you miserable kitten! Get down here! Get down here at once!"

Now, if Agnes would have adopted a slightly softer tone, and commented on how bad that monstrous creature was to make such a naughty sound, there was at least a 15 percent chance

Pooky would have (slowly) obliged and climbed down from her impossible position. Instead, crouched in the tree's leafy confines, Pooky simply gave Agnes an unblinking stare.

Agnes growled. She lifted her fingers to summon her broomstick, but stopped snapping when she spied it swaying lazily back and forth a short distance away, emitting a steady stream of snores.[55]

With no other choice, Agnes hiked up her muddy skirts, sloshed through the mud, and began shimmying up the tree trunk herself. Perhaps feeling a bit sorry for Agnes, Pooky slithered on her belly a wee bit closer, but when another even louder roar erupted, she froze. She bent low, as if about to spring up again!

"No!" Agnes said. "Don't do it! Don't even thinking of jumping onto some other tree. You get one save and one save—"

"Birdie? Birdie, is that you?" a voice called out.

Agnes clamped her lips shut. She and Pooky looked at each other and then looked down. Just a few trees away, wandering around in the mud and swatting at the green, smelly fog was

---

55. Though broomsticks tend to be an obedient and patient sort, they have one highly notable quirk: they are egregiously cranky if woken from a deep sleep. This is not the sort of cranky you may have experienced from your little brother when he tucks the blankets ever more tightly around himself, squishes the pillow over his head, and grumbles, "Go away." This is instead the sort of cranky that involves a wee bit of bristle thumping and possibly some potent magic gone awry. In short: it is never worth it to disturb a sleeping broomstick.

dinner—er, Ralph! Birdie's friend! But where was Birdie?

Agnes watched with disdain as Pooky's fur resumed its normal position, i.e. it was no longer standing on end. She even vibrated a bit and made googly eyes at the boy because that blasted little turncoat had nestled on his lap the *entire* miserable broom ride to Castle Matilda and looked pleased as pie at his return. Agnes wasn't. She wanted nothing to do with that rowdy kid. She plastered her finger against her lips and sent Pooky a dire, witchy warning. Until she could be certain Birdie was around, too, they would remain quietly planted in that tree for as long as it took, thank you very much.

Crack!

Creak!

Snap!

Or maybe not.

With everything that had gone wrong in the past twenty-four hours, Agnes didn't even try to avoid it. She didn't try to grapple her way back to the tree trunk. She didn't try to wriggle her fingers in time and dash off a half-baked spell. Nope, she just fell. Agnes, Pooky, and the branch broke clean away from that tree and crashed down with an enormous muddy splash a mere six inches or so from Ralph.

Ralph jumped at least two feet in the air. "Ah! It's you!" he exclaimed.

"Hmph, it's you," Agnes said, slowly ambling to her feet.

"What are you doing here? Are you trying to finish me off?"

Ralph darted backward as if trying to escape Agnes's wicked grasp.

But Agnes hadn't lifted more than an eyebrow in his direction. "Stop flitting around so. You're giving me a headache, and you're going to injure yourself. I also don't know how many times I need to say it, but in case fifty wasn't enough, I repeat: I never wanted to cook you or finish you off or anything else of the sort!" Agnes blew out a little puff of air. She straightened her collar. She tried to put on the closest expression to pleasant she could muster without throwing up. "Now, if you could just point me in the direction of Birdie, I'll let you get back to whatever it was you were doing."

But Ralph just stared at her.

Agnes cleared her throat. "Do you have a hearing problem?"

"No, I just, well—"

But Agnes didn't wait for Ralph to finish. She brushed past him. She looked around him, behind him, and even in the trees up above. Her shoulders hung slack when she finally turned to face him and asked, "Where is she?"

Ralph swallowed. "Birdie's gone. She went back to the manor."

"Back to the manor? As in back to Foulweather's Home for the Tragical? Where Octavia is? Why would she do such a thing?" Agnes lunged close and grabbed the front of Ralph's shirt. "Why would you let her do such a thing?"

"Because it was her choice. She wanted to go back. Mistress Octavia threatened to put Cricket in the Drowning Bucket, and

Birdie went back to save her."

Agnes threw her hands up into the air. "But how? How does Birdie think she's going to beat a Council member?"

Ralph's cheeks flushed a soft shade of pink. "Well, I suppose she was hoping I could help with that."

"By lollygagging around in the Deepest, Darkest Bog, miles away from the manor?"

"I'm not just lollygagging!" Ralph said. "I was on my way to see the Blue Dragon when you fell out of the sky."

Agnes's eyes lit up. Agnes licked her lips, and she took a few stalking footsteps in Ralph's direction. "Yesssss," she hissed while drumming her fingers together.

Ralph began to fidget. "You, uh, look pretty scary when you do that. Can you stop, please, because a moment ago our conversation seemed almost productive."

"Oh, it's productive, all right," Agnes said. "Because someone's got to help Birdie, and you're going to be my ticket to see the Blue Dragon."

"No, wait, I think you misunderstood. I didn't say *we're* going to see the Blue Dragon. I said *I'm* going to see the Blue Dragon."

"Yeah, and the Blue Dragon's not supposed to take kindly to solo visitors. He prefers the buddy system. That's you and me."

Ralph paused. He looked down at his bare feet. Finally, he said in a quiet voice, "No thanks."

"'No thanks'? Don't be a fool! I'm not asking you out to tea! From what I hear, that Blue Dragon will roast you before you even get close!"

"Well, um, funny you should bring up roasting since you very nearly roasted me a few hours ago!"

"Stop being such a baby and get over it!"

"Being cooked is hard to get over!" Ralph yelled.

"Well, fine, then—"

"MWAAAAAAAAAAAARGH!" the Blue Dragon roared.

The ground shook. The leaves on the trees trembled. And thick green fog wafted up to Agnes's knees.

Ralph's eyes widened. Both he and Agnes looked up toward the canopy of trees being tossed to and fro and shoved this way and that way as if something very *big* was approaching.

"MWAAAAAAAAAAAARGH!" the Blue Dragon bellowed again as yet another thick wave of smelly green fog tumbled near.

Agnes bent close to Ralph. "Look, kid, if either one of us is going to have any chance of helping Birdie, we have to work together."

Boom, boom, boom. The ground began to shake.

"What do you suggest we do?"

A shadow crossed over Agnes's face. "The same thing Birdie and I would have done if she was here with me. We have to act like we're BFFs."

"You and me?" Ralph exclaimed.

Agnes thrust her crooked hand in front of his face. "Hold my hand!"

Ralph's mouth gaped open. "But—but what if you try to nibble on my finger or something?"

"Don't be ridiculous! Just hold my hand. Do it! NOW!" Agnes roared.

"Oh, dear" came a voice from up above.

Agnes and Ralph froze. They looked up. They looked straight into the dangerously long snout of none other than the Blue Dragon. The Blue Dragon looked from Agnes to the boy. Two thin tendrils of green smoke—the same smelly green smoke blanketing the Deepest, Darkest Bog—snaked out of his nostrils. He tilted his magnificently long head. His electric blue scales gleamed. He thumped his endless tail along the ground, and great, knobby boulders rolled forth like pebbles. Agnes had dealt with her fair share of dragons before, but never one so extraordinarily large as the Blue Dragon.

Agnes gulped.

Ralph made a sound not unlike a whimper.

When the Blue Dragon bent his head near, Agnes and Ralph actually did grab ahold of each other's hands.

"So it is you," the Blue Dragon said. "I must admit, after twelve long years of dreaming of this moment, I never once imagined it would be anyone like, well, the two of you."

Agnes stiffened. She grappled for something, anything that would make sense. "'Twelve long years of dreaming'?

Dreaming of what? Of—of peanut butter?"

"Peanut butter?" Ralph exclaimed.

"Peanut butter?" the Blue Dragon said with a swoon. "Oh my, it's been simply ages since I've had peanut butter! But no, that's not at all what I've been waiting for." The Blue Dragon batted his long, fringed eyelashes. "Why, I've been waiting to be saved, of course!"

Ralph gasped. Agnes snarled. She dropped Ralph's clammy hand like a hot potato and crossed her arms against her chest. "But we're not here to save you! You're supposed to save *us*. Well, not us, really, but Birdie. You're supposed to save Birdie!" As Agnes raged, Pooky took the opportunity to poke her head out from Agnes's sleeve and give the dragon a once-over. Despite the Blue Dragon's astonishing size, she tried very hard not to look a bit impressed.

"Birdie?" the Blue Dragon repeated. "Who's Birdie? Is *he* Birdie?" he said, gesturing at Ralph.

"No, but I get mistaken for her more often than you'd think," Ralph said with a pointed look in Agnes's direction. "My name's Ralph."

"Oh, well, hello, Ralph." The Blue Dragon glanced at Pooky. "And who may I ask is that?"

Agnes crossed her arms against her chest. "That's Pooky."

The Blue Dragon tried to lower his voice to a whisper, but dragons don't whisper very well. "And have you considered that your Birdie may have wound up inside of Pooky's belly?"

Pooky rose up on all four legs with a nasty hiss. Agnes blew out an exasperated sigh. "Birdie is not an actual *bird*; she is a person. She is a little girl."

"Oh, I find children quite delightful!" the Blue Dragon exclaimed.

"Yeah, well, today she's going to die."

The Blue Dragon hiccupped. "That's awful! Just terrible!" A moment later, his eyes widened. "Oh my! And that is why you are here? You—you thought I would help save the life of your Birdie? How did you think I could possibly do such a thing?"

"I was told you had the power to change people." Agnes paused, and she lowered her voice. "I thought you might be able to change me."

"But aren't you, uh, well . . . I hope I'm not being impolite by saying so, but you look to be, uh, well, uh—"

"A wicked witch?" Ralph finished for him.

"Yes, that's right. What he said." The Blue Dragon cleared his throat. "Why would a witch want to change? No one in Wanderly *ever* changes except by Council decree."

Agnes fluffed out her skirts. "Look, if you can't give us the help we're looking for, there's no need to stick around this miserable, stinking place a second longer."

The Blue Dragon jerked upright. "You think it stinks?"

"Worse than the Dead Tree Forest," Agnes said with a sharp nod. "Worse than my socks after I've had a bout of toe fungus and haven't scrubbed 'em in the creek for a month. Worse—"

Ralph gave Agnes a swift poke in the ribs. "How 'bout you tone it down a bit, huh? Look at him!"

"Bah! Who cares about something like hurt feelings! That sorry sap of a dragon is a waste of our time, and time is the one thing Birdie doesn't have!" Agnes whirled around on her heel and snapped her fingers for her broomstick that had finally woken up and sailed faithfully toward her. But right before she could climb aboard, something fell atop her head.

Plip-plop!

Agnes looked up.

Plip-plop! A big, fat drop of green splashed into her eye.

Plip-plop! Plip-plop! Plip-plop!

"Oh, what a terrible, horrible, no good, very bad day!" the Blue Dragon wailed. "Your Birdie is going to die; no one has come to save me; and I shall always stink!"

Beside Agnes, Ralph lifted his black gown up and over his knees. The swamp mud mixed with the dragon's tears was becoming awfully soupy. And it was rising fast. Pooky floated by on a hollowed-out tree log, and Agnes snatched her up in the nick of time.

"Do you have any idea what it is like to be full of smelly green gas? No dragon wanted a thing to do with me on Snaggletooth Isles, and when the gang of magicians came for me, even my own colony threw a never-ever-come-back party! The magicians trapped me here, but I think even they've grown tired of my smell because I haven't seen a single one in ages!"

"But how is it possible to trap a dragon?" Ralph asked.

"Just look," the Blue Dragon said with a miserable sniff. He lifted high the arch of his massive wings. But when he strained and flexed, nothing happened. His wings couldn't unfold. They had been bound together with invisible and unbreakable thread so that he couldn't do what dragons did best.[56] The Blue Dragon couldn't fly.

"If you can imagine, it gets even worse," the Blue Dragon continued. "The lonelier I get, the more smelly gas I seem to produce. Add to that the ridiculous rumors you mentioned, that somehow I have the power to change people when—ha!—I can't even make my stink go away! Oh, it's no wonder no one but the two of you has ever bothered to come looking for me. And now I shall have no hope left. Now I ought to just curl up in a little ball so the smell can finally do me in."

"Just a thought," Agnes said, "but if you were really looking for someone to come and save you, why not tone down the scary noises?"

"You mean, my super-specific-exhaustively-practiced roar? But I thought . . . The magicians told me that . . ." The Blue Dragon paused. "I suppose it's not Wander-speak for 'help,' is it?" Upon seeing Agnes's expression, the Blue Dragon burst into

---

56. Since we have discovered together the great value of true things, it seems only fair to mention that this fact is *likely* true. As was mentioned before, dragons go to great lengths to avoid the citizens of Wanderly. It's possible their best attribute is something as nuanced as tap-dancing or archery, and we just don't know it yet. But certainly all can agree that to achieve such significant aerial heights while boasting of an enormous size is no small thing.

another loud, sobbing round of tears.

"Are you happy?" Ralph said, glaring at Agnes. "Why don't you insult him again and see if we can get the whole bog to flood!"

"We were tricked!" Agnes exclaimed.

"But it's not his fault. He didn't advertise the whole change thing." Ralph paused. His face fell. "All he's ever wanted to be is . . . free."

Agnes rolled her eyes. "So what?"

"I think we have to help him."

"No, we have to help Birdie. Birdie's my BFF, not that big lug!"

"But Birdie would want us to help him."

"Then why don't you stay and help him?"

"Because you're the witch. You're the one with magic."

"Gah! Will none of you ever understand that dark magic is not the helping sort of magic?"

The Blue Dragon's big snout dipped in between Ralph and Agnes. "Pardon me, but did I eavesdrop correctly? Are you, a *wicked* witch, really thinking of saving me? How is that possible? How does such a thing—" The Blue Dragon's eyes lit up, and he surged closer to Agnes. "Hey! Maybe you don't need to be changed after all. Maybe you were never really wicked to begin with! Did you ever think of that?"

Before Agnes could squash flat his theory by ticking off all the very many egregiously wicked things she'd done through the years, the Blue Dragon's snout twitched. His tail began to thump, and his whole body trembled so violently the trunks of the trees knocked about and the leaves clattered like tin cans.

"Oh—oh—oh no!" the Blue Dragon yelped.

Agnes reached back and yanked Ralph toward her through the sloshy swamp soup. "What is it?" Agnes said. "What's happening?"

But the Blue Dragon's snout wrinkled up. His oversize teeth gleamed! He sucked up a huge, gulping gasp of air.

"WA-WA-WA-WA-WACCCCCHHHHHHHH-HOOOOOOOOOOO!"

The Blue Dragon sneezed a sneeze unlike any other sneeze.

And out tumbled a flickering, raging ball of smelly green flames. The flames licked up the trunks of the trees and toasted the leaves. They dove down to the floating logs and scared them as if they were filets mignon. Without a single shout of warning, Agnes sucked up a breath and dunked her, Ralph, and an irate Pooky beneath the swamp slush.

By the time they surfaced, with green mud dripping off their noses and dribbling down their chins, the fireball was gone. But so was something else. The one thing Agnes had been unable to grasp for.

The Blue Dragon bent near. In the palm of his giant hand, nestled among his shiny blue scales and razor-sharp claws, was a small heap of ash. "I-I'm so sorry," he whispered. "I have terrible allergies. It happens without warning. I hardly meant to. I—"

"AIIIIIIIIIIIIIIIII!" cried Agnes as she surveyed what was left of her broomstick. Agnes raced along the Blue Dragon's snout and butted her big, witchy nose against his gawking eyeball.

"You singed my ride!" she said. "I've had that broomstick since I was thirteen—*thirteen*! It did everything I wanted it to! It knew when to hush up; it knew when to be delightfully disobedient; it knew when I needed a little pick-me-up; and it knew how fast to fly to keep my hair properly frizzed. But worst of all, that was how I was going to get back to Birdie! And now it's gone! You ruined it! You ruined *everything*!"

Agnes's feet slid out from underneath her. The brim of her hat slid down to her nose. Pooky crawled out from her bell sleeve, and with a very pointed swish of her tail and backside, began using the dragon's snout as a scratching post.

"I—I suppose this means you aren't much interested in rescuing me anymore, doesn't it?" the Blue Dragon asked softly.

Agnes huffed and Agnes puffed. A few hissing and spitting noises slipped off her razor-sharp tongue, but before she could properly berate the Blue Dragon, Ralph spoke instead.

"Actually, it means that is exactly what she's going to do."

Agnes ripped her hat off and tossed it into the air. "No! No! I'm DONE! I never wanted to help him in the first place. He's nothing more than a crybaby who deserves to sit here in his stink!"

"Maybe," Ralph said. "But Birdie deserves to live. And that's why you're going to free him and"—Ralph took a deep breath—"that's why he's going to fly us back to Foulweather's Home for the Tragical. He'll get us there as fast as your broomstick would have. You still can't brew that laughing potion you were after, but, well, he's a dragon! A *huge* dragon! That ought to count for something."

The Blue Dragon couldn't shake his head fast enough.

"Ack! I mean, eek! I mean, no way!" The Blue Dragon took a breath. He slid Agnes down the tip of his snout and gently pushed her in Ralph's direction while depositing the remnants of her broomstick into a little vial Agnes capped with a snarl. "In other words, thank you very much for the offer, but I've heard quite enough about this Birdie of yours and her impending death. I don't like the sound of that Tragical place, and I'm not a fan of any sort of foul weather. Indeed, this whole episode has proven to be terribly anxiety inducing, and perhaps I'm more accustomed to a life of complete and total isolation than I thought. So, good luck to you, and ta-ta!"

Agnes plunked the vial beneath her pinafore and placed her hands on her hips. "Sorry, Blue. The kid's right. You owe me big-time. And anyways, you said yourself you've been dreaming of this day for twelve long years. If I can figure out a way to free you, then the least you can do is figure out how to scare Octavia Foulweather silly."

The Blue Dragon gulped. "But I'm not scary. I'm gassy."

"You're still a dragon!" Agnes said.

"Real dragons aren't gassy."

"Well, you're certainly not a *fake* dragon."

"How can you be so certain? The Chancellor says—"

Agnes stomped her foot on the ground. Her cheeks caught fire. Her hands tingled, and she shrieked at the top of her lungs, "If one more person tells me one more time that the Chancellor says this or the Chancellor says that, I'm going to SCREAM!"

Ralph cleared his throat. "You are screaming. Already. Just saying."

Agnes hissed in Ralph's direction before turning back to the Blue Dragon. "Be a gassy dragon!"

The Blue Dragon met Agnes's gaze. "Be a good witch," he said.

Agnes's eyes widened. How maddening! What an impossibility! There was nothing good about a witch. Didn't the Blue Dragon know anything?

But her small stony heart beat faster.

Her small stony heart beat out words.

Words Agnes had been collecting. Words that made Agnes wonder. Words that were good . . . weren't they?

I like you. Trust. Friend.

Agnes was sure she never used to have anything good inside of her. But that was before she met Birdie. That was before she became a friend. And now that good had become a part of her. Oh, it was a meager offering to be sure, and nothing compared to the decades of dark deeds that trickled through her veins, but maybe a wee bit of light would be enough; maybe a wee bit of goodness could find a way to shine even in someone like Agnes.

Agnes felt the familiar crackle and pop of magic. It raced up her bones and warmed itself in her fingertips. A shiver rippled down her spine, and she wet her lips in anticipation. She thought of the best thing she knew. She thought of friendship. And she loosed her magic on the Blue Dragon with a great and mighty whoosh!

The impact knocked Agnes to her knees. She hovered low with her face inches from the mud.

And the Blue Dragon rose up. The Blue Dragon flapped his wings.

The Blue Dragon was free. . . .

Agnes was too.

The Blue Dragon flapped his wings over Agnes. The leaves of the trees rippled back and forth in celebration, and Agnes's purple hair whipped about. Still on the ground, she turned her face up.

The witch marveled.

"Look at me!" the Blue Dragon exclaimed. "Look at *me*!"

Ralph laughed out loud. He revved up his hands and feet as if fully prepared to take a flying leap onto the back of the Blue Dragon, but he paused. He looked over his shoulder and held out his hand to Agnes.

"Come on," he said. "We better hurry up before he takes off without us."

Agnes nodded, but then, at the very last moment, yanked Ralph hard enough that he plopped down in the mud beside her.

"Sucker!" she said with a gleeful snort. She pressed her hand on his head for leverage and launched herself into the driver's seat atop Blue. Once Ralph lifted his scowling self out of the swamp sludge, and Pooky nestled into Agnes's lap for a long overdue snooze, Agnes dug her heels into the Blue Dragon's scaly sides.

"Yee-haw! Spread your wings, Blue. It's time to go save Birdie!" she bellowed.

And so they went. Despite the unlikeliest of circumstances, and the strangest of companions, for the first time in over a decade, the Blue Dragon soared with the Winds of Wanderly whistling beneath his wings.

An Extraordinary Explosion of Glitter

irdie knelt beneath the glow of a candlelit sconce.

It glowed brighter, stronger than normal. As if the manor were preparing for battle.

Birdie knew she had precious little time before Cricket's life would be dangling from the Drowning Bucket. But there was one last thing she had to do. And quickly!

Birdie pulled her nubby pencil free from her pocket and flattened out the final sheet of paper tucked within her gown.

Dear Ms. Crunch,

I can't believe we finally got to meet. You're a lot like what I pictured. But possibly even more impressive-looking. I'm not trying to butter you up. Because, honestly, I can't imagine there's any amount of buttering in the whole world that will make up for what I've put you through.

Ms. Crunch, I didn't want to leave you behind at Castle Matilda.

I really, really didn't.

But I was so confused. And Ralph was so . . . nearly cooked. I came all that way to save him, and it just wouldn't have made sense to put his life in danger a second time. Ralph doesn't remember a whole lot of what happened, except he did say he thought you never meant to hurt anyone. Especially not me. Considering Ralph's not a big fan of witches, this is especially meaningful.

Anyways, I'm back at the manor, right where I started. I'm about to take Cricket's place in the Drowning Bucket, because it was always supposed to be me in there. It's funny how all this time I've been fearing my Tragic End, but now that it's here, it's not nearly so scary as I imagined it would be.

I owe a lot of that to you. For a long time I thought it was your magic making things different, but now I realize it wasn't just about storm clouds and spiders, but about friendship. Friendship changes things just like magic does, and maybe even more. Your friendship changed me.

And that's my main reason for writing. Because even if things look the same on the outside, everything is different on the inside. And it turns out that's what matters most of all. I hope it's the same for you, Ms. Crunch. I hope now you know you're more than just a witch. I hope you never ever forget it. I know I'll never ever forget you.

Your BFF (I hope it's okay to call myself that),
Birdie

PS: If you think of it, maybe you can check in on the other Tragicals from time to time? That's probably asking a lot, but if Mistress Octavia gets nastier after I'm gone, they're really gonna need somebody.

Birdie swiped at her eyes and tried not to think about the look on Ms. Crunch's face when Birdie left her behind at Castle Matilda. She folded the letter for safekeeping, tucked it into her black gown, and slipped down the hallway in the direction of the dormitory. Birdie intended to move quietly, but the manor wouldn't have it. The manor celebrated Birdie's return as if she were the star of a parade. The candles flickered, the curtains wriggled, and the echo of Birdie's footsteps was magnified like a round of thunderous applause. If Birdie hadn't been trying to steer clear of Mistress Octavia, it would have been terribly flattering, but all she could think to do was move *faster*.

And so she picked up her feet. The manor spurred her along. Before Birdie knew it, she was skipping. She skipped right through the Dark Hallway and past the row of Council portraits knocked so far askew they could barely see straight. She skipped right past the library with the boarded-up window, where a little wisp of the Winds of Wanderly swept alongside her. She skipped right up to the dormitory with the dim light Sir Ichabod always kept burning and pushed against the door Mistress Octavia never bothered to lock. By the time Birdie burst into the room, her chest was heaving, her cheeks were glowing, and not one thing about her looked the slightest bit Tragical.

The other children were gathered in the center of the room, piled on two separate beds, holding tight to one another. Cricket was at the center of it all, and when she saw Birdie, a cry escaped her lips.

She rolled off the bed. She held a hand out in Birdie's direction.

"Birdie," Cricket asked. "I-is it *you*?"

Birdie rushed toward Cricket and threw her arms around her. "Yes, and it turned out just as we hoped!" Birdie paused and looked at the other Tragicals. "Because of each of you, I found my way to the Annual Witches' Ball. And Ralph is safe now."

Cricket looked around Birdie's shoulder. "Safe?" she echoed. "But where is he, then?"

"He—he's bringing help. He should be back here any minute, I'm sure."

"You didn't stay with him?" Cricket asked, wide-eyed. "Did Mistress Octavia send someone after you? Did the witches drop you off? Did—"

Birdie placed her hand on Cricket's arm. "Cricket, it was me. The Council cloak took me here because I asked it to."

"But why?"

Birdie cast an appreciative glance in Francesca's direction and said to Cricket, "Because friends are meant to be together."

"No," Cricket cried, shaking her head to and fro. "Mistress Octavia—the Drowning Bucket! You were supposed to be safe. All of this was going to be okay because you were supposed to be free!"

"What makes you think that's not still true?"

Cricket looked up at Birdie with tears in her eyes. "Because you're *here*."

"Being free isn't just about where you are; it's about what you believe. Mistress Octavia can do all sorts of things to us, but she can't change what we know is true. And no matter what she says, no matter what she does, *we're not nobodies*. We're children. We're friends. And I don't think Wanderly ever meant to write us out of the story."

The door to the dormitory crashed against the wall.

The lantern fell clean off its hook, and a puddle of wax spilled onto the floor. Miraculously, the flame did not go out. If Mistress Octavia had eyes to see, she would have gladly snuffed it with her boot, but she did not. Instead, she stormed right past the lantern with her nostrils flared. Birdie placed herself in front of Cricket and scooted them both backward.

Mistress Octavia pricked her finger hard into Birdie's chest.

"You noisy little thief!" she hissed. "What an audacious return you've made. Now give me back my cloak!"

Birdie swallowed. She reached beneath the collar of her gown. The brilliant purple fabric spilled out of her hands, and Mistress Octavia snatched it away. "I-I'm sorry. I think it might be a bit broken," Birdie said.

Nevertheless, Mistress Octavia slipped it across her shoulders, and her eyes narrowed. "Did you bring that ridiculous witch with you? Is she here somewhere?"

"It's only me, ma'am. And I was hoping you might change your mind about my punishment."

Mistress Octavia sucked up a sharp breath. "Change my mind? Oh, but I already have. And it's all so utterly tragical! With your return, not one but two will meet their dooms. Today, you *and* Cricket will go down in the Drowning Bucket! Today will be a Tragic End for you both!"

The Tragicals gasped.

A wave of cold washed over Birdie. It was what Sir Ichabod had predicted; it was the precise tragedy he was trying to save her from. But the reality of it made her knees buckle.

"Please," Birdie whispered. "Please. Cricket didn't do anything wrong. It was me. I was the one who did everything. You don't have to punish her when I'm standing right here! Let it be me. Just me."

Mistress Octavia smiled her awful smile. "This *is* just about you, Birdie. All because of you. No one cares for Tragicals. No one. And because you so obviously care for Cricket, she has to die too. If you bothered to take the rules seriously, none of this would have to happen. Now, come along, children, it would be rude to leave our guests waiting."

Francesca's head snapped up at the unfamiliar word. "Guests?" she said. "But we never have gu—"

"Shut your mouth, you little traitor!" Mistress Octavia hissed. "And line up! All of you! Slouch your shoulders and trudge!"

The children filed into line and trudged down the hallway as they had so many times before. At the helm, Mistress Octavia kept her eyes fixed forward, but she lashed out at the walls with her broken broomstick every now and again as if she sensed the manor's disloyalty. With each mighty whack, the children flinched.

Except for Birdie.

All Birdie could think about was who the guests might be. Had Mistress Octavia finally convinced the Chancellor to come and visit the manor? Or would it be a reporter from the *Wanderly Whistle* eager to see a Tragical meet their doom? Whoever it would be, Birdie was trying to stay focused. She was trying to plan. She was trying not to despair because until she and Cricket were scuttling toward the Black Sea inside of the Drowning Bucket, she had learned the value of time.

The children climbed up the ladder leading toward the trapdoor.

Mistress Octavia used her broken broomstick to push the door open, and the raucous sound of hissing and spitting tumbled near. As the children climbed up the ladder and onto the Plank, Birdie could see the guests weren't Council members or reporters, but a nasty handful of witches from Castle Matilda.

A shrill, wild cackle erupted behind Birdie, and she wondered if Ms. Crunch had come back too. If in the hour Birdie needed her most, Ms. Crunch would come through for them all! But when Birdie whirled around, she didn't catch a single glimpse of Ms. Crunch's unruly purple hair, jaunty hat, or exceptionally large and warty nose.

Mistress Octavia called over her shoulder, "See any one you know, Birdie? I daresay you have done me a service by so foolishly returning. It would have been heartbreaking to send these unusually patient witches home without a full meal. They're starving, you know. My only condition was I drown you first before they dig in!"

Several of the younger children began to cry. Great, big, sniffling tears rolled down their sunken cheeks. The witches surrounding the Plank squealed in delight, clicking their heels beneath their broomsticks and pumping their wicked fists in anticipation. The older children, with trembling chins, stretched their hands out to the younger ones. Soon, all the Tragicals were linked like a tightly wound chain. At last, they had learned what to do. They had learned how to comfort one another. They had learned they were stronger together.

And just like that, Birdie remembered the letter in her

pocket. The last letter she would ever send to Ms. Crunch. However unremarkable a single letter seemed, Birdie knew better than to underestimate anything surrendered to the Winds of Wanderly. Birdie reached her hand toward her gown, but Mistress Octavia ripped Birdie and Cricket away from the line of Tragicals and shoved them in the direction of the Drowning Bucket.

At the end of the Plank, the Drowning Bucket lunged against its metal chain. It clashed and clanged three hundred jaw-dropping feet above the swirling Black Sea. Cricket buried her damp cheeks against Birdie's gown.

"I'm so scared, Birdie! I'm so scared!" Cricket whispered over and over.

"Faster! Walk faster!" Mistress Octavia screeched.

"Faster! Faster!" the witches hissed in unison, all of them floating with narrowed eyes gleaming eerily.[57]

"Birdie, what are we gonna do? There must be something we can do!" Cricket said.

Birdie bit her lip. Mistress Octavia leaped onto a small platform near the Plank that held the Drowning Bucket's pulley

---

57. Though these famished witches still appeared properly terrifying, it shouldn't go unnoticed their eyes were a bit bloodshot, their clothes a bit rumpled and stained, and several of their long witchy bootlaces were sloppily untied and even half chewed because—in light of Birdie's marvelous plan at Castle Matilda—they had endured a nearly endless (and wholly unsuccessful) night of animal wrangling. So much so that they unanimously agreed there would be no more "live" prizes at the next Annual Witches' Ball (or ever).

system. Mistress Octavia placed her hands upon the wheel and barked, "Get in! Get in, *now!*"

Cricket shook her head vehemently back and forth, and Birdie placed her hands on Cricket's shoulders. "Remember, fear isn't what's most important. Friendship—friendship is bigger. We have each other. We're together. And I promise I won't let go of you."

"Wait!" a hoarse voice cried out.

Birdie and Cricket turned toward the trapdoor. Sir Ichabod's large nose poked free, and he swung himself onto the Plank. His medallion thumped heavy against his chest as he scrambled down the Plank in their direction. None other than Sprinkles, who had also been hiding in the dungeon since the spinning wheel incident, was positioned proudly on Sir Ichabod's shoulder.

"Go back to your hiding spot, Tragical!" Mistress Octavia hissed at him.

All around, the witches jeered in agreement.

Sir Ichabod tucked his long, scraggly hair behind his ears. Though he trembled, he met Mistress Octavia's gaze. "No," he said.

"No? No? But you can't tell me no!" Mistress Octavia shrieked.

"I am not just a Tragical," Sir Ichabod said. "I never was. I am a grown-up, and I won't let you hurt these children. Not anymore."

And, as if it were the simplest thing in the world, the medallion slipped free from Sir Ichabod's neck.

Sir Ichabod's face was alight! But before he had even a moment to celebrate, the green-haired witch with the awful tooth swooped near and shrieked, "Actually, you look a whole lot more like a billy goat than a grown-up to me!" With a lazy twirl of her crooked finger, she transformed Sir Ichabod into exactly that.

"No!" Birdie cried out. "Sir Ichabod! Sir Ichabod, is it still you? Can you still hear me?"

The billy goat swimming in Sir Ichabod's tattered gray garments turned its head miserably in Birdie's direction. "Baaaaa," it bleated pitifully, while a wide-eyed Sprinkles bounded down the Plank, scrambled bravely over Mistress Octavia's boot, and soared through the air where he landed in Cricket's waiting hands.

Looking terribly pleased with herself, Rudey Longtooth let out a hideous cackle. "Don't feel too badly for him, dearie! Better to be a goat than to be dead like the two of you scrumptious little morsels!" And she punctuated her words with a mighty whack from her broomstick against Birdie's and Cricket's backsides. A whack that sent Birdie, Cricket, and Sprinkles flying helplessly through the air and tumbling smack-dab into the center of the Drowning Bucket. Beneath their weight, the Drowning Bucket squealed in delight.

"Take it home, Council sister!" Rudey screeched.

Mistress Octavia didn't waste a moment. She bent down deep and cranked the Drowning Bucket's pulley with all her might. With nothing but her Tragic End ahead, Birdie scrambled for her letter. It was her last chance to tell Ms. Crunch that together they had discovered a new kind of magic. That, in all of Wanderly, it was *friendship* that had the power to change a Tragical and a witch. And all that time, it was waiting in something as ordinary as the tip of a nubby charcoal pencil and a blood-red quill pen.

Birdie wrenched the letter free from her gown. She opened up her palms and released it to the Winds of Wanderly.

"Wh-what are you doing?" Cricket whimpered.

"Being a friend," Birdie said.

And with that, the Winds of Wanderly swept onto the scene. They seized upon Birdie's letter. With one heavy gust, the letter soared straight into the thick gray clouds that never lifted off Tragic Mountain. And suddenly, as if an entire bottle of ink was spilled from the heavens, the clouds were doused an ominous shade of *black*.

Cricket gripped Birdie's hand tighter. "Birdie, do the Winds always do this sort of thing to your letters?"

Birdie's mouth hung open. Mistress Octavia cranked harder and got to kicking her pointy boot at the Drowning Bucket's pulley because it still hadn't budged an inch. The witches twittered atop their broomsticks. And all around, the Winds began to race.

Harder. Faster. LOUDER.

Birdie turned up her chin and stared as the black clouds began to toil and churn. They puckered and shuddered, and with one great and mighty rumble, they burst open and rained down buckets full of—

"ARGH! I got me a paper cut!" an orange-haired witch howled. "Even worse than that, this paper's got *words* written on it!"

"Whatcha talkin' about, Frances? We don't even know how to read!" the witch hovering beside the orange-haired Frances shrieked.

"Well, I recognize my *A*, *B*, *G*s—especially when they're bent on slicing me up like a fruit platter! Maybe this plan is as doomed as the Tragicals! Maybe we ought to get outta here!"

As the witches began to race about, the words from the sky continued to fall. Shreds of paper blanketing the gray and dreary exterior of Foulweather's Home for the Tragical in white. Making it look shining and new like the start of a brand-new story.

Along the Plank, the other Tragicals bent down in wonder. They scooped their hands through the paper. They filled their hands up to overflowing with words. Words they began to shout out.

"Your friend!" Mildred said.

"I like you!" a boy called.

"Thank you!" Benjamin shouted.

"Hello!" a girl exclaimed.

Cricket tugged on Birdie's hand. Her eyes shone bright. "Birdie, it's you! The things you have written! And it's just like that picture I drew— Oh, Birdie, the sky's raining words! It's magic!"

But the shreds of paper drew to a sudden halt. They froze in midair. Each and every one of them began to tremble and twitch. And then in one giant burst, they exploded in a blinding shower of sparkling pink glitter.

"AI-EEEEEEEEEEE!" the witches cried in unison.

"All I see is cute! All I see is pretty!" a witch wailed.

"It's stuck to my black dress! I can't brush it off! I-I-I'm *sparkling*!" a witch howled, waving her hands wildly through the air.

Another witch threw herself down against her broomstick. She wrapped her arms and legs around it while shouting, "I dink dit's don dy dongue! Det dit doff! DET DIT DOFF!"

Two more witches zoomed by, lying completely prone on their broomsticks, as if the impact of so much sparkle had cast them into a deep sleep. One red-faced witch took to punching her way through the curtain of glitter without an ounce of success. And finally, the green-haired witch hollered, "No meal could possibly be worth all this! MOVE OUT! MOVE OUT!!"

And the witches flew away.

And Mistress Octavia looked worried. And a fair bit splotchy.

Tumbling on the heels of the swiftly fleeing witches was the one thing Mistress Octavia couldn't protect herself against: *giggling*.

Despite her rapid-fire burst of emphatic shushing, the children were simply beside themselves. For every time they thought of the terrible witches being frightened away by something as infinitesimally small as glitter, they exploded into another bout of giggling, because who would have ever imagined?[58]

Not Mistress Octavia. Indeed, she was getting itchier by the moment. But even that annoyance paled in comparison to the look on her face when the curtain of glitter thinned out and a voice rose above all the rest. The unmistakable voice of a witch.

"Hello!" Ms. Crunch bellowed.

Only Ms. Crunch wasn't alone. Ms. Crunch was soaring on the back of the Blue Dragon, and seated behind her was none other than a grinning Ralph.

Birdie gasped and threw her arms around Cricket. "Cricket, they've come back! They've come back for us! This is so much more than avoiding our Tragic End. This—this is *good*." And, with the Winds of Wanderly ruffling up her hair, and Cricket's hand locked tight in her own, Birdie called out, "We're over here, Ms. Crunch! We're right here!"

And Ms. Crunch swept down and rescued them, the way Birdie always believed she would, while the other children jumped up and down along the Plank, for once looking not a single bit like Tragicals.

---

58. And this, right here, might be the truest explanation of why witches are so dreadfully wary of children. If you think back to your preschool days, or if you are lucky enough to have a younger brother or sister, consider what happens when you hand a three-year-old an open container of *glitter*? So you see, whether in your world or mine, even the smallest of children are extraordinarily well-equipped to deal with the fiercest of foes.

Something's Brewing on Tragic Mountain

Birdie had never flown on the back of a dragon before.

Much less one as extraordinarily large as the Blue Dragon.

She never imagined dragons to be a weepy sort, but fat green tears rolled repeatedly off the Blue Dragon's long fringed lashes while he mused softly, "So this is the Birdie we came to save. Oh, and to think I almost wasn't a part of it!"

Beside Birdie, Ralph nodded and said, "You can say that again, Blue."

To which the Blue Dragon cleared his throat and obediently repeated in a much louder voice, "So this is the Birdie we came to save. Oh—"

Ralph waved his hands in the air. "No, no, Blue! I didn't actually mean you were supposed to say it again." But Ralph was smiling. And when he snuck a glance in Birdie's direction, she smiled back. Despite the fact that Ralph had returned to Tragic Mountain, surely he too was freer than he'd ever been before.

Cricket and Sprinkles, meanwhile, were busy administering a hearty dose of comforting pats along the Blue Dragon's rough scales. "There, there, Mr. Dragon. Don't cry. Everything is all right now." To which the Blue Dragon's generously sized heart swelled at least two sizes larger.

But the Tragicals on the Plank were shouting. The Tragicals on the Plank were trying to get their attention. And standing before them, with her eyes fixed on Ms. Crunch, was Mistress Octavia. Mistress Octavia lifted her hand. Mistress Octavia began to flick her wrist with the practiced swish that never failed to make Birdie flinch.

And Birdie remembered Mistress Octavia's secret.

Her heart caught in her throat. She tried to drum up the words. She wanted to shout at the top of her lungs, "SHE USED TO BE A WITCH! SHE USED TO BE A WITCH!"

But there was no need.

The swirl of magic—*real* magic—that crackled off the tip of Mistress Octavia's fingertips said it all.

The only consolation was she flat-out missed. The inky black ribbon Mistress Octavia aimed at Ms. Crunch plummeted harmlessly into the Black Sea. Foul aim or not, Ms. Crunch was steamed. Without missing a beat, she bent near the Blue Dragon and commanded, "Make yourself a moving target. No matter what these children tell you, don't bring them near the Plank."

"I—I—I," the Blue Dragon tried to say while swallowing profusely. "I mean, *whaaat*?!"

"For crying out loud, just keep everybody outta the way!" Ms. Crunch roared.

She prepared to leap off the Blue Dragon's back, but Birdie grabbed on to her arm. "Please don't go! Mistress Octavia was already awful, but Mistress Octavia with magic is—is—is . . ."

A shadow flickered across Ms. Crunch's eyes. But then, as if remembering something, she set her jaw. "Nothing is impossible. Now let go so I can put my witching to good use!"

Birdie uncurled her fingers one by one, and Ms. Crunch leaped onto the Plank with a great and mighty crash.

Ms. Crunch and Mistress Octavia glowered at each other.

"I've had enough of you! You and your magic are ruining the years of misery I've poured into these Tragicals!" Mistress Octavia hissed.

"Actually, I think *you've* had enough of you. Or at least enough of being a big, fat phony. Ha! What are you exactly? A Council member? A Tragical? A wannabe witch?"

Mistress Octavia's eyes flashed. She lifted her hand and executed another swift swish. The children threw their hands over their eyes in terror. They waited for an awful shriek to erupt from Ms. Crunch, but when all was quiet, they peeked open their eyes and gasped. Ms. Crunch looked dumbfounded. The crisp, clean lines of her jaunty hat had been transformed into an elaborately feathered concoction that was nothing short of ridiculous. Even more intriguing was the fact that Mistress Octavia's name was singed into the velvet brim.

"FOULWEATHER," the hat screamed.

Mistress Octavia's nostrils flared. Ms. Crunch threw the hat onto the Plank and began stomping on it with her witchy boots. "Is that all you got?" she asked. "That hat's hideous, but it sure isn't enough to do me in."

Mistress Octavia raised her hands again.

"Watch out!" Birdie cried from atop the Blue Dragon. Ms. Crunch managed to duck and dive seconds before another blast of magic swirled free. This time, however, Mistress Octavia's magic didn't sink harmlessly through the sky, but singed itself into the Plank, again bearing her name.

"FOULWEATHER," it taunted.

Mistress Octavia stomped her feet. She jiggled her hands. She shot out several more swishes of magic that flew willy-nilly around the Plank.

Francesca Prickleboo's black buckle shoes ballooned into a pair of floppy red clown shoes. "FOULWEATHER," they honked. [59]

The Drowning Bucket at the end of the Plank transformed into a festively colored piñata fit for a birthday celebration. "FOULWEATHER," it ballyhooed, swinging merrily about.

"Argh!" Mistress Octavia exclaimed. And she rushed forward.

---

59. The Francesca Prickleboo of a mere few days ago might have taken one look at her humiliating new shoes and plummeted straight off the Plank in utter distress. But things are quite different when one has friends. And ofttimes an event that threatens to be devastating merely becomes yet another experience to endure *together*. And perhaps even find something to snicker about along the way.

She rushed forward in the direction of the *children*. Ms. Crunch stood firm, but the toe of Mistress Octavia's pointy boot caught on a loose nail, and as she tumbled down, her hands fell upon her Council cloak.

Her magic wound its way into the brilliant purple fabric.

"FOULWEATHER," the threads boldly proclaimed.

Mistress Octavia shook her head from side to side as if she found the rising sight and sound of her name deafening.

"Ha!" Ms. Crunch said. "Your own magic tattles on you! You can't cast a single stinking spell without it spilling the beans. How could you possibly think that's a good idea?"

"I don't," Mistress Octavia said with narrowed eyes. "It must be a side effect of the potion."

"What sort of harebrained potion is that?"

"One that squelches my magic. The Chancellor says that it . . . it is a *necessary* requirement for maintaining this prestigious position."

Ms. Crunch snorted. "Prestigious position my big toe. You hate these kids!"

"I hate bad endings more! And that's what's at stake for me if these brats don't sign their Tragical Oaths! Now get off my mountain before I ruin you!"

Ms. Crunch's eyes flashed. "Ruin me? But you already seem quite busy ruining yourself."

"What's that supposed to mean, old hag?"

Ms. Crunch bent toward Mistress Octavia. She lowered her

voice to a growl. "Let me spell it out for you. You have stepped outside the bounds of your Chancellor-approved role. You used magic. And the evidence is written all over this manor and on that ridiculous Council cloak of yours. You can't go anywhere without advertising to all of Wanderly what you've done. The Chancellor will have no choice but to punish you."

Mistress Octavia's face flushed a peculiar shade of red. "No, that's—that's just not possible—"

"Ha! You're a Council member, no less. You of all people should know the rules! Tell me, what happens, exactly, during a Council detention?"

Mistress Octavia took a few deep breaths. And then, ever so slowly, she smiled her awful smile. "Maybe you can let me know. Too bad I won't be around for mine!"

Mistress Octavia jumped to her feet! She seized the broken broomstick that had fallen against the Plank, and the children cringed the way they always did when it was wrapped tight in her spindly fingers. But this time she did something astonishing with it. She did not raise it in the air and shout her frustrations. She did not run at Ms. Crunch and try to thump her on the head with it. No—instead, she stuck it beneath her bottom, sat lightly atop it, and zoomed off through the sky with a wild cackle!

. . . And zoomed off through the sky with a wild cackle!

. . . . . . And zoomed— Oh, I'll just be honest, Mistress Octavia didn't zoom off more than six inches away from the Plank because both you and I know it is nearly impossible to get very far on half a broomstick. Indeed, the sight of Mistress Octavia, looking as frumpled and frazzled as ever before, swaying ever so slightly back and forth on a broken broomstick was so pitiful, for a moment, Ms. Crunch almost looked a bit sorry for her.

But certainly not enough to let her off the hook.

Ms. Crunch wriggled her fingers in the air, and a magical rope entwined itself around Mistress Octavia's wrists and ankles. Mistress Octavia fell helplessly against the Plank, and her broken broomstick fell down, down, down until it crashed into the ever-raging Black Sea and was swallowed up once and for all.

"Baaaaa!" Sir Ichabod bleated. He trotted up to Ms. Crunch with the heavy medallion dangling from his teeth.

"Ugh! I thought you said Tragicals weren't allowed to have pets?" Ms. Crunch called out to Birdie, who was still seated safely on the Blue Dragon.

"Ha! That's Sir Ichabod," Mistress Octavia hissed from the Plank.

Ms. Crunch snorted. "Sir Ichabod, huh? That ought to make Pooky good and jealous! I've never heard such a fancy name for a pet, and what's it doin' with a medallion?"

"Ms. Crunch, that is Sir Ichabod the *butler*," Birdie called out. "And that medallion's not an award, it's a curse."

"A curse?" Ms. Crunch said. "What sort of curse?"

"Whoever wears it has to pick ten thousand blueberries a day, is forbidden to leave Tragic Mountain, and must obey the person who places it around their neck."

"All that, huh?" Ms. Crunch said, rubbing her hands together. "What a bargain! It would be a shame to leave a perfectly good curse lying around."

As if reading Ms. Crunch's thoughts, Mistress Octavia began wriggling backward along the Plank like a worm. But it took merely the slightest stretch on Ms. Crunch's part to wrap that medallion clean around Mistress Octavia's neck with a smile wide enough to show off all her crooked teeth.

Mistress Octavia howled.

Ms. Crunch crossed her arms and tapped her witchy boot. "Well, that's not a very nice thank-you, now, is it? Here I've gone and saved you from who knows what at the hand of the Chancellor, and all you have to do in return is pick ten thousand blueberries a day and do whatever I tell you."

"I despise those blueberries!"[60] Mistress Octavia spat out. "Why don't you just turn me in and be done with it?"

"Because these kids have been bugged enough! I don't trust the Chancellor as far as I can throw him, and who knows what

---

60. You may be worrying an endless sentence of blueberry picking is not nearly enough of a punishment for the likes of Mistress Octavia. But have you ever happened to eat a pickle-bologna-and-jelly sandwich? Have you ever tasted a hot-dog milkshake topped with a dollop of sour cream and sprinkled with pepper? That is how Tragic Mountain's blueberries smelled to Mistress Octavia. And she had to pick ten thousand *a day*, and perhaps forever. I hope this makes you feel a bit better.

sort of harebrained replacement he'd find?"

Mistress Octavia sneered. "You aren't a witch at all, you know that?"

"All I know is the Chancellor's precious roles don't seem to be making a whole lot of sense anymore. And soon he's not going to have a clue who or what he's dealing with." Mistress Octavia's eyes widened, but Ms. Crunch snapped her fingers in the air. "Blue! Oh, Blue!" she called out.

The Blue Dragon swept near to the Plank. Ms. Crunch plucked Pooky off his outstretched wing, while Ralph, Birdie, Cricket, and Sprinkles slid gently down. The Blue Dragon turned his great fringed lashes toward Ms. Crunch and let out a string of soppy sniffles.

"Stop that," Ms. Crunch said.

"But I can't! The danger seems to be nearly over—which I am quite happy about, mind you—but I fear that also means all of this is about to end."

"Shows how much you know. In fact, your work is just beginning."

The Blue Dragon lifted up his head. "It is?"

"Yes, and you'll start by depositing our new blueberry picker somewhere along the side of Tragic Mountain. I am placing you in charge of her."

"Me?" the Blue Dragon said with a gulp. "In charge of *her*? But how?"

"You're a dragon, remember? You're big. And you're stinky. That counts for a lot."

The Blue Dragon bent near to Agnes and lowered his voice to a dragonly whisper, "But she seems a bit nasty," to which Mistress Octavia promptly snapped her teeth at him, and he shuddered.

"Of course she is! If she wasn't, we wouldn't need your help. You've got the power to change people, remember?"

The Blue Dragon's mouth fell open. "But—but—but none of that was really true. It was all a made-up story!" He lifted a bushy eyebrow at her. "Don't *you* remember?"

"Hogwash!" Ms. Crunch said. "We made it this far, didn't we? Now, stop your dawdling and take her away, Blue!"

The Blue Dragon stretched wide his mighty wings. With a new and decidedly determined tilt to his head, he reached out his claws and snatched Mistress Octavia up by her scrawny waist. She screeched and she shrieked, but soon, she was gone. And for the time being, the children felt something they had never felt before: they felt safe.

Back on the Plank, Birdie knelt beside Sir Ichabod. She leaned her cheek against his rough fur and patted him in between his nubby horns. "Ms. Crunch, I don't suppose you've got magic left enough to turn Sir Ichabod back into himself, do you? Even though he's been freed from his curse, that can't mean much considering he's still a goat."

"Enough magic?" Ms. Crunch said. She paused to exchange a knowing glance with Pooky seated beside her. "Of course I've got enough magic left! I've got magic oozing out of my eyeballs. The real question is what *kind* of magic. As far as the good kind, I don't have a whole lot of that. But I suppose it's worth a shot."

Ms. Crunch lifted her hands but then stopped. "If I were you, I'd move it," she said, gesturing for Birdie, Ralph, and Cricket to join the other children along the Plank.

As the children ran past her, to Pooky's wide-eyed horror, Sir Ichabod tried to gallop right along with them. Fortunately, Ms. Crunch caught him by the horn and tossed him back out in front before nary a delicate kitten paw could be trampled. "Don't be a ninny!" she chided Sir Ichabod. "We're doing this for you after all."

And she promptly turned him into . . . nothing.

"Oh no!" Amelia cried out, throwing her small hands over her eyes. "He's disappeared! He's gone!"

Looking the slightest bit smug, Pooky pranced over to investigate.

"Wait! Hold on just a minute there. I see him!" Ms. Crunch said. "He's that pipsqueak slug crawling about. I guess I better try again."

Ms. Crunch wriggled her fingers and turned him into . . . *CRASH!*

A rhinoceros exploded onto the scene, wearing an astonished kitten! The Plank groaned; it began to split and crack. The children squealed and grabbed on to one another while Ms. Crunch wiped a bit of sweat off her brow. "Oh, goblin's goo!" she said before closing her eyes and bending her knees and turning him into . . .

"Sir Ichabod!" Birdie cried.

And it was.

Sir Ichabod slumped along the Plank, looking terribly exhausted, but whole and complete.

"Sir Ichabod, you're back!" Birdie said, rushing to his side. "And you've broken the curse! But how do you suppose you did it?"

Sir Ichabod's eyes shone, and his voice was thick. "It was just as you said, Birdie. I stopped believing I was merely a Tragical, and I acted instead like who I knew I could be, like who I always was." Sir Ichabod paused and turned toward Ms. Crunch. "I owe you a great debt of thanks, as well."

"Hmph," Ms. Crunch muttered. "Were you paying attention to the part where I turned you into a rhinoceros?"

"Yes, and the slug, too," Sir Ichabod said with a grin and a wink in Pooky's direction.

Though Birdie had never seen Sir Ichabod exude such joy, Pooky didn't seem to appreciate it one bit. For there was nothing to be taken lightly about changing from a billy goat to a slug to a rhinoceros and back to a person all in one breath! Judging by Pooky's unabashed stare, she would be keeping a close and careful watch on Sir Ichabod for quite some time.

Ms. Crunch shrugged and got to shimmying and shaking her black garments all about. She dug her hands into her pockets. She fished out a few vines of black licorice and a perfectly moldy slime sandwich and tossed them over her shoulder. Finally, she located a small vial full of ash and prepared to uncork it.

"What's that, Ms. Crunch?" Birdie asked, with Cricket and Ralph by her side.

"Evidence the last twenty-four hours was a total disaster! This here is all that remains of my broomstick. With Blue watching over Octavia, it's my only way back to the Dead Tree Forest. It shouldn't take more than a few household ingredients to cobble back together, but I'll need a minute or two to raid your pantry." Ms. Crunch spun on her heel and marched toward the trapdoor.

But Birdie put her foot down. She gulped. Ever so softly, she said, "No."

Ms. Crunch continued to bustle around a few wide-eyed children. "Yes, well, like I said it should only be—" She paused. She turned to meet Birdie's gaze. "Did you just tell me *no*?"

Birdie's heart began to pound. It was an awfully scary endeavor to tell a witch no. But Ms. Crunch wasn't just a witch. She was her friend. Birdie had never been more certain of it. She nodded.

Ms. Crunch's eyes gleamed black as coal. "So you're telling me that I hauled my witchy self to your awful mountain, got stuck on more than one occasion with that kid"—she jabbed her finger in Ralph's direction—"had to hightail it out of Castle Matilda with hundreds of hissing witches spitting at me, went traipsing after a mopey dragon, pulled you and your little friend out of the Drowning Bucket, and you're telling me I can't spend a few minutes inside your creaky old house?"

"Y-you said it yourself, Ms. Crunch. All those things you did.

Things you did for me. Even when I let you down. Even when I left you behind. You never gave up on me." Ms. Crunch opened her mouth in protest, but Birdie barreled on. "I know we've got room for all your things, and I bet we could even park your entire haunted cabin on the front lawn, but Ms. Crunch"— Birdie's eyes filled with tears—"I really don't want you to go away. I could search all of Wanderly and never find another friend just like you."

Ms. Crunch swallowed. Hard. "I warned you about using that F-word in person. It makes me feel itchy, it makes me feel—"

"So this time I'm kidnapping *you*."

Ms. Crunch's head snapped up. Birdie cleared her throat and corrected, "Er, witch-napping you."

"That's not a thing," Ms. Crunch said. "No one wants a witch."

"I do," Birdie said. She looked around at the other children. Despite the fact that Ms. Crunch was the spitting image of all the terrible witches they'd read about in stories, they were trying to smile. Trying to nod. Trying to see what Birdie had seen from the very beginning. Because friends see more than what's right in front of them. "*We* do," she corrected herself.

Ms. Crunch's cheeks flushed. The ends of her purple hair began to curl. She was having a hard time spitting out words. "Well, then, you—I mean, all of you—are . . . are even more Tragical than the Chancellor's led everyone to believe! Whoever heard of a witch caring for orphans?"

Sir Ichabod took a step forward. "Speaking of the Chancellor, I daresay Birdie might have a very necessary idea. I fear we shall only be able to cover up Mistress Octavia's absence for so long. When the Chancellor realizes she's gone, if there is no one here to protect the children, what shall become of them?"

Birdie shivered. She thought back to Mistress Octavia's Room of Sinister Plotting. She thought back to the plaque beneath the Chancellor's portrait. She thought back to Mistress Octavia's letters soaring chaotically around the room. *Dear Uncle* . . . Even if the Chancellor never bothered to visit, family was family, wasn't it? And the Chancellor already despised the Tragicals; surely the overthrow of Mistress Octavia would be the perfect excuse for revenge.

Ms. Crunch crossed her arms against her chest. "If you're that worried, why not ship them off Tragic Mountain?"

"Because it would be mere weeks, maybe even days, before the Council finds and returns them. Or worse."

Ms. Crunch jutted her chin into the air. "Why does it have to be me?"

"Perhaps the better question is, why shouldn't it be you?" Sir Ichabod said.

Birdie took several steps in Ms. Crunch's direction.

"What do you think you're doing?" Ms. Crunch said.

"I already told you. I'm witch-napping you. And . . ." Birdie paused. She cleared her throat. In her strongest and most authoritative voice, she continued, "And you should think twice about putting up a fight. There's no reason for this to get ugly."

"Ugly, huh?" Ms. Crunch said, wrinkling up her face, twitching her hairy warts, and sticking out her squiggly tongue.

But with Ralph and Cricket following closely behind, Birdie kept moving forward.

She thrust her hand out in front of her.

She slipped it into Ms. Crunch's gnarled, crooked one.

And Ms. Crunch, for once, was speechless.

"Come on, now," Birdie said, pulling Ms. Crunch toward the trapdoor leading into Foulweather's Home for the Tragical. "It's long past time we all went home."

"Home?" Ms. Crunch croaked.

"Home," Birdie said.

And that is exactly what they did.

The witch, the butler, the one-eyed kitten, and the children formerly known as Tragicals slipped into the manor one by one. The manor let out a long, happy sigh, and the Winds of Wanderly twirled through the sky, pausing merely once to close the door behind them ever so gently.

Hello, again. [61]

---

61. You truly are an impeccable reader. I can likely count on my hand the number of readers who would turn the page *after* the last page. Bravo!

I bet you thought I would say goodbye.

Books, however, never say goodbye. Not merely because after so much time spent together, the idea of farewell makes us hopelessly teary, but for the quite obvious reason that we haven't any legs and can't budge an inch on our own.

And so, my story rests wholly in your hands.

You may wish to lend me to a friend, potential friend (books are fantastic conversation starters), or even a so-called enemy (let us not forget how things turned out with our favorite tattletale, Francesca). You may wish to grab the nearest sheet of paper (I hear in your world paper is readily available without a single restriction!) and pen a brand-new tale because words, whether you happen to live in a storybook kingdom or not, have a magic all their own. You may wish to talk about me with your family (pet snails make extraordinary listeners, by the way) or write a letter to someone far, far away like Agnes did.

I know you will make the right choice.[62]

---

62. Indeed, there is no wrong way to enjoy a book. Books take as much delight in being creatively read as in being creatively written.

And once you have finished, I shall still be here.

Waiting.

Always and ever ready to say:

"Hello."[63]

---

63. If you wish to test me on this, simply flip back to the page where our adventure together first began.

ACKNOWLEDGMENTS

Much like Agnes's first letter, this book began as little more than a hope cast into the wind. It is my great joy that the incomparable Molly O'Neill answered. Molly, thank you for taking a leap of faith on me. Neither Birdie nor I would be the same without your astounding talent, wisdom, kindness, and wholehearted generosity. Of course, as Pooky would adamantly insist, an extra special thanks to Captain Von Smooch, who is tops among all "feline literary assistants."

Thank you to my brilliant editor, Stephanie Stein, who kindly read this story, believed it could be a real book, and then magically transformed it into one! I have no doubt that among fairy godmothers in Wanderly, you would be the very best. Thank you for making my lifelong dream come true.

My deepest thanks goes to the entire team at HarperCollins. Thank you for pouring your talents and time into this book. I am especially grateful to cover designer Jessie Gang and artist

Melissa Manwill, who captured Birdie so perfectly it still brings tears to my eyes. Thank you to copy editors Jon Howard and Jeannie Ng for their extraordinary attention to detail. Much thanks to Erica Sussman for supporting and believing in this book from the start. Thank you to Vaishali Nayak and Jacquelynn Burke for their dedication in connecting this book with readers. Thank you to Kristen Eckhardt for so diligently overseeing production from beginning to end. And thank you to Louisa Currigan for keeping all the very many strings tied so neatly together.

Thank you to the entire staff at Root Literary Agency. You inspire me every day with your passion for books, their makers, and their readers. And special thanks to Heather Baror for her work in bringing books into children's hands all around the globe, giving Birdie wings!

I am ever so grateful to the one-of-a-kind Liesl Shurtliff for her kindness, generosity, and support. Liesl, as a writer I have learned much from you, and as a reader I am utterly delighted by your stories.

Mom and Dad, I'm not sure it's possible to thank someone for an entire lifetime of love and support, but please know how much I love you both. Mom, thank you especially for your contagious passion for books and love for others—it helped shaped my dreams and my heart.

And thank you to my little family. This book, and this dream, would be absolutely impossible without you. Jerad, you are my best friend and my forever love. My favorite place will always be right beside you. Ellie and Violet, I love you so much it makes my mama heart burst! Thank you for being the best daughters ever simply by being you.

Finally, thank you to each reader who has chosen to journey alongside Birdie, her friends, and one rather chatty book. As Sir Ichabod would say, a book is not truly a book until it has found a reader, and you, dearest readers, are so much more than this writer ever hoped for.